Praise for *Life, Death and Cellos*

'a **very enjoyable read**' Marian Keyes

'*Life, Death and Cellos* is **a witty and irreverent musical romp**, full of characters I'd love to go for a pint with. I thoroughly enjoyed getting to know the Stockwell Park Orchestra and **can't wait for the next book in the series.**' Claire King, author of *The Night Rainbow*

'*Life, Death and Cellos* is **that rare thing – a funny music book**. Rogers knows the world intimately, and portrays it with warmth, accuracy and a poetic turn of phrase. **Sharp, witty and richly entertaining.**' Lev Parikian, author of *Why Do Birds Suddenly Disappear?*

'With its **retro humour bordering on farce**, this novel offers an escape into the turbulent (and bonkers) world of the orchestra.' Isabel Costello, author of *Paris Mon Amour*

'**Dodgy post-rehearsal curries, friendly insults between musicians, sacrosanct coffee-and-biscuit breaks, tedious committee meetings: welcome to the world of the amateur orchestra**. Throw in a stolen Stradivarius, an unexpected fatality and the odd illicit affair and you have *Life, Death and Cellos*, the first in a new series by Isabel Rogers.' Rebecca Franks, *BBC Music Magazine*

ALSO BY ISABEL ROGERS
Life, Death and Cellos

ISABEL ROGERS

BOLD
AS
BRASS

THE *Stockwell Park Orchestra* SERIES

This edition published in 2019 by Farrago,
an imprint of Prelude Books Ltd
13 Carrington Road, Richmond, TW10 5AA, United Kingdom

www.farragobooks.com

ISBN: 978-1-78842-138-6

Stockwell Park Orchestra

Conductor

First violins

Second violins

Violas

Cellos

Double basses

French horns

Flutes

Clarinets

Oboes

Bassoons

Trumpets

Trombones

Tuba

Percussion

To Pearl's tea urn and custard cream stash....

Chapter 1

'Schoolkids?' David took another swallow of beer and looked aghast. 'Are you mad?'

Eliot Yarrow grinned, not entirely placatingly. 'Look around. Stockwell Park Orchestra in all its boozy glory. What do you see?'

What David saw were familiar people lolling round their regular pub after a rehearsal. It's what they did: play music, then drink and laugh. What else is there?

'I see brass players who seem to be able to afford three pints but complain when Rafael asks them about their latest orchestra sub.'

'Forget about Rafael's accountant brain for a minute,' said Eliot. 'I haven't done the maths,' – he flicked a glance at David to check his tic hadn't returned – 'but I reckon our average age is north of fifty. And we are mostly (how can I put this?) middle class.'

David looked round again. 'Classical musicians do tend to be, well, I suppose, like me,' he said.

'Exactly!' said Eliot. 'It's not your fault. But if we don't start getting some younger players, in a few years' time we could be looking at arthritic attempts on less challenging Mozart rather than something exciting.'

Erin, Charlie and Ann returned from the bar with refills, manoeuvred themselves over stools and around cello cases and sat down at the table, expertly balancing full pints and sliding some over to Eliot and David.

'What's this?' said Erin. 'Who doesn't think Mozart's exciting?'

'I do. He's not,' said Charlie.

'I'm not getting into this again – you were wrong before and you're wrong now,' replied Erin. 'Eliot, what's going on? You can't decide things while the cellists get you a beer. That's just rude.'

Eliot drained the last of his old pint and lined up the next. 'Cheers. I was mentioning to David it would be a great idea to get involved with some local schools. You know, reach out.'

'Reach out?' said Erin. 'We're not American.'

'He'll be "dialoguing" next,' said Charlie.

Eliot blew a raspberry at them. 'Get some kids along to play with us. See what talent is on our doorstep already, and show the ones who don't think they like it that we're not all grumpy bastards in dinner jackets.'

'Stockwell Park Orchestra: Not All Grumpy Bastards In Dinner Jackets,' said Ann. 'Strapline for the flyer right there. Head teachers will batter down our doors.'

'We don't all wear dinner jackets,' Erin pointed out. 'It's not 1953. Someone let the girls in.'

'Watch out, or he'll be getting us to play in roll-neck sweaters,' said Charlie. 'With maybe "bright floral blouses" for the ladies. What do you reckon, Eliot? Shall we mix it up a bit?'

Eliot grinned. He was not ready for the nylon-tastic fire hazard that would be invoked, and Charlie knew it.

'It's a good point, though,' said Erin, ignoring the red-blouse-to-a-bull being waved in front of her. 'Leaving aside the Mozart-hating thing (which is, may I say, completely wrong and probably illegal) and the fact that we're not all in our dotage yet—'

'Oi!' said Ann. 'I'm enjoying mine. Don't spoil it.'

Erin carried on: '– we probably *should* open up our gene pool a bit.'

'Steady on,' said Charlie. 'Nobody said anything about breeding ourselves into the modern world.'

David cleared his throat. The conversation was veering again, as it usually did with musicians in a pub. It had the wayward enthusiasm of a spaniel on the scent of a particularly absent-minded squirrel. 'I'm not sure we—'

'It's OK, David,' said Eliot, shooting a look at Charlie. 'No breeding. No florals. Just, I dunno, let's get some musical kids into some of our rehearsals and see how they like it.'

'A community outreach programme,' said David. 'I think that's what it's called.'

They drank in silence for a moment. Eliot watched them mull over his suggestion. David was frowning, but his whole body regularly fell into the resting creased look of an origami heron so there were no clues from that. Charlie was staring at Erin thoughtfully, though whether it was the mention of breeding or floral blouses that made him so pensive was unclear. Erin herself drank deeply from her pint and considered the idea. Ann raised her eyes and looked straight at Eliot, smiling. She had the advantage of decades of parenting skills behind her, as well as many cello lessons given to kids. She knew exactly what could be involved.

'Are you sure you know what you're letting yourself in for?' she said. 'I'm not saying no, but small kids are bloody exhausting.'

Eliot laughed. 'If you're asking if I have any experience at working with kids, then no, not really. I'm not a dad. Though I *am* a pretty accomplished uncle. But hey, I wasn't thinking of primary school age. Unless we're talking serious prodigy territory, I reckon we'll need teenagers if they're going to be a decent standard.'

'And you think teenagers are easier?' said Ann. She rolled her eyes and laughed. 'No – don't get me wrong. I think it's a great idea. It'll be… interesting.'

David raised his head suddenly. 'Will we all need to be DRB checked?' From the blank looks he got around the table, it appeared nobody knew. He sighed. 'Well, I suppose I could look into it,' he said. 'There could be a lot of… issues.'

'Not insurmountable ones, I hope,' Eliot said. 'Shall I mention it next week? Come to think of it, why don't we start with pupils at the school we rehearse at? Are they the right age? Has anyone met any of them?'

'Sunbridge kids? Nobody's ever seen them,' said Charlie. 'Most of them have pissed off round the corner to deal drugs by the time we tip up to rehearse.'

It was true. Sunbridge Academy had not found the transformation from inner city comprehensive in special measures to beacon of excellence as easy as the new management team had hoped. The impressive sign over the gate made the most of its brief: there were bold yellow sunbeams firing out over a bridge that appeared to invite pupils to skip over the River of Limitation and cavort in the lush Fields of Opportunity beyond. The implication of sunny uplands positively screamed out of the background abstract artistry. Stockwell's exhaust fumes were committed to sooting over the sign's hopeful wavelengths of light, but the battle was young and flying electric cars are apparently only a decade away, always.

The main change the orchestra had noticed since the rebrand had been that the brown plastic chairs in the school hall had been replaced with identical chairs in primary colours, and the lingering lunch smell that sometimes drifted from the cafeteria was more likely to be of chickpea fritters than mince and carrots.

'They won't all be drug dealers,' said Ann. 'But I'm guessing their budget is squeezed as much as any school these days. They might not even have a music department any more. If they have any specialist teachers at all, they'll probably visit from the regional office. It'll be all peripatetics and hubs.'

'Well, it's a start. We can try,' said Eliot. 'There are other schools round here too, though, aren't there? Oakdean College is – what – about half a mile away?'

'Those posh kids wearing duffle coats that smell like wet sheep on the Tube when it rains?' said Charlie. 'Who shove past you at the ticket barriers braying about how they just beat Harrow at water polo or real tennis or peacock shooting?'

'Now they *will* have a music department,' said Ann.

'They do,' said Erin. 'Their head of music came up to me after the Elgar last term and asked if I could do an assembly for them and play something on the Strad.'

Everyone turned to her in surprise.

'Oh yeah?' said Charlie. 'We've been playing round here for years but it takes a Strad to tempt them out? Typical.'

'I haven't agreed yet,' said Erin, suddenly defensive. 'I muttered something about diaries.'

Ann studied David. His angular frame was becoming more concave, as if he were trying to hide himself behind his own ribcage.

'You have a son, don't you?' she asked him. 'Does he go to school round here?'

David took another swallow of beer and nodded. He looked apologetically at Charlie. 'He's one of the damp sheep, I'm afraid.'

'Oops,' said Eliot quietly from behind his pint.

'He's only ten, though,' said David. 'In the prep school. It's quite separate from the seniors, even though they're on the same site. I hope he's never barged in front of anyone at the ticket barriers.'

'A little lamb, rather than a fully grown sheep then,' said Ann.

Charlie grinned. 'Of course not. Sorry, David. I hope I didn't—'

David shook his head. 'Not at all.'

'Thank God for that,' said Eliot. 'So. Why don't we ask both Oakdean and Sunbridge to see if they want to join in our new and beautifully named community outreach programme? If the rest of the orchestra seem to think that's OK, of course. Can I just ask them informally next week, David, or do we need a full committee meeting or something?'

Although Eliot hadn't been conducting Stockwell Park for long, he had already heard alarming rumours about how dull their committee meetings were, and also that the conductor was expected to attend. He intended to put off that experience for as long as he could.

David thought for a moment. 'I think something like this might be put through on the nod, as it were. Unless it transpires there are significant financial implications, in which case Rafael would undoubtedly—'

'Well, let's make sure there aren't,' said Eliot quickly. 'I just want to get a few kids along. A sort of recruitment drive, if you like. Future-proofing us. Rafael would like that, surely?'

David remembered Rafael's recent spreadsheet juggling to keep the orchestra alive, and shuddered. 'I'm sure he would,' he said.

'OK then. Erin can go into Oakdean, as she already has an invitation.'

'Maybe I should take Charlie with me,' Erin said. 'To challenge his inverted snobbish assumptions?'

Eliot laughed. 'I don't mind. But two cellos? Or do we want to give them a variety of instruments, to give them a feel for it?'

'They'll know their way around an orchestra,' said Ann.

'They've probably got four different ones,' said Charlie. 'Plus a baroque one that only plays on period instruments at old pitch.' Erin kicked his ankle. 'Sorry, David. Ow.'

'Three, actually,' said David, with a small smile. 'One full, one chamber and one that plays jazz. Oh, and the wind band. So actually, yes, four, sort of. You were right.'

'Good grief,' said Charlie. 'I was bloody joking.'

'Right then, I'll just have to ask for volunteers to go into Sunbridge and drum up some punters there,' said Eliot.

'Good luck with that,' said Charlie.

'That's next week's problem,' said Eliot, and finished his pint.

Chapter 2

The late January drizzle fell lightly around Charlie and Erin as they walked from Stockwell tube station to Oakdean College, as if it knew Charlie's left-wing ire needed cooling if he was to avoid a scene. He had promised Eliot he would behave, and prioritise the mission above any personal urges to strike a blow for the masses in a south London minor public school nobody had heard of. To convey his utter contempt of the inherently unfair private education system, he was wearing his most socialist donkey jacket and a wool hat with a peak to keep the drizzle off his face. He had even remembered not to shave.

Erin was in her usual jeans, leaning away from the weight of her cello case as she stepped round puddles on the pavement.

Oakdean College bore the drizzle stoically, its redbrick walls mottling damply here and there where Victorian guttering and drainpipes could no longer stretch to reach each other as they had done in their effortless youth, when Albert still lived and the Empire was briskly nicking stuff from all round the world and pretending it was in the name of civilisation. In any case, sons had to be educated and Oakdean – while not exactly welcoming them with open arms – provided them with a decent enough schooling and a perfunctory sort of brisk Victorian care, which involved quantities of cold water and stern moral lectures.

One likes to think such institutions mellowed as they weathered the twentieth century and stumbled into the twenty-first, what with summers of love and winters of discontent, and punk. Oakdean, however, was a small oasis of stone and brick and saggy drainpipes in the ever-changing maelstrom south of the river. Over decades, it had (like many schools of a similar kind) developed its own eccentric habits. Most children play conkers. The majestic oak tree in the front quad that gave the school its name provided acorns that had regularly put out the eyes of some of the most promising youth since 1853. Far from banning the game, Oakdean had refined and developed its rules, and every year held The Acorning: a knockout tournament that often did precisely that. At Oakdean, a glass eye was a badge of honour.

Erin and Charlie walked through Oakdean's open gates: tall iron arrangements that had been carefully replaced as exact replicas long after the originals had been melted into patriotic Spitfires. Entwined into the upper reaches of the bars were the words *PARVIS E GLANDIBUS CRESCUNT QUERCUS MAGNAE* ('from small acorns grow mighty oaks') moulded in oak leaves and tendrils of an unspecified exotic-looking vine. The artist, though clearly enjoying himself, had been no botanist.

The busy traffic noise started to fade as soon as they had gone a few yards into the school grounds, cocooned as they were by thick stone walls and an enormous rhododendron hedge that ran around the entire perimeter. Their feet crunched over gravel as they aimed for the main door just visible beyond a stalwart oak tree in the centre of a grass-covered quad. The gravel drive looped gracefully around the tree before making its way back to the gate.

'Fuck me,' said Charlie, not quite under his breath enough to be classified as trying to behave. 'We're still in Stockwell, right? Only I think we might have teleported to an Oxbridge theme park.'

'Keep your voice down,' said Erin. 'You promised. Plus they've probably got hidden mics to root out subversive conversations.'

'It looks well Brexit.'

They skirted the carpet of snowdrops under the oak and approached the door, which was suffering the incongruity of a shiny steel video entry phone right next to its original bell pull with as much dignity as it could manage.

'Which one do I use?' said Erin.

'Depends which century you want to try, maybe?'

'Twenty-first it is then.'

She pushed the buzzer, which squawked loudly like a surprised incorrect quiz answer, and waited.

Nothing happened.

'I really hope they've got a butler,' said Charlie. 'And we get to hear him clomping along the corridor for hours before he gets to the door.'

Erin peered at the small video screen, which steadfastly remained dark.

'And maybe some mutant kids,' continued Charlie conversationally. Erin snorted with laughter, just as the screen lit up. She immediately tried to fold her face into a serious musician expression, not altogether successfully.

'*Yes?*' said the screen. There was no corresponding face: just a square light.

'Oh, hello,' said Erin. 'Er – we're from Stockwell Park Orchestra? We're here for your assembly?'

'Hi!' added Charlie, leaning round Erin and looming towards the screen. 'Two cellists, at your service.'

'*Ah.*' The screen glowed. '*Yes. Come in.*'

The door unlatched with another loud buzz, and Erin pushed it open. They stepped inside onto the polished wooden floor of a hallway that smelled of slightly burnt coffee and lilies. A woman was already emerging from a room on their left, her heels tapping smartly as she approached. She removed her glasses and let them dangle vertiginously over her bosom from a chain round her neck. She inspected Erin and Charlie sternly at close range.

'Which one of you is the Stradivari?'

There was a small pause. Erin felt her nose begin to tickle from the lily pollen, and pinched it to ward off a sneeze. The pause stretched.

Charlie stuck out his hand. 'Good morning. I'm Charlie, and this is Erin. I can't tell you how much I've been looking forward to our visit to Oakdean. And you are…?'

The stern woman faced Charlie, raised her chin and, seeing Charlie's hand was still firmly in mid-air, clasped it gingerly. 'Good morning. Mrs Batten. Assistant to the Headmaster.'

Charlie shook Mrs Batten's hand while Erin coped with half a dozen sudden sneezes, managing to keep them controlled as tiny squeaks. Mrs Batten eyed her as if such a bold display of bodily functions should not be exhibited in her hallway.

'So, where would you like us?' asked Charlie. 'Don't mind Erin. She's allergic to… things.'

Mrs Batten pressed her lips together and gestured to the far end of the hall. 'This way, please. The assembly will be through there.' As they walked, she stepped to one side to pop her head round another door, leaning forward so Charlie and Erin could only just make out her saying, 'The gentleman with the Stradivari has arrived. I'm taking him through now.' They glanced at each other with raised eyebrows.

'You're with the Stradivari gentleman now,' Charlie whispered. 'Have some respect.'

Before Erin could reply, Mrs Batten was with them again, and together they walked into a large, wood-panelled room. Tall sash windows ran along the far wall, looking out onto playing fields and tennis courts and rain. In the distance, the rhododendron hedge was just visible, keeping Stockwell and modernity at bay.

'You'll be playing at that end,' said Mrs Batten to Charlie. 'Do you require anything else?'

'No – we've brought stands with us, thank you,' said Erin.

'And copies of the *Socialist Worker*,' murmured Charlie, almost inaudibly.

Mrs Batten glanced at Erin briefly, then returned her attention to Charlie. 'The Headmaster will join you presently. The boys arrive in five minutes.'

She nodded, as if satisfied with imparting correct information, and left.

'I'd better adjust my Romulan cloaking device,' said Erin. 'I think a bit of me showed just then by mistake.'

'Jesus,' said Charlie. 'Almost think I'd have preferred the Sunbridge yobbos. This place is mental.'

They walked to the far end of the room, set their cello cases down and started unfolding two music stands. A loud and jovial greeting boomed from the door behind them, and they turned to see a small, balding man in his sixties striding towards them. He wore a tweed three-piece suit which had just enough lime green stripe in its pattern to evoke grouse moors and Labradors. His smile was wide as he bore down on them with right hand extended, his left arm swinging enthusiastically at his side to hasten his arrival.

'Good morning, good morning! I'm delighted to welcome you to Oakdean,' he cried as he approached. 'The marvellous musicians from Stockwell Park Orchestra, I presume?' He laughed heartily at his own original wit, and finally docked his hand into Charlie's and pumped it with great fervour. 'We have been looking forward to your visit with great anticipation,' he said, clasping ever more firmly as he laid his left hand over Charlie's to entomb it within a headmasterly glove of welcome, his gaze riveted on Charlie's cello case.

'Happy to be here,' said Charlie, noticing the headmaster's eyes were slightly different colours. 'I'm Charlie. This is Erin.'

The headmaster stopped shaking Charlie's hand and turned to Erin, taking hers gently and making the smallest of bows. 'Charmed, my dear. I am Dr Irving.'

Charlie raised his eyebrows at Erin over Dr Irving's head and mouthed *Oh my God*.

Dr Irving turned back to Charlie. 'With what sweet music will you be delighting us? Some Bach, perhaps? I am particularly fond of the cello suites.'

'Well,' said Charlie, 'we thought, since we'd brought two cellos, we might break out some duets. Shostakovich, and maybe a couple of Bartoks?'

'Yes, yes. Naturally,' agreed Dr Irving, refusing to dial down his enthusiasm. 'And we are all on tenterhooks to see the Stradivari.' He laid his palm lightly on top of Charlie's cello case as if he were a priest giving a blessing.

Erin decided enough was enough. 'Well, actually, Dr Irving—'

'Ah! Here come the boys now,' said Dr Irving, as boys in single file began to enter the hall from a couple of corner doors. 'Come right down to the front, boys! That's it.'

Erin caught Charlie's eye and shrugged. They set up their music stands and chairs, and licked their thumbs to wet the small circles of black rubber they laid on the floor to hold their cello spikes in place. The hall filled with the long limbs of middle-class teenagers fed diets of consistently high protein and self-assurance. They ran their fingers through floppy hair and slouched on chairs. A few wore eyepatches.

When the hall had filled up, Dr Irving cleared his throat in the manner of one accustomed to their phlegm commanding silence within a thirty-yard radius.

'Good morning, boys.' There was a murmur of response. 'This morning Oakdean is graced with the presence of a piece of history. Antonio Stradivari made a few hundred violins, and those that survive are worth millions. Only around sixty of his cellos still exist, and we are looking at one here today!' He scuttled sideways and indicated Charlie's mid-brown twentieth century French cello. An excited ripple travelled through the watching boys.

'Well, actually,' said Charlie, 'this one is—'

'And we are privileged to be visited by two fine musicians from the Stockwell Park Orchestra which – as you might be aware – rehearses a mere acorn's throw away, on the premises of Sunbridge Academy.'

The ripple that went through the boys at that point could more accurately be described as condescending. Perhaps snobby. Even raucous. Dr Irving raised his hands placatingly, but indulgently.

'Be that as it may,' he continued, as the hisses and giggles subsided, 'be that as it may, we have two fine musicians here today to wave the flag, as it were, for Stockwell Park. With a Stradivari!'

He backed away and led a small round of applause. Charlie and Erin stared at each other. Erin stood up.

'Hello. I'm Erin, and this is Charlie. We're very pleased to be here to talk a bit about what goes on in Stockwell Park Orchestra, and hope we might persuade some of you to come along and try us out.'

There were some snorts from the back of the hall.

'Sod it, Erin,' said Charlie softly. 'Let's just play something and bugger off.'

Erin nodded. 'We'll play a couple of duets for you now, and perhaps afterwards you might like to ask us some questions.' She sat down and sorted the music on her stand in front of her. 'This is *Präludium* by Shostakovich. It should have a piano accompaniment, but sounds almost as lovely without. Hope you enjoy it!'

As they played the Shostakovich, Dr Irving's face developed a beatific glow. He closed his eyes and swayed happily in his front row seat until a piece of chewed paper hit him on the back of the neck. A group of boys in the mid-section of the hall were immediately entranced by Erin and Charlie's playing so when he turned, furious, one eye swivelling to spot the culprit, he saw nothing but innocent musical appreciation. For the rest of the duet, he never really regained his former calm, and twitched whenever he heard anyone shift in their seat behind him.

By the end of the Bartok duets, there were half a dozen pellets of damp, chewed paper scattered behind Dr Irving's chair, where they had ricocheted off his nape. He had two spots of high colour on his cheeks, and was blinking fast. Nevertheless, he leapt to his feet to lead the applause, a smile clamped to his face as Erin and Charlie stood up.

'Superb! Superb!' he cried. 'Bravo!' He made another small bow towards Erin. 'And brava, naturally!'

'Naturally,' said Charlie, making his own small bow to Erin.

'Fuck off,' whispered Erin, smiling at the applauding boys like an experienced ventriloquist.

'Perhaps we might implore you to say a few words about the Stradivari?' said Dr Irving, walking towards Charlie as the hall settled into silence.

'Of course,' said Charlie, turning to the boys. 'It belongs to another cellist in Stockwell Park Orchestra, who

21

unfortunately can't play it at the moment because of injury, but that's a whole other story. She has kindly lent it out so we can all benefit from its glorious tone and scope. Erin – over to you!'

Erin smiled and took a step forward. 'Thank you, Charlie. This cello is more than three hundred years old…'

Charlie snorted. As Erin spoke, Dr Irving's face transformed itself from shock to disbelief and worry, finally settling on a strained politeness. Charlie grinned at him.

After a few minutes, Erin looked around the hall. 'Well, I've said a bit about the Strad, and our orchestra. I hope some of you might want to come along to a few rehearsals this term – we're planning a special concert featuring young people from our local area. How many of you play instruments?'

Nearly all the boys raised their hands.

'That's great,' she said. 'And of those, how many orchestral instruments?'

Half the hands went down.

'Piano is always popular,' said Charlie, almost sympathetically. 'I play that too, but you can't get as much look-in with an orchestra.'

'Unless you play a concerto,' called a boy from the back.

'Shut up, Jacob,' said another boy. 'You can't even play "Chopsticks".'

The mood soon turned ugly.

'That's all Rupert can play on his upright.'

'It's simply not authentic if you don't use a harpsichord—'

'Just because your dad bought you a whole set of viols—'

'Viols to the vile—'

'His *embouchure* is flabby—'

Silence was restored with one of Dr Irving's throat clearances. He glared at the boys, then turned back to Erin, manfully looking her right in the eye. 'I'm sure our music department can coordinate which boys might be suitable to spread their wings, as it were, beyond the rhododendron.'

'That's great, thank you,' said Erin. 'Any other questions, boys?'

One of the chewed paper-aimers raised his hand. 'Are there many… ladies in your orchestra?'

There were guffaws and a couple of whistles. Erin and Charlie looked at each other.

'There are a few,' admitted Erin. 'Obviously I'm rare, as a cellist. Usually ladies play small things they can easily lift, like the piccolo or triangle.'

'She does waste a lot of time having to arrange her skirts to sit side-saddle in concerts,' said Charlie. 'Mate. Are there any real questions?'

Aside from a sheepish murmur that blew round the hall like a susurration of dry leaves, there appeared to be none.

Dr Irving stirred. 'Well, boys, I think we should thank Erin and Charlie one last time for visiting us.' He led the final round of applause, and the boys began to file out. 'Exquisite playing, my dear,' he continued directly to Erin. 'And on such an instrument. Marvellous. Marvellous.'

He stayed while they packed their cellos away and the hall emptied, rummaging absent-mindedly round the back of his collar and brushing away stray bits of paper starting to dry onto his jacket.

'Head & Shoulders, mate,' said Charlie as they started to walk to the front door, nodding at the white pellets of detritus around Dr Irving's feet. 'Works wonders.' He then sped up to leave Erin to be personally escorted by a now positively fawning Dr Irving. They were ushered outside just as Erin's nose began to tickle again, and the door shut on Dr Irving's repeated thanks and promises to attend future concerts.

Charlie put his cap on. The drizzle fell.

They walked together towards the gate, starting to giggle helplessly.

'What the *fuck* was that?' said Charlie.

'It was… surreal,' said Erin. 'The head of music seemed quite normal when he came up to me last term. I had no idea.'

'Yeah – where was he today then? Dobbed us right bloody in it.'

'And what was with the eyepatches?' said Erin. 'Did you notice?'

'Yeah. Reckon Irving's got a glass eye too. Maybe it's a cult.'

'Maybe it's triffids. Let's hope nobody turns up next week.'

'I took a morning off work for this. Christ.'

'You'll get your reward, Charlie. Connecting with the community, innit?'

'Yeah, right.'

They scrunched their way towards the Tube as the clocktower of Oakdean College struck the hour, frightening some sheltering pigeons back out into the rain.

Chapter 3

Charlie might have thought Sunbridge Academy easier to visit than Oakdean, but Carl and Marco had their own problems. As Charlie and Erin walked back to the Tube station, Carl and Marco were in the Sunbridge foyer just as the bell sounded for morning break. They were immediately surrounded by a deafening swirl of blazer-wearing kids making their collective break for freedom, despite the drizzle. As the tide of youth rose higher, Marco clung to Carl's reassuring bulk. Carl's trombone case bore the brunt of the force like the iron bow of an icebreaker, and they leaned into the current together, Marco burrowing into Carl's back, mewing occasionally but definitely trying not to swear at anyone specific. After cursing a conductor to death a few months earlier from his seat in the violins, Marco wasn't about to make that mistake again. Also, it was only three years since he'd been a pupil at Sunbridge, and he wasn't at all sure if some of his bullies were still around, three years taller and eager for another fight.

After a couple of minutes, the torrent calmed. Carl returned to an upright position from his forward brace, and called to Marco, 'You alright back there?'

Marco removed his hands from where they had been clutching fistfuls of Carl's coat, and took some deep breaths. He wasn't sure if he was having a panic attack or some kind of flashback. On regular rehearsal nights he felt perfectly fine, but this sudden throng had taken him right back to his tortured schooldays, rocketing up his adrenaline. 'Yeah. The place hasn't changed at all.'

'What – you came here?' Carl laughed. 'You kept that quiet.'

'David thought it would be a good idea if I did the visit. You know, to show the kids what was possible, kind of thing.' Marco blinked rapidly. 'And my mum said it would do me good to come back and face my – um—'

'What?'

'Um, "*demônios*" was her exact word.'

'Huh?'

'Demons.'

'There are demons in Sunbridge?'

'There were.'

'Good job I'm here then,' said Carl. 'Stick with me, pal. You'll be OK.'

They made their way over to a glass-walled office, inside which they could see some administrating happening. It wasn't immediately clear where the door was located in the expanse of smeared glass: Carl put his trombone case down and was pacing about patting his hands over it like a trapped mime artist when a voice called from behind them.

'The cleaners complain about greasy handprints, but what can you do when a posh architect decides "educational vision" means acres of glass and a couple of beanbags?'

They turned to see a woman standing with folded arms, wearing leggings, a tunic and Doc Martens.

'Miss Edwards!' said Marco. 'We were just—' He looked around the foyer in case the stampede began again.

'Hello, Marco,' she said, smiling. 'I didn't realise you'd be part of the detail. Brought your bodyguard, I see. Probably wise.'

'Oh, this is Carl,' said Marco. 'Trombone.'

Carl nodded. 'Hi.'

'Nice to meet you, Carl. I'm Kayla, head of music,' she said, stepping forward and shaking Carl's hand. 'No standing on ceremony round here. Even Marco can call me Kayla now, if he likes. Whaddya think, Marco? Is three years enough?' Marco looked horrified, and she laughed. 'Well, maybe not. See how you go. Look, I was just about to grab a coffee – do you guys want one, before we start?'

'Sounds good,' said Carl, and Kayla led them around the glass office box to the staffroom behind another glass door, this one smokily opaque: another revealing detail about the architect's assumptions about the relative needs of teachers and admin staff. She opened it onto a warm fug of steam, old teabags and microwaved cinnamon porridge. The room was full of people all trying to use the single kettle before the bell rang for the end of break. Tempers were fraying.

'They've nicked my soya milk again. Christ.'

'Oh, who got the pint mug out? They'll use all the water!'

'Clean spoons – bloody hens' teeth.'

'Does he have to have cinnamon every damn day? Stinks the place out.'

'Sugar? Where's the sugar?'

'Well, refill it and whack it on again quick. Come on.'

'Have you seen my soya milk?'

Kayla turned to Carl and Marco. 'They spent a fortune on the makeover when we turned into an academy. Still only one lousy kettle. Go figure.'

Carl didn't think it was an appropriate time to tell Kayla about Pearl's capacious urn, which she produced from the back of a cupboard in the main hall every week at orchestra rehearsals.

Marco was transfixed, his eyes wide. Every muscle fibre with a memory in his body screamed he was in a forbidden place. Staffrooms existed behind doors that were closed to small, nervous pupils like him.

A thunk of something heavy smashed against the thick glass door behind them; Marco jumped clear of the floor and managed to land close to Carl's reassuringly solid bicep. They turned to see the indistinct side of someone's face squashed against the glass like a specimen under a microscope slide. As they watched, the face slid slowly downwards and eventually peeled off the glass, leaving another smear for the cleaners to deal with later.

'Christ,' Kayla muttered, and went to open the door, but since it opened outwards it quickly became clear whoever's face had slid down it was attached to a collapsed body acting as an impromptu doorstop. She poked her head through the gap. 'Oh, it's you. Can you…? That's it. Thanks.' The gap widened slightly and she stepped through.

Carl looked at Marco. 'Normal?'

Marco nodded, and gulped. 'It went into special measures when I was here, and then there was this whole academy thing, but I don't think it's working.'

'Early days, early days,' said a bright voice from the kettle throng. A woman with vibratingly enthusiastic hair walked towards them, carrying a brim-full steaming pint mug in what appeared to be triumph. 'It's only our second term – Rome wasn't built in a day!' She stuck out her hand. 'Rosalind Banks. Deputy Head. Part of the new Academy management team! You must be the orchestra people Kayla was telling us about! How exciting!'

Carl and Marco each shook her hand, trying not to react to the faces being pulled behind her by the rest of the staff. Marco in particular felt her exclamation marks rain down hard.

'Shouldn't you go and, er—' Carl nodded to where the blurred outline of Kayla could be seen helping Squashed Face from collapsed to vertical.

'An efficient manager delegates!' said Rosalind. 'Kayla is a trusted member of our team and I know she will deal with this effectively.' She beamed at Carl as she walked through the door. Her silhouette stepped daintily round Squashed Face, and she was gone.

When the door had safely clicked shut, a parrot-like chorus of '"An efficient manager delegates!"' broke out, and Carl and Marco turned to see the group of remaining teachers swap eye-rolls and muttered oaths. They all jumped when the door opened again, but relaxed as they saw it was just Kayla returning.

'Sorry about that,' she said, walking towards the kettle again. 'At least it wasn't concussion this time. Oh, Gerald?'

A man standing on his own in the corner was startled away from his cinnamon porridge. 'Mmm?'

'You have Jaden for chemistry next, don't you?'

Gerald nodded. 'Was that him, on the door…?'

'Yeah. Look – just keep an eye on the Bunsen burners, yeah? They've threatened to flamethrower him. And we know how the school jumpers go up.'

Gerald began spooning porridge in more quickly, just as the bell went.

'Right, come on,' said Kayla, to Marco and Carl. 'Coffee. Quick.'

By the time they had made their drinks, the incoming tide of kids had already passed by, so Marco felt safe to walk through the foyer holding a coffee in one hand and his violin case slung over a shoulder. They passed the hall where the orchestra rehearsed on Monday nights, round a few corners of corridors, past banks of lockers and coat hooks, noticeboards and artworks on the walls, until Kayla led them into a classroom half-full of shouting teenagers who were chasing each other round the desks.

Marco looked around. Nothing had changed since he'd been here three years ago. Kayla's bashed-up keyboard still stood by the window, one side propped up with a couple of textbooks because the bottom of one of its legs had been broken off. There were rows of plastic crates along one wall, labelled 'maracas', 'chime bars' and 'recorders'. A bongo pyramid balanced precariously behind the door. His reverie was cut short when a finger cymbal flew through the air like a small metal frisbee and caught the side of his head.

'Ow!' He put his hand up to his face. It came away with a smear of blood.

Carl took a couple of steps towards the kids, who instinctively shrank away from his sheer bulk like a shoal of fish will bend away from a shark.

'Tracie Scott,' said Kayla, a knife edge in her voice without having to shout, 'throw one more thing in my class and I swear you'll be in the Head's office before you take your next breath.'

There was instant silence. Tracie Scott looked half-repentant, half-defiant.

Kayla took a deep breath and addressed the whole room. 'These are the musicians I was telling you about last time, from Stockwell Park Orchestra. Carl, who plays trombone, and Marco, violin. I *had* hoped they might want to play a bit of music for us, and maybe encourage a few of you to go along to the orchestra to see if you like it.' She looked at each of the kids, ending up with Tracie, who shifted her weight from one leg to the other and looked at the floor. 'I wouldn't be at all surprised if they decided to turn round right now and leave. Tracie, do you have anything to say that might change their minds?'

Tracie muttered something to her shoes.

'Pardon?' said Kayla.

Tracie raised her head. 'Sorry, miss.' She looked at the trickle of red on Marco's cheek. 'Sorry. Didn't mean for it to hit ya.'

Marco fished in his pocket for a tissue and wiped the cut. 'That's OK. Quite mild, really. Just like old times.'

'Was you here?' Tracie looked astounded.

'Yeah,' said Marco. 'Feels like I've never been away.' He grinned.

Carl relaxed a bit, and put his trombone case down.

'Marco was one of my most promising pupils,' said Kayla, to the class in general. 'He arrived here as a scrawny twelve-year-old—'

'And left just as scrawny,' said Carl.

The class laughed nervously, not yet knowing if Carl was completely under control.

'Yeah, well, luckily playing the violin doesn't need a whole lot of muscle,' said Kayla. 'And that he *can* do. During the five years he was here, I watched him get better and better – what grade did you get to in the end, Marco?'

'Seven, while I was here,' said Marco, still dabbing at the cut on his face, which was clotting nicely. 'Did grade eight in my first year at college.'

'Well, there you go,' said Kayla. 'And your perseverance was brilliant. Despite the setbacks.'

'What – did the bullies break your arms?' asked Carl, smiling. The class joined in. Kayla folded her arms and flashed a look of concern at Marco.

'Er, no,' said Marco, putting the tissue back in his pocket and straightening his shoulders. 'Just my fingers.'

'Christ,' breathed Carl.

'Anyway, they mended.' Marco waggled his fingers to demonstrate. 'So that's good.'

A murmur of admiration ran through the watching kids.

'So,' said Kayla. 'Moving on. What are you two going to play for us?'

Carl laughed. 'Since there aren't a whole load of trombone/violin duets, we thought we'd give you a couple of solo spots and see where we go from there. Is that OK?'

'Brilliant!' said Kayla, and wandered to the door. She poked her head out, called a few names, and a minute later half a dozen more pupils came filing into the room and sat down as if nothing was amiss. A faint aroma of recent smoke drifted off their clothing.

While Carl got his trombone out of the case, the others arranged themselves around him, some sitting on desks, some on chairs. Tracie crept round the far side, retrieved the finger cymbal, and replaced it in the drawer. Kayla pretended not to notice.

Carl gave a few experimental parps on his trombone, then burrowed around in his case for a couple of mutes. The pixie mute went straight into his bell; the plunger he held in his hand while he started to play 'Over the Rainbow'. He wandered round as he played, not needing any sheet music, and leaned in and around the listening pupils as his phrases wrapped themselves between the tables and chairs. When he reached the repeat of the chorus, he upped the tempo and went into a set of variations. A couple of the people who had come in late started to tap their hands on the desks. Carl raised his eyebrows at them and – frankly – shimmied over so, by the end of the tune, most of the kids were tapping out rhythms on whatever they had nearby, clapping, or moving their feet. Carl brought the whole thing to a close with a virtuosic riff all the way up and down his slide, just to prove the trombone was as dexterous as any other instrument in the right hands.

The class erupted into instant applause as he finished, whooping their appreciation. Kayla grinned and joined in.

'Ta,' said Carl. 'So, who here plays trombone?'

Tracie raised her hand, rather sheepishly.

'Huh. OK. Who else wants to learn now?'

All the hands shot up.

Carl laughed and returned to his case to put his trombone away. 'All yours, mate,' he said to Marco, chuckling. 'See if they're interested in your squeaky twiddling now they've heard a real instrument.'

Chapter 4

And so, the following Monday evening, the orchestra rehearsal was joined by a dozen or so new players. Eliot got there deliberately early, to welcome whoever turned up and try to finesse them into a spot where they might feel comfortable. He knew there were a few established players who were, shall we say, yet to be convinced of the efficacy of his community plan – he had heard as much in the pub – but with David's backing, they had agreed to give it a go.

Erin smiled at Eliot as she arrived.

'What news from the recruitment drive?' he called, as she walked over from the door.

'You mean, did I manage to stop Charlie blowing the place up in some left-wing guerrilla plot?'

'Well, that too.'

Erin stood her cello case on the floor and started shrugging out of her coat. 'He was very well-behaved, considering. Oakdean is seriously weird.'

'I've never been behind the hedge,' confessed Eliot, looking a bit guilty he'd asked her to do it. 'You do hear rumours…'

'Well, once they'd got over their incredulity that a girl can operate under her own free will, they liked what we played, I think. Some of them genuinely sounded as if they wanted to give it a go here. Some others' – Erin stretched one hand out horizontally and tipped it from side to side – 'were a bit iffy, to say the least. There's a strong possibility one of them could turn up with his complete set of viols and insist we do a period performance of Vivaldi or something.'

'Christ,' said Eliot. 'Well, thanks again for doing the outreach thing. I owe you.'

Erin laughed. 'Let's discuss terms after we see what the results are.'

Carl walked in and heard Erin's final remark. 'Ten quid says I get more than you,' he said as he went past. 'Had them eating out of my hand.'

'You didn't threaten them, did you?' said Erin.

'Didn't have to,' said Carl. 'Played them some proper music. It was like being the fucking Pied Piper.'

'Tell me you didn't swear at them,' groaned Eliot.

'I'm not bollocksing stupid.' And with that, Carl was gone.

'I'm beginning to regret sending Carl,' said Eliot, looking at the huge retreating back view of a trombone player who made the rest of them look like hobbits.

'He didn't swear.'

Eliot and Erin turned to see Marco standing next to them.

'He was brilliant, actually,' he went on. 'Got them all joining in and that. Should think a load of them will want to come along. I know at least one trombone, and maybe some string players? Dunno. We decided to leave it open, like you suggested, Eliot.'

'Great stuff,' said Eliot. 'Can't wait to see who turns up.'

More players drifted in, and then a group of kids wearing Sunbridge uniforms were herded into the hall by Kayla, instantly hiking the noise level up by twenty decibels. Tracie carried a beaten-up trombone case; a few others had violin cases, and one was empty-handed.

Kayla made her way over to Eliot, who was standing by the rostrum and therefore looked more like the conductor than anyone else.

'Hi,' she said. 'Are you in charge? I gather from Marco and Carl you're willing to set up some youth auditions?' She lowered her voice. 'Brave man.'

Eliot shook her hand. 'Hi – yes. I'm Eliot. The conductor. Although, now I've said that out loud it does make me sound like a slightly fey Viking warrior.'

Kayla laughed. 'Kayla Edwards. Head of Music here. Or head of what's left of music here, let's be honest. But this lot,' – she gestured at her group protectively – 'this lot are great. And looking forward to this opportunity.'

'And the credits, miss. You said we'd get coursework credits.'

'Yes, Tracie. I did. I promise.'

Eliot raised his eyebrows. Kayla raised her chin.

'Don't knock bribery as a teaching aid till you've tried it,' she said.

Eliot heard the glint in her voice and the years of funding cuts it sharpened itself on. He looked at the Sunbridge kids and grinned. 'Hi, everyone. Welcome to Stockwell Park Orchestra. Thanks for letting us use your hall every week. Why don't we find you all a place to sit and somebody nice to sit next to? Have any of you played in an orchestra before?'

Everybody shook their head.

'Great!' said Eliot. 'That means I'm the best conductor you've ever met. I'm winning already. Now – I can see a few violins – can you go over to Marco and he can sort you out. And you' – he looked at Tracie – 'can sit with Carl. Carl!'

Carl waved from his seat behind the cellos, and Tracie walked round to him, looking apprehensive.

'You didn't bring any finger cymbal ammo, did you?' called Carl as she approached, and she smiled.

'Nah.'

'Good. Over here then.'

'That just leaves… you,' said Eliot, looking at the girl who wasn't carrying anything. 'Where shall we put you?'

'This is Irie,' said Kayla. 'She wants to try out as a percussionist, if that's OK?'

'Of course!' said Eliot. 'Max is just setting up over there, behind Carl and Tracie.'

Irie nodded and walked round the edge of the orchestra to where a percussionist was wheeling timpani into place.

'Fantastic,' said Kayla. 'Thanks so much for this. We just don't have the resources for an orchestra on site here. There are regional things, of course, but competition for those is so high, my kids don't stand much of a chance.'

'Don't thank me yet,' warned Eliot. 'This is an experiment. My idea. Let's hope we can get something off the ground, though, because that would be brilliant. If we can't get local kids interested in us, we'll be pensioned off in a few years and that would be such a shame.'

Erin and Charlie had by that time sat at the front desk of the cello section, and saw the hall doors open behind Eliot. Erin cleared her throat pointedly, and jerked her head. Eliot turned.

What could only be described as a phalanx of Oakdean College boys marched into the hall, led by Dr Irving. Leather-soled shoes slapped their expensive way across the lino. Dr Irving pressed forward towards Eliot, raising his hand and smiling at Erin as he approached. Half a dozen tall adolescent boys lanked behind him in loose two-by-two formation, each wearing a dark wool coat and school scarf. Some of them had patches over one eye. They all carried instrument cases of varying shapes and sizes.

'Christ, here come the cyborgs,' muttered Charlie to Erin.

'Shh,' she hissed back, trying to smile at Dr Irving at the same time.

'Cyclops! I meant Cyclops.'

'Charlie!'

'Though they do have that steampunk vibe about them. Maybe they're part-clockwork.'

Dr Irving came smartly to a halt just short of Eliot, shot his hand out and started pumping Eliot's up and down as if he were trying to crank a vintage car.

'Good evening, good evening,' he cried to the hall in general. 'How wonderful to be here. I have brought my small band of merry boys, as you see.' He flung his left arm behind him to indicate the merriment of his troupe. They turned their faces to him languidly, still imprinted with the bored distaste that had fastened itself on them as they walked through the non-oak-lined Sunbridge foyer. Several of the eyepatches seemed to glitter.

'Lovely to meet you, er—' said Eliot, trying to disentangle his hand from Dr Irving's perpetual motion machine of an arm.

'Dr Irving,' said the man himself, renewing his handshake at double speed now it involved an actual introduction. 'Headmaster of Oakdean College. I've had the pleasure of meeting the delightful Erin before.' He inclined his head towards the cellos. 'And these' – he turned to indicate the boys – 'are some of our highly gifted music scholars.'

'Eliot Yarrow.' Eliot finally achieved separation. 'Welcome. And this is Kayla Edwards, Sunbridge Academy's Head of Music.'

Kayla offered her own hand. 'Hi.'

Dr Irving's gaze swept down to Kayla's Doc Martens, and rose slowly, taking in her preferred choice of teaching uniform: leggings and a comfortable shirt. His smile conveyed a complex mix of stiff politeness and ineffectually camouflaged disdain. 'Charmed, I'm sure.' He clasped her hand, gave it a single shake, and dropped it immediately. The boys behind him sniggered.

'You got off lightly,' whispered Eliot to Kayla, as he massaged his Irving-compressed right hand.

'You think?' said Kayla.

'Yes, well. Let's get this show on the road. Boys!' Eliot smiled at the group behind Dr Irving. 'Welcome. Thank you for coming.'

'Hope it didn't interrupt your swan-plucking evening,' breathed Charlie. He might have said more, but was silenced by a glare from Erin.

'What instruments have we got?' said Eliot.

'Ah, yes.' Dr Irving bustled into action. 'Caspar and Rufus here are violins. Sebastian, viola. Rupert, cello.' He beamed at them and then turned back to Eliot. 'They represent Oakdean's pinnacle of musical achievement, carrying on our fine tradition of developing sensitive chamber music players. Last summer they embarked on a tour of the Far East, playing at a number of our most prestigious foreign embassies. To myriad ambassadors, indeed – isn't that right, Caspar?'

Caspar turned his head so his one eye faced directly at Eliot. 'Yah. A little trip we put together. Sort of ad hoc arrangement. Seemed to go down pretty well, actually.' Eliot smiled politely through Caspar's speech, nodding and trying to catch the odd word as it flashed past without the usual signposts of consonants or vowel change. His comprehension wasn't helped by copious and ill-concealed ripples of laughter emanating from the orchestra. Even Kayla's lips were twitching.

Caspar flicked his head back to get his floppy hair out of his face, which was odd because it had only been covering the eyepatch. He ran his hand through it anyway.

'And here we have Tarquin, who plays the French horn,' Dr Irving said.

The laughter threatened to erupt again.

'OK – if you guys want to make your way over to the relevant section, and we'll find you a seat,' said Eliot, 'that would be great. And that leaves…?'

'Hector, on the trumpet,' said Dr Irving.

Charlie and Erin seemed to find something incredibly interesting on the floor under their stand, and leaned down to inspect it together, their shoulders shaking.

'Right,' said Eliot, trying to keep a straight face, and turned to the brass sections. 'Extra horn and trumpet coming through! Be nice. Find a seat for them.'

'Marvellous, marvellous.' Dr Irving beamed. 'I hope you don't mind me staying to listen, do you? Keep an eye, you know.'

Eliot nodded.

'Just the one,' said Charlie. 'Ow!'

'Behave,' mouthed Erin.

'And Kayla – are you sticking around?' said Eliot.

'Of course!' said Kayla. 'Usually I have to stop Tracie doing anything stupid, but it looks as if Carl has got everything under control, so I can relax.'

'I've seen Carl in action,' said Eliot, 'and, believe me, nobody does anything stupid around him. Well, not twice, anyway.'

The orchestra shuffled seats and made room, and finally everyone was sitting down and facing more or less the right way. Dr Irving took a chair and placed it in front of the violins, where he commanded a good view of Caspar and Rufus. Kayla sat on the other side of the hall, near to where Tracie sat with Carl in the trombone section.

Eliot spread his arms wide.

'Hello, everyone, and a huge welcome to our guests. As you'll see from the music on your stands, we're going to play Sibelius 2 this evening. I chose it because it has some cracking tunes, loads of parts for extra trumpets and trombones and, for anyone who hasn't played it before' – he smiled at the Sunbridge pupils – 'the key signature isn't particularly scary. D major. A friendly key. I thought we could sight-read straight through this before the break, and see how we go. If you have a new person sitting next to you and they get lost, give them a bit of help, won't you? I'll stop if it gets hopeless, but if we can plough on that would be great. How are we sorting brass parts?'

Neema, the first horn player, put her thumb up. 'Tarquin is bumping my part to start off with.'

'Second trombone assistant good to go,' called Carl, grinning at Tracie.

'Great,' said Eliot. 'And I can see our violins are flourishing – brilliant.' Caspar and Rufus exchanged a pained glance from their respective seats in the first and seconds. They had each been seated next to a Sunbridge violinist, who were wide-eyed and sitting on the very front edge of their chairs. Marco gave them an encouraging nod.

'And violas – all OK?' said Eliot.

Pearl called from her place on the back viola desk. 'Plenty of room here, yes. We've tucked Sebastian here in front of us. And I can still nip out before the break to check the urn's up to temp.'

A muted cheer rose from the orchestra in general. Pearl's role was never underappreciated.

'And we've given Rupert to Ann,' said Erin conversationally, turning round to give a cheery wave to Ann at the back of the cello section. Ann's lips twitched. She gave a brief hint of raised eyebrows but it disappeared before Rupert looked at her.

'Great,' said Eliot. 'Off we go, then.'

He raised his baton, gave an empty bar to show the pulse, and the strings set off in the triple-time, easy lolloping way Sibelius 2 begins, like a cowboy on horseback appearing over the horizon, only more Scandi. The whole orchestra set off as if it were cantering a dragon along a frozen fjord towards the adventures Sibelius had planned up ahead.

Chapter 5

As she had promised, ten minutes before the break Pearl slipped out through the viola section to fulfil urn duties, turning sideways between the busy *tremolo* bows as if that would somehow make her Rubenesque figure fit through a smaller gap. Pete, her desk partner, was scrunched forward on his chair, frowning at the music. He had reached the stage in the piece where he moved his viola from side to side while keeping his bow relatively still: always a sign he was nearing exhaustion. The trumpets blasted triumphant chords over the whole string section, who were valiantly scrubbing out their *fortissimo tremolo* because composers enjoy combining a full upper body workout for the strings while pointing out casually that the brass can scythe through that scrub with a couple of lungfuls of raspberry-blowing.

Max was letting Irie have a terrific go on the timpani in the last movement: he had put her in sole charge of one drum, with the simple instruction to whack it as hard and fast as she could with both her sticks whenever he pointed at her, and stop when he stopped pointing. She stood with her feet planted square, grinning hugely, her eyes glued to Max. She was a slight girl, dwarfed by the enormous drum in front of her, but attacked her task with such determination amid the deafening slab of noise of an orchestra at full throttle that Eliot turned to catch Kayla's eye, grinning. Kayla grinned back, and put both thumbs up.

As the final chords thumped out, Pearl was already pouring the first coffees and opening packets of biscuits.

'Well done!' said Eliot, beaming at everyone. 'And I hope that gave an idea to our newer players of how the piece goes. I think we all made it to the double bar together, just about. Congratulations!'

There were smiles and small pockets of applause and congratulatory nods all round, as the players started to lay their instruments down temporarily in open cases and drift along the corridor towards coffee.

Eliot walked over to Kayla, who was still smiling.

'At the risk of coming over all Brucie, didn't they do well?' he said.

'They did! I could see a couple of them get lost a few times, but considering that's the first time any of them have had any orchestral experience, I think they did brilliantly.'

Eliot nodded to where Irie was having an extra lesson from Max on how to do a drum roll on the timpani. 'She's hooked already. I was thinking of playing *Night on the Bare Mountain* this term too, as it has loads of brass and an insane amount of percussion in it. Irie will enjoy that.'

An insistent fluttering of applause approached, and they turned to see Dr Irving strut towards them while clapping high above his right shoulder, as if he were executing a paso doble. He, for once, said nothing, apparently preferring to convey his enthusiasm through the medium of dance.

'Not bad, was it?' said Eliot, resisting the urge to bunch up the lower part of his jersey and flamenco the other way.

Dr Irving let his arms fall to his sides. 'If I may say so, that was a fine attempt at one of the great symphonies. A fine attempt. Enhanced, I might add, by our Oakdean *miracula*

42

musicorum.' He glanced at Kayla. 'I'm sure Caspar and Rufus showed your... protégés the musical ropes.'

Eliot wondered, not quite for the first time that evening, if his plan had been a good idea after all. 'Er – I saw a lot of hard work going on in all sections,' he said hastily, as he saw Kayla's chin rise. 'Shall we have a coffee? I'm parched.'

He walked out of the hall between them, trying to keep the conversation on a non-confrontational footing.

'Caspar is a great talent,' Dr Irving continued. 'A *great* talent. I shouldn't be in the least surprised if he chose to insert himself into the musical field, post-academia, so to speak. Perhaps a *concerto grosso* might lend itself to the programme this term? To hear Erin's Stradivarius played once more, now that—'

'Well, I'm not sure how much flexibility we have with our programme this season,' said Eliot.

They had by then reached the queue for the coffee. Erin herself was in front of them, and turned to meet Eliot's eyes as she overheard.

'Ah! The delightful Erin herself!' purred Dr Irving. 'I was just intimating to Eliot how—'

'Well, I wouldn't want to hog the limelight for two concerts on the trot,' she said quickly. 'After all, this isn't what Eliot's outreach programme is for. Wouldn't you agree, Kayla?'

'I would,' said Kayla. 'At the moment, I'm just grateful to you lot for giving us this opportunity. Although, also, I wouldn't mind paying good money to know where Pearl keeps her urn during the week and how much money I'd have to give her for sub-letting rights.'

'That,' said Eliot gravely, 'would be more than my baton is worth to divulge.'

They kept pace with the slow swirl of musicians eddying towards caffeine, picked up their cups and allotted two biscuits (ginger nut/plain digestive combo that evening), and peeled off to let the efficient refreshment of an entire orchestra of sixty-odd players continue. Kayla ended up next to Erin, Charlie and Marco. They stood in the foyer amid knots of other people, blowing steam off their coffees to try to bring them down to a drinkable temperature within the next ten minutes.

'This outreach thing of Eliot's is great,' said Kayla, 'but – and I'm not trying to upset any apple carts here – do the Oakdean boys need any exposure to orchestral playing? From what I've heard, they do a lot within their school as it is.'

Charlie swallowed a mouthful too quickly, and nodded through the pain of a mildly scalded throat as he replied. 'Christ, yes. Erin and I did the visit. Well, Erin made me go—'

'I did not!' said Erin. 'You volunteered. I just made you promise not to be a socialist revolutionary while you were there.'

'Yeah, well,' continued Charlie, ignoring her, 'Irving was all over me when he thought I had the Strad. I think it hit him hard that a frail lady could be responsible for that kind of instrument. It was like visiting the 1950s.'

'I don't think they get much opportunity to talk to women,' said Erin. 'Poor loves.'

'Or anyone who isn't white,' said Kayla. 'And what's with the eyepatches?'

'Fuck knows,' said Charlie. 'We should maybe ask David – his son goes to the Oakdean junior section. To be trained up in the ways of our one-eyed, overcoat-wearing overlords.'

'Let's hope he doesn't have to donate an eye,' said Erin, but then decided to change the subject. 'What do you play, Kayla? Must be something, if you're Head of Music. Fancy joining us too?'

'Ha! Well, I'll see how my lot cope with this evening first. I'm a keyboard player really, but a bit of double bass too. Mostly jazz, but I know how to hold a bow if required.'

'Well, we could definitely do with you adding some oomph to the basses in that Sibelius,' said Charlie. 'Bit of support down there. We've only got two regulars. One of them decided to take it up when he retired last year. The other one's even older and can barely see the music on the stand.'

'Charlie!' said Erin, jabbing her head sideways towards both bass players standing nearby.

'It's OK,' said Charlie. 'Their hearing isn't what it was either.' He looked at Kayla. 'You can see why we need new blood.'

'You're not really selling the section to me, though.'

'Ah. Yes. Point taken. But you get to chat to Ann at the back of the cellos. She's good value. But then you have to sit next to Carl. Swings and roundabouts.'

The players began to go back to the hall, some surreptitiously carrying half-full cups to hide under their chairs for the second half. The orchestra had received stern letters from the school caretaker about coffee spills, and David had forbidden any unlidded cups in the hall. The bond between a musician and their hot beverage is a strong one, however, and so long as they kept it out of sight of David's place at the end of the row of horns, they carried on sneaking them in, reasoning that since the brass regularly left little puddles after rehearsals from emptying out all their curly plumbing, the occasional drip of coffee wouldn't do any harm. There is a difference between mopping distilled water and a sugar solution, though, and the caretaker was close to Having Words.

As people settled in their seats, chatting, and began to ready their instruments, they heard Pearl's voice call from the corridor.

'Oh! Who's got… where's the…?'

The squeak of her sensible shoes hurried to the hall doors, and her worried face peered round, searching for David. She bustled round Eliot's back and whispered to David as he was blowing warm air silently through his horn to warm it up. His eyebrows lowered into a frown as he listened. Then he stood, rested his horn carefully on his seat, and together they walked out of the hall.

Eliot raised his eyebrows and shrugged. 'Shall we do a bit of work on the first movement? Cellos, I want a real sense of forward motion when we start, so get some momentum going in those pulsed bows – oh, hello! Is there a problem?'

Pearl and David had appeared next to him.

'There could be,' said David, cautiously.

'The basket is empty,' explained Pearl. When Eliot's face did not immediately register his understanding of this concise description of the disaster, she tried again. 'The little wicker-type basket with the money, by the urn? Well, it's plastic really, but looks like wicker. I got it from that pub that was selling off a load after they'd over-ordered for their chicken-in-a-baskets. People are tofu burgering now, apparently. Anyway, yes. People drop their money in for the coffees and teas and biscuits and whatnot, and, well. It was full. And now it's empty.'

'Oh. I see,' said Eliot, who had waited politely until she had finished. 'Um – could this wait until later?'

David cleared his throat. 'I thought perhaps we could enquire if anyone had – tidied it away for us?'

Murmurings began to spread through the orchestra.

'What's happened?' Tarquin asked from the horns.

'Someone's nabbed Coffee Lady's funds by the sound of it,' said Caspar, just in front of him, in what he perhaps hoped was a subtle whisper but came out as a fully projected sneer on account of the fact this was the only way he knew how to speak.

'It'll be one of the Sunbridge oiks,' said Rufus, over the head of one of the Sunbridge oiks sitting next to him, who was called Danilo.

'Fuck off,' said Danilo.

'Uncouth as well as light-fingered,' said Caspar. 'Typical.'

'You can fuck off too,' added Marina, who was next to Caspar. 'You posh gits are all the same—'

'Before this discussion escalates,' called Eliot, 'perhaps we could establish some facts? David and Pearl have a small announcement.'

The argument at the back of the violins mutated into silent, jabbing gestures. Gwynneth (first oboe) and Carl, who were fluent in sign language and often carried on long-distance conversations during rehearsals, were impressed at the potential shown by the novices.

'Ah, yes,' said David. 'Sorry to delay the rehearsal. Pearl wondered if any of you had, ah, relocated the basket of coffee money?' He put his hand up to his eye and hoped his tic wasn't about to restart.

'I would appreciate it,' said Pearl, 'because although many hands do make light work, I think this could be a case of too many cooks spoiling the broth.'

The orchestra digested this metaphor mélange politely.

'Nobody?' said David, looking carefully at the air above all the teenagers in turn, not catching anyone's eye. 'It would be a great help to know if it was tidied away, that's all.'

Kayla glared at Tracie, but was met with a wide-eyed shrug.

Dr Irving folded his arms and looked pointedly at each of the Sunbridge pupils.

The silence dragged out.

'Well,' said Eliot eventually, 'perhaps we could crack on now, and if anyone remembers putting it anywhere they could let Pearl or David know at the end. How's that?'

'Of course,' said Rafael (second bassoon and Stockwell Park Orchestra treasurer), 'Pearl operates her catering budget independently of the main orchestra finances. Any loss incurred could necessitate a restriction of provision downstream.'

'You mean no coffee next week?' said Carl. 'Bollocks to that.'

The whole orchestra stirred in alarm.

'And I had hoped it might have been a custard cream week,' said Pearl, sadly. 'I do try to rotate them in, if funds allow.'

They rehearsed the Sibelius in a rather preoccupied way for the rest of the evening. Caspar and Rufus exchanged looks over the heads of the Sunbridge violinists. Tarquin, in the horns, shot accusing glances over at Tracie playing trombone, until Carl spotted him doing it and bristled so protectively Tarquin shrank down next to Neema; she wondered why he was practically in her armpit during their next chord.

It felt like a long time before they got to the pub.

'You regretting this idea?' Charlie asked Eliot, as they settled themselves round a table in the corner. 'Have we let a load of street urchins loose and soon we'll find all our pocket kerchiefs turning up in Victorian novels?'

Eliot took a long swallow from his pint, smiling. 'Not yet. But it's a shame that happened tonight. Wonder who did it.'

'Maybe Pearl has just mislaid the money,' said Erin. 'You know, stashed it underneath some spare packs of digestives in that Mary Poppins carpet bag she's got.'

'Unlikely,' said Charlie. 'She is the world's most reliable purveyor of beverage/biscuit combos. Never seen her taken by surprise. Even when we had those extra singers a few years ago for *Carmina Burana* and they turned out to be on a vegan retreat or something and she had to source organic non-dairy carrot cake at a moment's notice.'

Eliot looked impressed.

'What we need is an undercover cop,' said Ann.

'I don't think we can draw on Her Majesty's forces to locate a bit of loose change,' said Erin.

'I don't want it to fester, though,' said Eliot. 'The kids won't want to come back if they all think we think they're criminals.'

'Team Cyclops won't worry,' said Charlie. 'They won't have doubted their right to be anywhere, ever.'

They laughed into their drinks.

'You couldn't have picked two more different schools if you'd tried,' said Ann. 'Maybe we should have done them one at a time.'

'Nonsense,' said Eliot briskly. 'It's good for us all to mix it up a bit. Nobody learns anything if you never step out of your little circle.'

'Thank you for that inspirational TED Talk,' said Charlie. 'In fact, I wouldn't be surprised if the Cyclopses nicked the money themselves to frame the Sunbridge kids.'

'Thought you were going to work on that reverse snobbery of yours,' said Erin.

'And stop calling them Cyclops,' said Eliot. 'It's bad enough trying to get their attention as it is – don't make me laugh at them too. I can flail around as much as I like, but if I'm on their eyepatch side, there's no way their peripheral vision can pick me up.'

'You'd think they could organise the ones with missing left eyes to play violin, and right eyes to play cello, at least,' said Charlie. 'They'd stand a chance then.'

'There was that policeman who found Fenella's Strad,' said Ann, ignoring Charlie. 'He came to the concert, remember? Seemed very nice.'

'Yes, he came up to speak to me afterwards,' said Erin.

'Along with the rest of the audience,' said Eliot. 'Rightly so. What a performance. How is Fenella, by the way? Have you heard from her?'

'Not much. She keeps a check on how I'm looking after the Strad, of course. She's gone to stay with her mother until the physio rehab's finished on her wrist.'

'And the policeman?' said Ann.

Erin smiled. 'Yeah. Noel Osmar. We had a good chat, actually. It was the very first time he'd ever gone to a classical concert.'

'Well, he's not going to pop along to check out our petty cash mystery,' said Charlie. 'It's hardly 999-level crime.'

'No, you're right,' said Erin. 'We'll have to sort this ourselves. Although he did give me his card…'

'Aye aye,' said Charlie, raising his eyebrows. 'Steady on, girl. You've only just got rid of Conductor Whose Name We Must Never Mention Again—'

'Charlie!' said Ann quickly. 'As if it's any of your business.'

Erin blushed, and drank her beer. Eliot watched this exchange with a bemused expression.

'It's complicated,' said Erin.

'Too right,' said Charlie.

'Zip it,' said Ann.

'Anyway,' said Erin, glaring at Charlie, 'did I hear we're going to do *Night on the Bare Mountain* this term?'

'Yep,' said Eliot. 'If I can get a team of three trombones and a tuba together. I'm hoping that with some of these extras we can cobble together a full section. That girl Carl took under his wing this evening looked like a decent player. And we'll need loads of percussion. Did you see that tiny girl – Irie, I think – knocking six bells out of the timp? She was brilliant.'

'Doesn't that have harp in it too?' asked Ann.

The other players shifted in their seats uneasily. Eliot looked around, suddenly nervous and wondering if his enthusiasm would be revealed to be premature.

'Er – yes,' he said. 'Should I be worried about that? Don't we have a tame harpist on tap? You must have done repertoire needing one before?'

'Oh, we have,' said Ann. The others sniggered.

'Don't worry,' said Charlie, patting Eliot on the shoulder. 'We all saw the wonders you worked on Mrs Ford-Hughes. You'll be fine.'

Despite being pressed by Eliot, they refused to reveal any more details about the mystery harpist, and resolutely talked of other things until closing time.

Chapter 6

Before the following week's rehearsal, Eliot got a text from Kayla Edwards. He called her back, because he had never met Sunbridge Academy's new Deputy Head, Rosalind Banks, and didn't appreciate what an all-caps 'BEWARE: ROSALIND WILL AMBUSH YOU NEXT WEEK!' implied.

'Hi, Kayla. Eliot here. Um – thanks for the ambush heads-up. What kind are we talking here? Bear pits? Piranha tanks? "Pleased to meet you, Mr Bond" type of thing?'

Kayla snorted down the line. 'Yeah, sorry. It did sound a bit melodramatic. Though, if you'd met her, not so much. Ask Marco. She's part of this new management team here, and is hell-bent on dragging Sunbridge's reputation up – which I'm not against, don't get me wrong. But, you know, it's a bit beanbag-heavy. We've got acres of new glass and she makes damn sure that's polished. The stuff visitors and governors don't see – not so much. And the staff who've been here since whenever? We don't exactly register on her radar.'

'Ah. Gotcha.'

'Very fond of management-speak. Problems as opportunities, and all that. And a noticeboard full of Comic Sans, for God's sake.'

'Heavens. So what does she want from us?'

'Well, you know, orchestral placements for our talented kids will look really good on a glossy brochure. And she mentioned at the last heads of department team meeting that she wanted to host your concert here this term, and invite the governors along.'

Eliot processed this information silently. He was standing at his sitting room window, a Victorian bay looking out onto the street in a terrace of identical houses. His flat was on the first floor, and he was level with the anti-pigeon spikes on the street lights. An old helium balloon and ribbon had caught in the spikes closest to his window months before. It still flapped its deflated festivities in any passing breeze.

'Do you know, that might not be such a bad idea, though,' he said. 'I mean, I'm not sure how far we can endorse any glossy brochure she wants to use to sell Sunbridge, but I can easily divert her to David or Rafael to talk the technical stuff with her. But maybe having the concert in your hall instead of our usual civic hall booking – that might be great. Embed ourselves in the community and all that. That *was* my idea, after all.'

'And a brilliant one,' said Kayla. 'I just wanted to let you know about the Rosalind pounce. You know, pre-pounce.'

Eliot laughed. 'Yeah, thanks.'

'And, having met the Oakdean headmaster, I'm not sure how he's going to react to his boys slumming it with us and Sunbridge taking all the glory.'

'Oh bugger, you're right. Shit.'

'You're gonna have to get far more Machiavellian if you're going to make it in this cut-throat world.'

'You're right. It's not all waving my arms around, is it?'

'Try sitting in on some of our management meetings. You'd pick it up fast.'

The Sunbridge bell sounded, and Eliot could hear thundering feet even down the phone.

'OK, look – I'd better let you go. Thanks for the info. I'll get my head round it and maybe run things past David.'

'Cool. See you.'

True to Kayla's prophecy, Eliot was waylaid in the foyer by Rosalind Banks as soon as he arrived, early, for the next rehearsal. She saw him through the glass wall of the admin office where she had been specifically hovering, and burst through the door, practically skittering round the corner in her heels – hair and lanyard all aquiver.

'Mr Yarrow! May I have a quick word, if you have a moment?'

Eliot stopped walking and watched her approach, breathing a silent prayer of thanks to Kayla for her warning. Rosalind clicked rapidly towards him over the lino, her high heels bringing her face about level with Eliot's shoulder. What she lacked in height she made up for in hair and exclamation marks.

'Call me Eliot, please,' he said, holding out his hand. There was no point in ruffling any feathers that could be smoothed.

'Eliot!' Rosalind chirruped, shaking it. 'How lovely! Rosalind Banks. Deputy Head here at Sunbridge Academy. I wanted to extend you a welcome in person, and to convey our good wishes, on behalf of the whole Senior Management Team! We – the SMT – think it's wonderful what you are doing this term!'

Eliot smiled. 'Thank you. I hoped my outreach idea might spread our net a bit wider. Not that I've been with the orchestra that long – did you know my predecessor, Joshua?'

Rosalind disengaged her hand and looked serious. 'I did not. I gather his association was abruptly terminated. Though in fact I had not made his acquaintance in person.'

'So you don't usually hang around for our rehearsals, then?' Eliot was rather enjoying himself. 'Didn't think I'd seen any of the management team – senior or junior – lurking around this late before.' He smiled broadly, to diffuse the meaning of the words he had actually said.

'A good manager is judged by outcomes, not process!' she said, almost standing to attention.

'Of course. I didn't mean—'

'No, no. Of course.'

There was a small pause. Rosalind fiddled with her lanyard coquettishly. Eliot nodded and began to saunter towards the hall as other players drifted in. Rosalind squeaked and accelerated to his side once more.

'Mr Yarrow – Eliot? – if I may proffer a suggestion?'

'Yes?'

'Well, it's more of an offer really! We would like to make our hall available for your forthcoming concert. The SMT thought it could illustrate your orchestra's deep roots in the community, and concomitantly provide synergies for our developing mission statement!'

Her regression into management-speak was like someone's accent slipping back into their natural rhythms. Eliot realised that Rosalind spoke fluent corporate jargon, and only managed to overlay it with less stilted phrases with conscious will. It was as if a robot had just given away its true identity. If it were not for the exclamation marks mooring her to other humans, she would have floated free long before.

He carried on ambling towards the hall, with renewed admiration for Kayla's fortitude.

'Free of charge, naturally!' Rosalind's voice was dangerously close to a yodel.

'Well, that's a very generous offer,' he said. 'Thank you. It might depend on seating capacity and what-have-you – I'll ask David about it, if I may? He's the orchestra's manager and deals with all the technical detail that I can't get my tiny musician's brain around.'

Players were staring as Eliot and Rosalind approached the hall doors, close enough to catch the end of their conversation. Kayla was already talking to Carl and Tracie over by the trombones. She caught Eliot's eye as he came through the door, and pulled a mock grimace. Rosalind stopped short of entering the hall, as if a forcefield prevented her from travelling too far from the admin hub. She nodded at Eliot, smiled, and clacked back to her office, just as the marching feet of approaching Oakdean players echoed through the foyer. Carl chose to warm up his trombone at that moment by playing 'The Imperial March' from *Star Wars* in tempo perfectly matching the Oakdean strides, so when they swept through the doors into the hall they were greeted by an entire room full of corpsing musicians.

Dr Irving was again at the head of the pack, apparently feeling he ought to shepherd his charges the couple of hundred yards down the road in person, like the most un-street urban gang leader imaginable. He gestured to his troops that they could lose the formation, while Carl meandered his warm-up into less recognisable arpeggios.

Kayla walked over to Eliot, rosining her double bass bow. 'I see Rosalind caught you. Did she run the SMT's plan up the virtual flagpole to see which way the winds of opinion were blowing?'

Eliot laughed. 'She did indeed. Thanks for the heads-up. It's not such a bad idea, though, holding the concert here.' He looked at Kayla's bow with interest. 'Are you going to play? Fantastic.'

Kayla was about to reply, but saw Dr Irving draw himself up to his full height of 5'7" behind Eliot's shoulder, his face flushing into one spot of high colour on each cheek. They both heard his signature throat clearance. Eliot turned around.

'Holding the concert here? Did I interpret that small conversational vignette correctly?' He twitched his mouth into a smile and raised his eyebrows. The red on his cheeks intensified. 'I attended tonight's rehearsal with the express wish of conveying our offer of hospitality for that very same event. For what orchestra would not sound better in the acoustics of our Old Hall? The panelling alone—'

'Um – nothing has been decided yet,' said Eliot. 'Sunbridge merely thought that—'

'Yes, well, we all know the capacity of thought contained within the Sunbridge perimeter,' purred Dr Irving. 'However, the rich history and tradition of—'

'One-eyed toffs,' said Kayla quietly.

Eliot stifled a giggle. 'Look, Dr Irving, honestly, I'm not the one who'll be making this kind of logistical decision.' He turned sideways to Kayla and whispered, 'Thank God.' Facing Dr Irving again, he continued, 'David, our manager, will I'm sure be very happy to know we have two such generous offers. Ah – David! Over here?'

David, on his way from the hall door to the horns, diverted.

'Um – just a small pre-rehearsal heads-up,' said Eliot, widening his eyes at David and hoping to convey that it was neither small nor able to be contained as a pre-rehearsal blip. 'In the last five minutes I have been the happy recipient of not one but two offers of venue for this term's concert. I don't know how far ahead our Civic Hall plans are fixed irretrievably, but Sunbridge have said we can use this hall for free if we like.'

David looked from Eliot, whose lips were twitching in amusement, to the ramrod-backed, slightly quivering Dr Irving, and then to Kayla, who was rosining her bow with an energy fuelled by pent-up class struggle. David felt his cheek almost twitch as his old tic stirred, and put his hand up to calm it. Surely he was due an easy concert. Two in a row with sky-high cortisone levels just wasn't fair.

'Naturally, the Oakdean College facilities would be absolutely complimentary, to extend our long and well-resourced arm into the community,' said Dr Irving, adjusting his eyepatch with one hand. 'I just wanted to make that clear.' He drew a neatly folded handkerchief from his jacket pocket and dabbed at the corners of his mouth, which had collected white flecks of excited spittle.

'I reckon that bow's done, don't you?' said Eliot to Kayla.

She stopped rosining, and smiled. 'Yeah, probably.'

David sighed. 'Well, thank you to Oakdean and Sunbridge for their most generous offers.' Dr Irving bowed slightly.

'It's a management thing,' said Kayla, shrugging.

'I'll take it to the committee and I'm sure we can come to an appropriate decision,' said David. 'Meanwhile, shall we…?' He wandered off towards the horns again, and Eliot began to wriggle out of his coat and find his baton.

Kayla returned to the bass section, where she was greeted by Ann on the back desk of the cellos, and cheery waves from Charlie and Erin at the front.

Dr Irving remained at Eliot's side.

'Was there something else?' asked Eliot, laying his coat over the back of a chair.

'Yes. A small addition to the portfolio of advantages Oakdean can perhaps offer.' Dr Irving leant conspiratorially towards Eliot. 'I'm not sure if you are aware of the connection our institution has with Sir Marmaduke Blythe?'

'The composer?'

'Indeed.' Dr Irving smiled. 'Young Tarquin over there' – he gestured to the horns – 'is in the delightful position of having Sir Marmaduke as a godparent. We have been graced on several occasions with his presence at opportune events at Oakdean. Indeed, last summer, we were fortunate enough to secure a visit from him at our Speech Day. He delivered a most affecting address. And, of course, wrote an original bagatelle for our senior orchestra.'

'Of course,' murmured Eliot. 'How marvellous.'

'Needless to say,' continued Dr Irving, somehow finding the need to say it anyway, 'should the concert find its happy way to the Oakdean Old Hall, I am convinced that Sir Marmaduke would be delighted to contribute in any way he can.'

'Well, thank you,' said Eliot, trying to move away from Dr Irving as he heard the orchestra getting restless. The rehearsal was late starting, and patience was wearing thin. 'I'll certainly pass this new information on to David, and he'll be in touch.'

Dr Irving bowed once more, and turned to sit on one of the chairs around the perimeter of the hall. He nodded at Tarquin on his way, who looked triumphant.

'Hello, everyone,' said Eliot, putting his scores on his stand and opening one, pressing his hand along the spine to make the pages sit flat. 'We thought after last week's fantastic read-through of the Sibelius, we could have a look at *Night on the Bare Mountain*. Because we have all you guys along to help us,' – he beamed at the visiting schoolkids – 'we'd get something that makes you earn your keep and should be good fun to play. We've got three trombone parts in this, so, Tracie, you get one of your own this time!'

Carl gave a confident thumbs up, and grinned at Tracie next to him. She looked nervous, but pleased.

'And there's a shedload of percussion too,' said Eliot. 'As well as the timps, we've got tubular bells, cymbals, drums and a tamtam, so we'll keep Irie busy too.'

'I can't play them all!' whispered Irie to Max.

'Don't worry,' he whispered back. 'I'll help.'

'We haven't got a harpist with us this week,' said Eliot, trying to ignore the ripple of sniggering that went round the players.

'I think David's lined one up for nearer the concert – is that right, David?'

'Yes,' called David. 'All sorted.'

'Oh, and before we crack on – sorry, I know we're late already – I just wanted to suggest we could do a special piece for this concert, using our guest artists.'

The guest artists perked up and listened attentively. Some of the Sunbridge ones even stopped chewing their gum for a moment.

'What about something like *Fanfare for the Common Man* to kick the whole thing off?' asked Eliot. 'That has three trumpets and three trombones, four horns and a tuba, plus a load of percussion again. And it will knock the audience's socks, and possibly ears, off. What do you reckon?'

The brass and percussion sections cheered. The strings and wind were split between those who enjoyed sitting a piece out, and those who resented sharing the limelight. Caspar and Rufus in the violins seemed especially disgruntled and glared at Dr Irving. He nodded at them and made 'calm down' gestures with the flat of his palms, indicating that plans might very well already be afoot in that area.

Gwynneth raised her hand. 'Is this a spontaneous idea, or… you know, only I know Rafael and David have spreadsheets and things.' Her Welsh accent wrapped itself around the word 'spreadsheets' like fog round a damp washing line in Merthyr Tydfil.

'Don't worry,' said Eliot. 'I've already run it past the committee. I'm not springing a mutiny.'

Pearl, the third member of that committee, and the one Gwynneth hadn't mentioned, nodded busily from the back of the violas. If there was one thing Pearl could do with utter competence (as well as providing coffee and biscuits), it was nodding enthusiastically when she heard other people's ideas.

It was what made her an ideal committee member. You can't have a roomful of Chairs. Underlings are the oil in the cogs of industry. Or, in Pearl's case, the full-fat milk in the flat whites of musicians, as she liked to think of it. Pearl's was not the steadiest mind in which to store metaphor, but it was one of the most inventive.

She made a mental note to prepare for superfluous strings and wind during future *Fanfare* rehearsals. An unemployed orchestral player is one in need of an extra cuppa.

Chapter 7

Later that evening, the pub was busier than usual. Erin, Ann, Charlie and Kayla had commandeered a corner table they could stash cello cases next to without obstructing the whole room. Since Kayla kept her bass in her Sunbridge teaching room, she was travelling light. Eliot fought his way to the bar to get the first round in, but Carl and the other trombone players were in front of him. Eliot wisely hung back behind the wall of muscle that was the trombone section at play, and made way for them as they turned, each cradling three full pints. They were great advocates of time and motion studies.

By the time he got to their table with the drinks, the conversation was already trying to make sense of the evening's events.

'That's twice now. I think if the cash goes missing again after this, Pearl will really have a breakdown.' Charlie shook his head. 'She was distraught tonight.'

'But it's not just that,' said Ann. 'My spare strings. A whole set – they were in my case.'

'And I know I haven't been bringing the Strad to orchestra – I mean, that's a bit of overkill,' said Erin. 'But I can't even think of it now.'

'I feel awful about this,' said Kayla. 'Hope to God it's not any of my kids. I mean, there are a few you wouldn't trust as far as you could spit, but I reckoned the ones I'd actually got to come along were OK.'

'Drinks!' said Eliot, piloting the tray onto the table from above their heads. 'Any breakthroughs in the mystery disappearances?'

'Don't take the piss, Eliot,' said Erin. 'Ann's strings were worth about two hundred quid.'

'Fucking hell,' said Kayla. 'Really?'

Erin nodded.

'I don't understand,' said Ann. 'It took a week from nicking some loose change to swiping a full set of spare strings. I mean, that's pretty specific swag. They must know someone to get rid of them, otherwise it's just nicking for the hell of it. And it's a pretty strange thing to go for.'

They all drank as Eliot sat down at the table and opened a couple of bags of crisps.

'Is it the kids, do we think?' he asked nobody in particular. 'If so, I'm a prize mug for inviting them along in the first place. I thought I was doing some good.'

'You are,' said Kayla. 'And if it turns out to be any of mine, they'll be paying for it for as long as it takes, believe me.'

'Well, it's a weird coincidence if it isn't,' said Charlie. 'I mean,' – he turned to Kayla – 'sorry, but it is.'

'I know, I know,' said Kayla miserably.

'In which case,' said Ann, 'I mean, not that we're assuming Eliot is a prize mug, you understand' – she smiled at him – 'but which kids? The posh, rich, *Lord of the Flies* types, or the free school meals lot?'

'Who knows,' said Erin.

'We were all out drinking coffee in the break,' said Charlie. 'Nobody was on guard.'

'Nobody thought we needed to be on guard,' said Erin.

'Ah… bollocks,' said Eliot. 'This isn't going to work, is it? And I really wanted it to.'

'I knew it was too good to last,' said Kayla.

'Hang on,' said Ann. They all straightened and gave her their full attention. She put her pint down on the table. 'It can't have been one thief, though. My strings were taken – I guess – in the break while we were in the foyer having coffee.'

'And rich tea biscuits,' said Charlie sadly. 'Pearl did say there weren't going to be any custard creams for a while.'

'Shut up, Charlie,' said Erin. 'Go on, Ann.'

'And then, when we were all back in the hall getting ready to play, Pearl's money was nicked.'

'Were they all there, though?' asked Eliot. 'I wasn't ticking them off a list. And I couldn't swear they were all back in the hall promptly.'

'And I didn't notice either,' said Kayla.

'Damn,' said Ann. 'I thought I was doing some proper detecting then.'

They slumped back in their seats and drank mournfully. The noise level from the trombones' table rose: they had reached their third pint.

'What we need,' said Ann, 'is something to be nicked from the trombones, and then we'd have a ready-made vigilante force at our disposal.'

'Yeah – having seen what Carl is capable of, I wouldn't mess,' said Eliot, who had witnessed Carl's efficient ejection of his drunk and belligerent predecessor the day of the previous concert.

They all drank in silence. Around them, the pub was its usual mix of half-musician, half-regular punter, as it was on rehearsal nights. The regulars were used to the weekly invasion, and the bar staff appreciated the boost to their sales. On the whole, the musicians behaved themselves, no matter how drunk they got, and the staff weaved their way good-naturedly round bunches of cello cases and the odd trombone case that wouldn't fit under a table. Most tables were full, and there were a few drinkers perched on stools at the bar. It smelled of beer and peanuts, with an occasional whiff of pickled onion Monster Munch scything through everything when someone opened a packet.

A man sat alone at a small table on the far side of the pub. He was reading a book and was about halfway down his pint, oblivious to the hubbub of drinking and gesticulating going on around him. Every now and then he reached for his pint without looking up, took a swallow and replaced it on the table. He read quickly, but attentively. His paperback was worn, its thick spine already creased from being unsentimentally cracked flat. The corners of the soft cover blurred as layers of card threatened to separate and fray. One curled permanently.

The man's face could be described as resting careworn. His hair, which was short but didn't make a point of it, was starting to grey. As he read, creases flickered in and (almost, but never quite) out of existence around his eyes, and his posture, though relaxed, maintained an underlying promise of explosive potential, like an off-duty acrobat. He was a man who knew how to camouflage himself if required.

He reached the end of his pint, laid his book open, face-down, on the table to keep his place, and took his glass to the bar for a refill.

Charlie nudged Erin. 'Hey. Isn't that...?'

'What?' Erin looked over where Charlie was nodding. 'Who?'

'At the bar.'

'There are a lot of people at the bar, Charlie. Including Carl. What about him? We know he drinks. If you start counting trombone alcohol units, you're lost.'

64

'No, the guy on the right. Back to us. About half Carl's height, and wisely waiting until Carl gets his round in.'

'What are you two whispering about?' said Ann, turning round to look at what Charlie was trying to point out. 'Oh, isn't that... what's his face?'

'You're all being immensely helpful,' said Erin.

Eliot and Kayla joined the spectator sport of Spot The Mystery Person At The Bar.

'Turn round, guys,' hissed Charlie. 'I don't want him to see us all staring. Have a bit of subtlety.'

'Oh,' said Erin, with sudden recognition.

'It is, isn't it?' said Charlie.

'Yes, I think so.'

'Handy.'

'Why?'

''Ere we are, trying to solve a mystery,' said Charlie, in his best Poirot voice, 'and 'oo should turn up in ze, 'ow you say, nick of time?'

'Will one of you tell me what the hell is going on?' said Eliot.

Kayla was watching with bemusement. 'Seconded. Are all your trips to the pub like this?'

'I'm almost as new as you are,' said Eliot, 'and just as flummoxed. Spill, people.'

'It's that policeman,' said Erin. 'Who found the Strad, and then came to hear me play the Elgar.'

Kayla, Ann and Eliot immediately turned round to stare again.

'Guys!' pleaded Charlie in a stage whisper. 'Will you *the fuck* behave?'

They swivelled back obediently.

'Right,' said Charlie. 'Erin – get the next round in. Fall into conversation. Bring him back here.'

'What? Are you kidding?' said Erin. 'He's clearly off-duty. The last thing he'll want is to be bothered by some half-drunk musicians who fancy themselves as amateur sleuths.'

'Oh, go on,' said Ann. 'He did give you his card, didn't he?'

'He was just being polite,' said Erin. 'You know, if I needed any help with the Strad, or anything.'

'Or anything,' said Eliot. 'I think it's a great idea. What was his name?'

'Noel Osmar,' said Erin. 'Any minute now you'll be telling me to "glean what afflicts him". The guy deserves a quiet drink if he wants one.'

'Go on,' urged Charlie. 'I'd do it myself only he didn't give his card to me, and I didn't imprint myself onto his brain with my *incredible interpretation of Elgar*.'

'Shut up,' said Erin, into her pint.

Kayla, thoroughly entertained, watched the conversation being batted around the table. She leaned in and took a crisp from one of the open packets on the table. 'I vote Erin goes to talk to him,' she said, crunching. 'I'm sorry I missed the Elgar, now. Sounds as if you had quite a time of it last term.'

'You missed a treat,' said Noel from just behind her chair, where he seemed to have apparated. 'Hello, everyone.'

Erin spluttered and put her pint down, mopping her mouth. 'Hello! We were just, um…'

'Reminiscing about the wonderful Elgar. Quite right too.'

Eliot stood up and tried to emolliate the situation with some good old-fashioned British manners.

'Hi.' He proffered his hand. 'I'm Eliot. Conductor of said wonderful Elgar.'

'Of course,' said Noel, shaking it. 'Noel Osmar.'

'Erin you know already,' continued Eliot, smoothly assuming host duties, 'and this is Charlie, Ann and Kayla.'

Noel smiled and nodded at everyone.

'Would you like to join us?' said Charlie. 'We're here having our usual after-rehearsal ramshackle party.'

'If you're not – I mean – busy,' said Erin. 'We don't want to intrude.'

'Love to,' said Noel. 'I was just having a quiet pint. Hang on a tick while I get my book.'

He put his glass down and went back to his table on the far side of the room, making his way through the crowd with seemingly no effort.

'Cometh the hour…' said Ann.

'We can't ask him about that,' said Erin. 'Nobody likes talking shop on their evening off.'

'I didn't see him clock us,' said Eliot. 'He must have eyes in the back of his head.'

'Maybe he's doing undercover work,' said Charlie. 'Secret camera hidden in his book, you know. Maybe he's scoping this place out.'

'With the shit that goes down round here, highly likely,' said Kayla. 'Not the secret camera stuff, though. That's just daft.'

'Charlie has an overactive imagination,' said Erin.

'It's part of my charm,' said Charlie. He looked round at the raised eyebrows. 'It bloody is.'

'Here he comes,' said Erin. 'Maybe we should stop discussing him before he arrives?'

'I'll get more drinks,' said Ann, standing just as Noel got to the table. 'Same again? You OK for now?' This last was to Noel, who gestured towards his full pint and nodded.

Noel dragged an extra chair over and sat down.

'This your local, then?' asked Eliot.

'Sort of,' said Noel, smiling. 'I like to visit all sorts of places. I live just round the corner.' He looked around the room as he swallowed another mouthful of beer. 'It's nice.'

'Don't remember seeing you in here before,' said Charlie.

'Charlie!' said Erin. 'That sounds like we're inbred swamp-dwellers about to play banjo at him.'

Noel laughed. 'It's OK. I'm not a regular.'

'And you could have been in disguise,' said Charlie. 'You know. Undercover cop and all that.'

'Oh for God's sake,' said Erin. 'Sorry, Noel.' She glared at Charlie. 'He can't help it.'

'There's always plenty going on round here,' said Kayla. 'To keep you busy.'

'There is,' agreed Noel.

'We were actually discussing something along those lines just now,' said Eliot. 'Something we're keen to get to the bottom of. Me especially, since it seems to have been my reckless brainwave that kicked the whole thing off.'

'None of this is your fault,' said Kayla. 'I feel guilty too.'

Noel raised his eyebrows. 'Occupational hazard, sitting next to a police officer. We bring out the guilt.'

'No!' Kayla laughed. 'Not like that. I mean, it's probably my kids doing it.'

'Noel won't want to hear about this,' said Erin.

Noel, on the other hand, looked amiable and perfectly willing to hear about it. 'Go on. Is someone threatening to half-inch the Stradivari again?' He didn't tell them that he regularly launched the location software he had been given by the Strad's insurers, which accurately pinpointed its whereabouts. He liked to think he was keeping a watchful eye on it from afar. He already knew that the cello in the case beside Erin was not the Strad, as it was safely locked in her flat.

'Our stuff's being nicked,' said Charlie.

'It's my fault,' said Eliot. 'I thought it would be a great idea to get some local schoolkids along – you know, give them an idea of what we do and maybe get them keen to join – but it may be backfiring.'

'What kind of stuff?' said Noel.

'Cash, to start with,' said Kayla. 'So I'm guessing my kids – I work at Sunbridge Academy, you see. I reckon some of them saw it and, well, couldn't resist.'

'Pearl leaves it all out in a basket at coffee time,' explained Erin.

'Is Pearl the lady who served us all wine at the Elgar concert?' said Noel. The others nodded. 'I remember her. She had a most effective delivery system. I wouldn't have clocked her as one who was negligent with funds.'

'She's brilliant, but trusting,' said Charlie. 'It has worked like that for years, no problem.'

'But then tonight someone nicked my spare strings,' said Ann. 'Out of my cello case. That's quite specific.'

'Instead of the money?' asked Noel.

'As well as,' said Ann. 'At this expansion rate, we'll all be fleeced by Easter.'

'Have you reported it?' said Noel.

There was a pause.

'Well… no. Not yet,' said Eliot. 'I suppose we were kind of hoping last week was just a one-off, maybe even Pearl misplacing it, and we could all ignore it.'

'Did you see the Cyclopses accuse Kayla's lot straight away?' said Charlie. 'They were right in there. Posh gits.'

'Cyclopses?' said Noel. He was beginning to have the air of a man who regretted moving table.

'Oakdean College pupils,' said Erin. 'We've got some along from each school. A few of the Oakdean ones seem to be missing eyes.' She stopped, and shrugged. 'Now I say that out loud, it sounds really weird.'

'It *is* bloody weird,' said Charlie. 'They all are. Maybe Dr Irving takes a sacrificial eye from every tenth new boy. I wouldn't put anything past them.'

'But even *he's* only got one eye,' said Kayla. 'Sunbridge has got a lot of challenges, I know, but missing random bits of bodies ain't one of them.'

Eliot put his elbows on the table and his head in his hands and mumbled downwards. 'You know, when I thought of this, it seemed such a great idea. Yeah, let's get some local kids in, get them keen, let them play. Nobody thought it was going to involve organised crime and missing body parts.'

'Let's not run away with ourselves,' said Noel, smiling. 'We haven't had any reports of ritual maiming in Stockwell, I assure you.'

'Yeah, well, they'd keep schtum, wouldn't they?' said Charlie. 'They'll all be Knights Templar, or Masons, or Underground Teapot Smugglers or something.'

'This is Charlie,' said Erin to Noel. 'He's our resident class struggle agitator and conspiracy theorist. He gets worse after his second pint. Don't mind him.'

Charlie threw a folded crisp packet at her head affectionately. It hit Noel.

'Sorry, Officer,' he said, trying to look contrite.

'What you need,' said Noel, putting his glass and the folded crisp packet on the table next to each other, 'is a friendly police officer who can advise you on an informal basis unless and until you decide to make a formal report.' He smiled at them. 'Wonder where you're going to find one of them around here at this time of night.'

'I knew I liked you,' said Ann.

'Can we pay you in beer?' said Charlie.

'Isn't that bribery?' said Eliot.

'Oh, I wouldn't get into the technicalities,' said Noel, chuckling. 'In fact, I was hoping to run into you guys again.'

'Why, what've they done?' asked Kayla quickly. 'I'm not in their gang really. This is my first time.'

'Nothing, nothing! Relax,' said Noel. 'I just didn't have enough time to make everyone's acquaintance before Christmas, and wanted to. Honest.' This last was directly to Kayla, who was looking as if she was having second thoughts about her new friends.

'The first thing you can do is watch each other's backs,' said Noel. 'Think of it as a roving Neighbourhood Watch. But without the nimby overtones and unstated threat of violence.'

'I thought the police were all for Neighbourhood Watch schemes,' said Erin. 'Don't they help?'

'Let's just say I've visited my share of local meetings as a young officer,' said Noel, 'and they're usually run by a member of the huntin'-fishin'-shootin' brigade or a bored ex-squaddie, all of whom implied they had easy access to a small armoury if required and the bloodlust to use it. Any discussion of consequences and escalation were not their forte.' He took another swallow of beer. 'Or indeed illegality.'

Ann's throaty chuckle rolled out from her corner of the table. 'You're not recommending I dig a moat round my cello case and chuck a few piranhas in every time I leave the hall, then.'

Noel laughed. 'Er – no. But you could arrange between yourselves to spread out and keep your eyes peeled. Try to keep an eye out, you know. It's a start.'

'Good idea,' said Eliot. 'It doesn't help you, though, Ann. Sorry about your strings.'

'They're insured,' she said. 'Not a big deal really. The excess is a pain, but there you go.'

'Have you really not heard about all the missing eyes at Oakdean?' said Charlie to Noel.

The rest of the evening was spent companionably discussing a possible Stockwell eyeball stash and related conspiracy theories.

Noel discovered that, far from being the upper-class reactionaries he had sometimes suspected, some classical musicians could be refreshingly daft. They parted friends, swapping mobile numbers and promising to meet up again soon.

Chapter 8

Sir Marmaduke Blythe settled himself into an overstuffed leather armchair in Dr Irving's office and tried to persuade his buttocks that they were comfortable. He reached for the genteel bone china coffee cup and saucer Mrs Batten had put on top of a glass coaster inlaid with the Oakdean crest to protect the Georgian side table next to him (incongruously and inexplicably made out of walnut), and took a cautious sip. One never knew at Oakdean whether a beverage would be delivered at lava intensity or a less blistering temperature. Pain had long been an intermittent but constant Oakdean threat, and as an Old Acornian himself, Marmaduke Blythe was accustomed to its Russian roulette nature.

The coffee was pleasantly warm. He relaxed slightly, eyeing the small plate of biscuits next to his saucer as he replaced the cup. His guard was not entirely lowered.

It was Saturday morning. Sounds of a normal school morning barely made it through the closed panelled door (this *was* oak: the side table was one of a pair that had been a pointedly awkward gift in the 1890s yet, for reasons too expensively libellous to go into here, they had remained in the Oakdean headmaster's study ever since). Being an immersive boarding school, Oakdean timetabled lessons six days a week and chapel on Sundays. The hope was, from decades of trial and error, that boys whose every minute was allocated from early waking to sensible bedtime were generally less likely to indulge in the Loitering Sins. In practice, it meant the pupils learned to smoke a whole cigarette really quickly and only bothered to drink if it was a neat spirit.

Dr Irving sipped his own coffee as he sat on the other side of the fireplace, in an equally overstuffed armchair.

'Their manager should be with us presently,' he said, crossing one tweed-wrapped leg over the other and pinching away an imaginary Labrador hair. The logs in the fireplace settled in the grate, sending sparks up the chimney into the chilly February morning. 'I'm grateful for your making yourself available for this meeting at such short notice, Sir Marmaduke.'

'*Amici amicos adiuvant*,' said Sir Marmaduke, in a rumbling bass voice with such a powerful timbre it set his coffee cup trembling in its saucer.

'Naturally.' Dr Irving smiled.

'Tarquin getting along satisfactorily?'

'Indubitably. An Oakdean man, through and through.'

'Excellent, excellent,' said Sir Marmaduke. 'I shall write to his parents post-haste.' He reached for his coffee again, vocalising his ongoing approval of the situation by setting up a permanent nasal idling below the range of normal human hearing.

'I'm also grateful for your acquiescence to our preparations for the inspection,' said Dr Irving. 'As I'm sure you are aware, this modern tick-box culture necessitates some dreary trawling of our so-called "community links". Tedious, I know, but remarkably lucrative. And of course it looks marvellous on the boys' Oxbridge applications.'

'It is of mutual benefit,' said Sir Marmaduke, raising his hand as if to wave away any thanks. 'Refreshing one's *curriculum vitae* with respect to various… minorities and lowly charity cases is never unnoticed, in certain circles.'

'If we can get this concert here, flag it up to the governors in time and ensure it features prominently in the inspectors' timetable, we shan't need to divert any further funds or separate inputs for the next couple of financial cycles, at least,' said Dr Irving. 'Once the input has been noted, one can generate a rather satisfactory circular reference, I understand. Our Bursar does all the legwork, of course. I don't pretend to understand the technical details.'

They smiled at each other in complete understanding, as gentlemen have been smiling at each other in wood-panelled club rooms for centuries. All that was missing was the cigar smoke.

A sharp rapping was followed by Mrs Batten's head, neck and cashmered left bosom popping into the study round the edge of the door. Her spectacles swung into view a moment later as they traversed an arc on the chain around her neck.

'The gentleman from Stockwell Park Orchestra is here, sir. Shall I send him in?'

'By all means, Mrs Batten. By all means. Thank you.' Dr Irving stood up and strode towards the door, in time to clasp David's hand as soon as he set foot on the carpet. 'Greetings, David! Come in, come in!'

David was propelled into the room rather faster than he had anticipated.

'Good morning, Dr Irving,' he said, coming to a halt at the edge of the Persian rug. Dr Irving's study benefited not only from a luxuriously underlaid pure wool Axminster, but also a thick-pile Persian rug that almost entirely covered it. Together, the soundproofing qualities of rug, carpet and interlined velvet curtains had deadened the broadcast of various innovative methods of delivering corporal punishment right up until they had disappointingly (for Dr Irving) become illegal.

'Good morning indeed!' cried Dr Irving. 'Do come in, nearer the fire. I find the weather this morning a tad dreich, as our bekilted friends north of the border are wont to exclaim!' He bustled David towards the empty chair, and called after his secretary as she was closing the door, 'May we trouble you for another coffee, Mrs Batten?'

David found himself sitting opposite Sir Marmaduke, who regarded him with heavy lids over the rim of his cup.

'David, may I introduce Sir Marmaduke Blythe? Sir Marmaduke, this is David, manager of Stockwell Park Orchestra.'

David stood up again and leaned towards Sir Marmaduke, offering his hand. It was taken with the minimum amount of effort and dropped quickly. David sat down again, wondering if he should have brought some of the others for moral support. Although his son attended the prep department at Oakdean, David had not been in Dr Irving's study before. The prep school was corralled in an entirely separate building on one side of the grounds, and the two institutions were run on quite independent lines, each with their own headmaster. David decided not to mention his parental qualifications. As he learned more about the senior school, other options for his son grew increasingly attractive.

Dr Irving retrieved his cup from the table next to David, and perched on the club fender between the two armchairs. 'Thank you both for coming along to my – may one call it a daylight soirée?'

David glanced at Dr Irving and smiled nervously. He didn't feel qualified to say if one were allowed to call a morning meeting a soirée. Perhaps if one of the participants were a famous composer knighted for unspecified services to music, anything was possible. He raised his hand to his cheek: an automatic gesture when he felt his stress tic might be about to resurface.

Mrs Batten tapped on the door again, and brought David's coffee to his own personal walnut side table, together with a small milk jug and bowl containing irregularly shaped brown sugar cubes. It looked alarmingly like a bowl of ear wax excavations in assorted sizes. None of your easily stackable cheap Tate & Lyle white stuff here, David noted, as he thanked her and tried to manoeuvre one lump into his tiny cup with tongs that would not have looked out of place in a doll's house. The lump fell out of the tongs' grip too soon, splashing coffee wildly. David mopped the polished walnut with his handkerchief and sweated under his jacket.

Dr Irving exchanged a glance with Sir Marmaduke, but cleared his throat and pressed on. 'I should like, if I may, to posit some options for the forthcoming concert.'

David, having stirred the sugar into what was left of his coffee, took a sip. As the temperature registered, he opened his eyes very wide indeed, feeling the skin of his lips and tongue blister. Politeness dictated his agony could only be expressed through the medium of a small mewing sound as he swallowed, which ensured the burnt area extended down the back of his throat as well.

Dr Irving interpreted his lack of formal reply as acquiescing to his topic of discussion. 'I have alluded to some of our former, as it were, joint ventures. Sir Marmaduke has been generous enough to compose a number of gallimaufries for our *discipuli Euterpes* over the years.'

Sir Marmaduke rumbled into his armchair, which seemed to indicate pleasure.

'And now,' continued Dr Irving, 'in the person of his highly talented godson, Tarquin, Oakdean boasts a musician of singular promise.'

David began to get a horrible feeling of déjà vu. His cheek jumped.

The Marmaduke rumble gained momentum. 'The boy's a prodigy,' he said. 'Been waiting for the right occasion.'

'And there we have it,' said Dr Irving. 'Sir Marmaduke has offered to write a piece for French horn and orchestra, especially featuring Tarquin's talents, and we both feel that this term's concert would be an ideal showcase.'

David looked at each of them in turn. Two faces, each with only one working eye: Dr Irving's oddly matched glass one remaining immobile, Sir Marmaduke sporting a patch. They were deadly serious. 'You mean, you haven't written it yet?'

'Sketches, my dear boy,' said Sir Marmaduke airily. 'All in m'head.'

'Sir Marmaduke's compositions are famously Of The Moment,' said Dr Irving. 'That's what makes them so deliciously fresh.'

'Um – it's a very interesting proposition,' said David, careful to measure his words so as not to let any unforeseen loophole escape that they could pounce on later and retrofit into an agreement. 'I know Eliot has already suggested including—'

'Who?' said Sir Marmaduke, spearing David with his one-eyed stare.

'Our conductor. Eliot Yarrow. He's terribly good – came to us permanently at the end of last term.'

'Don't know him. Young, is he?'

'Ish. We're lucky to have him.'

'Hmm.' The Blythe armchair emanated its now-familiar rumble, and seemed content again.

'Anyway, he's suggested Copland's *Fanfare for the Common Man* in the concert, which would of course feature the horns prominently. I'd enjoy playing that alongside Tarquin – did you know I'm a horn player too?' David heard himself try to hoik the conversation up to an exchange-of-pleasantries-among-equals level, and wondered why he was bothering. Then he sniffed. He thought he had caught the whiff of something burning. Nothing he could identify. Then he wondered if his coffee injuries were more severe than he had first imagined. But surely that would be more barbeque-y rather than a dry sort of right-angled burning smell. He shook his head slightly, and pressed on. 'As you know, we rehearse in Sunbridge's hall anyway, and there *is* the argument that pupils from there might greatly benefit from culture being brought to their doorstep?' He added an upward inflection to sound as non-confrontational as he could.

'I think we all know what Sunbridge pupils would benefit from,' said Sir Marmaduke, and indulged in a sustained mutual chuckle with Dr Irving.

David reminded himself never to go on orchestral business alone again.

'Perhaps you could leave the idea with me?' he asked, diplomatically. 'I'll raise it with my fellow committee members, and be in touch?'

The burning smell intensified.

'Of course, of course,' said Dr Irving, rising from his seat on the club fender and effectively bringing the meeting to a close. 'Might we press you for an answer in the next few days? Sir Marmaduke will require appropriate notice.'

'Yes, of course. Delighted to meet you, Sir Marmaduke,' said David, leaning forward and shaking his hand again. It was not returned with any more warmth than the first attempt.

Dr Irving bounded forward to reach the door before David, and flung it open. As he passed, David saw a large scorch mark on the back of his tweed jacket. It was smoking slightly.

'Good day to you, David,' cried Dr Irving, entirely oblivious to the threat of mild conflagration.

'Goodbye,' said David, deciding not to try to warn him. Some situations were better exited from promptly.

His tic jumped merrily about in his cheek all the way down the drive.

Chapter 9

'You went there on your own?' said Charlie. 'Are you mental? Erin and I barely made it out alive, and we were watching each other's backs.'

David suddenly regretted not taking Eliot and Rafael aside somewhere private to tell them about his Oakdean visit, instead of trying to catch them for a quick word before the next rehearsal on Monday evening. The 'quick word' had been overheard by Charlie and Erin as they were getting their cellos out of their cases.

'Dr Irving asked me to pop in at short notice. I didn't want to bother anyone else on their Saturday morning,' said David.

'Never mind that now,' said Eliot. 'What did he want?'

'Something tells me it wasn't to offer an ongoing financial contribution to arts in the community?' said Rafael. 'Which is a shame.'

David looked hassled. 'He offered to host our concert there.'

'But he already offered that last week. Just after we'd had the same offer from Rosalind Banks for here,' said Eliot. 'She doesn't seem to be around this week.' He looked around nervously. 'Yet.'

'Indeed,' said David, 'but this time, he wanted to – ah – emphasise the offer. And he had reinforcements.'

'Did he get some of his lads to pelt you with chewed-up bits of paper?' said Charlie. 'They're good at that.'

'Er – no. I met Sir Marmaduke Blythe, who was also keen to make our concert at Oakdean go swimmingly, perhaps with a newly commissioned piece.'

'Oh God, yes,' said Eliot. 'He did mention something about him last week. I thought he was just padding out his offer.'

'Don't tell me Marmaduke Blythe is going to be this term's Mrs Ford-Hughes,' said Erin. 'I don't think any of us could take another concert like that.'

'You met One-Eyed Blythe?' called Ann as she walked in and put her cello case down, catching the tail end of the conversation. 'Isn't the old bugger dead yet?'

'Do you know him?' asked Eliot.

'Let's just say our paths crossed in the eighties, and leave it at that,' said Ann. 'In the days when he actually still wrote music. I thought he must have died – haven't heard anything about him for bloody years.'

'I hope he didn't expect the commission to come from us?' said Rafael. 'As in, paying for it.'

David looked trapped. 'Oh no. That wasn't mentioned at all. I don't think that was the thrust of it.' He swallowed. 'No, it was more about using their hall and maybe Sir Marmaduke could write a bit of something for Tarquin…'

'The plot thickens,' said Rafael. 'Who's Tarquin?'

'Ah,' said Eliot. 'I think I know this one. He said something about a godson…?'

'Yep,' said David.

'He must be one of the Oakdean kids who came to play with us,' said Erin. 'But which one?'

'I can't remember all their names,' said Eliot.

'I remember they've all got bloody weird ones,' said Charlie. 'The kind that run in families with Hapsburg jaws.'

'Well, you have to admit the names are not their fault,' said Erin.

The hall was filling with players, making any kind of private conversation impossible.

Ann laughed. 'Good luck navigating your way through this, boys. Why don't you explain it all to Pearl and give her the casting committee vote, and leave it at that?'

'She could certainly give coffee-making lessons to Dr Irving's secretary,' said David, who had been soothing his burnt throat with ice cream all weekend. 'Could we perhaps discuss this further after the rehearsal? I said I'd get back to Dr Irving within a few days.'

'Sure,' said Eliot. 'Sorry, my idea seems to have opened a can of worms. I'll know better next time. Meanwhile, let's get this show on the road.'

The Oakdean boys had arrived without Dr Irving, for once, and were finding the same seats as the previous week. Kayla and the Sunbridge kids were sorting themselves out on the other side of the hall. Eliot wondered if they were ever going to talk to each other voluntarily. Not for the first time, he feared he might have bitten off more than he could chew. He waited for all the players to find their seats.

'Hi, everyone,' he said, then looked at the schoolkids. 'Welcome back – good to see you liked us enough to return.'

Caspar and Rufus in the violins exchanged sneers with Sebastian and Rupert over in the violas and cellos respectively, which were not missed by Danilo, Marina and Reece from Sunbridge, who also played violin. Quiet mutterings of 'wanker' started to waft through the upper strings.

'Quite the happy band, aren't they?' murmured Charlie underneath Eliot's left ear.

Eliot twitched an eyebrow at him, but ploughed on. 'As threatened last week, I thought we could attempt to read through Mussorgsky's *Night on the Bare Mountain*. We've managed to get a set of copies – thank you to Pearl, as usual, for her outstanding admin skills.' He waited for the small appreciative murmur to die down. 'It only lasts about ten minutes, but packs it all in. Anyone know it?'

A lot of nods. None of the kids.

'Put it this way,' said Eliot, 'if you ever need some spooky incidental music for a horror film, you can pretty much use any excerpt from this. We're supposed to imagine witches flying around and Satan arriving for a party. Some of you of a certain age may have flashbacks to Maxell cassette tape adverts and inexplicable indoor hurricanes blowing flying ducks up walls. You young things will have to make it up yourselves. Brass: get ready to sacrifice a lung. Anyone within three seats of the piccolo may need earplugs once it winds up to full strength. And strings: think of it as a cardio workout. The harp will be along later. Let's go.'

Carl looked along the trombone section, nodding at Tracie. She nodded back, looking determined.

Tarquin, who had been shuffled along to play fourth horn along with David instead of bumping first for Neema, and took this as a personal insult, looked grumpy. David was planning to use this rehearsal to listen carefully to him, to see if he could discern any evidence of the musical prodigy he had been assured lurked beneath Tarquin's decidedly ordinary exterior.

Max had given Irie the stick for the tamtam and stationed her next to it. The suspended gong in its frame was almost as big as she was, but she was on the percussion team now and wasn't going to let them down. There were therefore three players lined up to play timpani, tubular bells, cymbals, drum and tamtam: percussionists are the most versatile of orchestral musicians, frequently counting bars' rest on three different instruments and leaping between them silently to get to their next entry. Max had delegated the timp-playing to his colleague, so he could cover the other three and direct Irie on the tamtam when required.

Eliot grinned, and straight away the violins were trying to get their fingers around the triplets which were flashing past them at a rate of knots at the specified *allegro feroce* tempo. Some were more successful than others, given there had been no easing in. Richard, the leader, was note-perfect and did his best to guide the rest of them behind him, but it has to be said there were variations of interpretation depending how far back along the desks the players were. In any case, it mattered little, since after four short bars the piccolo was three ledger lines up and blasting everything within a five-metre radius. A moment later and the triple trombones with added tuba were thundering through their chords, so no matter how hard the strings worked it was only ever going to be *staccato* window dressing. By the time the horns joined in with most of the percussion section, the hall was full of raucous over-blowing and enthusiastic teamwork and it was hard to believe they were only on bar twenty-two. Mussorgsky was never one to hide any light under nearby bushels; he was more of an 'if you've got it, flaunt it' kind of guy. And why not?

He was also the kind of guy to drop sudden pauses into massive orchestral texture that had got a head of steam up, which is dangerous even for professional musicians, but created the kind of pile-up among amateur players that takes a full halt, general picking up of overturned vehicles, assessing scraped knees and other injuries, and a diffused calming from Eliot before setting off again. They had several of those, but Eliot remained cheery and encouraging, sometimes yelling, 'Anyone hurt?'

After one particularly concertinaed enforced halt, the bassoons started off again with a perky Russian tune trying to be all insouciant and folky, as if there hadn't been witches circling on their brooms a moment before.

During another stop, Eliot called some encouragement over to the double basses, where Kayla was playing. 'You're doing great, basses! I know the odds are stacked against you – there really should be at least eight of you, but you three are sounding magnificent. Keep it up!'

A bit further on, when the whole orchestra had wound itself round another whirlpool and managed to dock into a *diminuendo* successfully, the eerily mournful sound of a lone tubular bell rang out through the hall. Apart from some quietly sustained flute, clarinet and bassoon chords, the only other sound was the cellos playing harmonics at the same pitch as the bell, which gave an equally other-worldly feel, since it was impossible to warm the note with any vibrato. The violins came into this lunar landscape with a sad little refrain for a while, and then Eliot tried to be both conductor and audio description at once.

'Here's where the harp comes in – a bit like this.' He did his best impression of the bit in a film where our hero falls back in time through the medium of a blurred scene change. 'You get the idea – it's only four bars, but it's a beautiful four bars.'

He tried singing it again for a similar four bars a page later, but then brought in a gorgeous clarinet solo that the first clarinet, Beatriz, played so beautifully that she drew appreciative foot-shuffling from the others afterwards. After a couple more bars of the hybrid Eliot-harp, Brian took over the solo on his flute but, being Brian, the ethereal beauty of it eluded him somewhat. It didn't help that he had nothing but high, quiet notes until the end of the piece, the flatness of which even Eliot's attempt to sing the last harp arpeggio into his highest *falsetto* failed to disguise.

'Well done, everyone,' he said, after a small cough to try to get his voice down into its normal register again. 'What do you reckon? I think it's rather fun.'

'You might not be saying that after those dozen bars of harp,' muttered Charlie.

Those within earshot giggled. A brief look of puzzlement drifted over Eliot's face, but the harpist mystery remained as cloaked as it had been in the pub. David, over in the horns and thus too far to hear but correctly inferring its nature, looked awkward. He wondered if he knew any backup harpists.

They rehearsed the Mussorgsky until the break. Pearl went out a few minutes early to sort out her urn, as usual. She had also taken preventative measures to foil the thieves. Instead of the plastic pretend-wicker basket, she had brought an empty ice-cream carton from home. She had cut out a slot in the lid big enough for people to put coins thorough, and then secured the box shut with gaffer tape. Not being easily thwarted, she had embraced this new security idea with gusto, and so not much of the original box was now visible under the interlocking swathes of tape. It was swaddled like a rather rectangular baby Jesus.

While the urn was reaching its final temperature, she put the box down on her table in the customary place used by her basket. She reached into a hessian shopping bag containing all her catering paraphernalia, and retrieved another roll of gaffer tape. Pearl, of all people, knew more than one way to skin a cat. She carefully stuck the end of the tape onto the box, unrolled a length of it, and let it hang over the side of the table. Reaching under the table from the other side, she caught hold of the roll and brought it up and over the box again, sticking the whole thing to the table. She repeated this manoeuvre a few more times, like a spider wrapping a fly, until the entire box was firmly attached to the table. The money slot peeked through layers of tape. If any thief wanted her loose change, they were going to have to up their game.

The noise of her ripping tape off the roll echoed back into the hall while the rest of the orchestra finished playing, sounding exactly like someone of Pearl's age breaking wind in a space in which they imagined themselves alone. Eliot had to stop the rehearsal slightly earlier than planned because nobody could concentrate. Of course, then nobody really wanted to be the first to approach the source of the noise, but the draw of caffeine proved too much in the end. Waves of revelatory 'ohhhh!'s could be heard as people saw what she had been doing.

Erin, Charlie, Ann, Kayla and Eliot hung back and tried to formulate a crime-busting plan that could be later endorsed by DCI Noel Osmar.

'Trouble is,' said Charlie, 'if we're too good at this preventative shit, we'll never catch 'em.'

'What we need to be is invisible and omniscient, then,' said Ann. 'Right you are.'

'What we should have done is sorted this out before now,' said Eliot.

'Well, we were drunk,' said Erin, not unreasonably.

'Speak for yourself,' said Ann. 'I was driving.'

'And your liver has been highly trained by years as a professional musician, we know, we know,' said Charlie.

'Come on, they could be eyeing up Pearl's basket already,' said Kayla.

'Look – you go and get me a coffee,' said Erin. 'Here's my 50p. I'll stay here and Keep Watch.'

As the rest of them went through the doors to the foyer, Erin sat sideways on her seat in the cellos and crossed her legs. Just as she was about to dig her phone out of her pocket, the doors opened again and an elderly man wearing an eyepatch came into the hall. He walked with a stick and leaned heavily on it. Erin heard him wheeze.

'Hello?' she called. 'Can I help? Are you looking for anyone in particular?' She wondered if she should assume the eyepatch meant he was in some way connected with Oakdean, or if that was horrifically prejudiced. Then she wondered if she was being gaslighted by part of a pirate outfit.

The man stopped halfway between the doors and the orchestra seating, frowning at her. His heavy wool coat hung open, revealing a long, bright green scarf. He drew himself up straight and sniffed.

'This Yarrow chap. Is he here?' he said.

His accent put him firmly in the Oakdean orbit, but Erin wasn't about to jump, just in case.

'He's getting a drink – he won't be a minute. Is he expecting you?'

The man ran his one eye down to Erin's shoes and back up to her face. Definitely Oakdean, she thought, folding her arms.

'Thought I'd catch him this evening,' he said. Then he glared with renewed vigour. 'Drink? Isn't he working?'

'Coffee.' Erin decided she wasn't going to pander.

'Ah. Well.' He grumbled a bit into the folds of his scarf and looked round impatiently at the doors.

They obligingly opened a moment later, but only to reveal Ann and Charlie returning with Erin's coffee.

'Fuck me, if it isn't One-Eyed Blythe!' muttered Ann to Charlie, then more loudly to the visitor, 'Sir Marmaduke! This *is* a surprise.'

She walked past him to give Erin her coffee, then turned to face Sir Marmaduke, who was squinting at her with no sign of recognition.

'Madam?' he said.

'Don't "madam" me,' she said. 'I last saw you wearing nothing but a thong, trying to scoop up loose change with your toes in the Trevi Fountain at three a.m. in September 1988. Then the *carabinieri* arrived.'

Sir Marmaduke's face elongated and paled as his jaw fell slack. He leaned on his cane. Cleared his throat. 'Annie?'

Charlie and Erin turned to face her too.

'*Annie...?*' they mouthed.

Ann shrugged, smiling. 'Yeah. So?' Turning to Sir Marmaduke, she said, 'Bingo. What on earth are you doing here?'

'Oh – need to see Yarrow. Time is of the essence, and all that. Where is he?'

'Here,' said Ann, nodding towards the doors, which were being opened by Eliot and Kayla.

'We swiped you some biscuits,' called Eliot, waving a handful aloft, and then saw his visitor. 'Hello. Sir Marmaduke, is it? I think I recognise you from pictures...'

Sir Marmaduke walked towards Eliot.

'He had more hair in those, I bet,' said Ann under her breath. 'Never one to willingly update his media profile.'

'What with that and the gammy leg and the one eye, he's quite the catch,' said Charlie.

'Well, he only ever had one eye,' said Ann.

'Presumably he had both before going to Oakdean?' said Erin.

'Will you three stop muttering?' said Eliot, handing out biscuits. 'I'm trying to welcome our impromptu guest. What brings you here, Sir Marmaduke?'

'Met your manager chap a few days ago,' Sir Marmaduke said, waving his cane around in the air vaguely, as if drawing a sketch of David to aid his memory.

'Yes, he did mention it,' said Eliot. 'Did he also mention we had already been kindly offered this hall for our concert, by Kayla's esteemed management colleagues?'

Kayla grinned and dunked her Bourbon.

Sir Marmaduke looked around the hall, taking in its grubby windows with their peeling paint surrounds high in the walls, the intense ocular throb of the new brightly coloured lino and assorted gym equipment lashed to one wall. 'Yes, he did. But Oakdean's Old Hall: now that would provide surroundings commensurate with a newly commissioned Blythe original! Whereas here—'

'We've got new lino,' Kayla pointed out helpfully.

Sir Marmaduke glared at Kayla. 'Here, you have a third-rate, tawdry school that can just about manage to drag the education of its Neanderthal pupils up to a level to enable them to service my Jaguar. And believe me, even that is beyond most of them. There's a reason the leaders of this country spring from educational establishments that put the emphasis on the correct criteria to mould an outstanding man. And people like you will never understand.'

'Whoa,' said Erin.

'He hasn't changed a bit,' said Ann.

'People like me?' said Kayla.

'Oh God,' said Eliot, and turned to Sir Marmaduke. 'Stop. For God's sake shut up. Before you say something… else. Look, it was my idea to get schoolkids in to play in our orchestra. I think Sunbridge pupils stand to gain an awful lot more from the experience than the already privileged Oakdean boys, even though it has been lovely having them here and mixing things up. So, on balance, I reckon having the concert here would back up everything I've been trying to do this term. Even though it's not actually up to me. The committee will take that decision.'

Sir Marmaduke was swaying alarmingly, clutching his cane but not letting it touch the ground and therefore assist with his balance. If someone had been drawing him as a cartoon at this point, there would probably have been smoke coming out of his nose and possibly his ears.

'Young man,' he said, 'I don't think you realise—'

'Oh, put a sock in it,' said Ann. 'You've been told "no". I know you're not used to that, but I knew you before you were Sir anything, and we both remember what happened in Rome.'

Sir Marmaduke's cane returned to the lino with a thud, and he stood there, wheezing slightly. The threat of publicising whatever had happened in Rome, before or after the Trevi Fountain thong incident, was clearly powerful enough to stall the Blythe ire, at least temporarily. He knew the unsavoury mental image of a thong-clad junior Blythe was now imprinted in the brains of Eliot, Charlie, Erin and Kayla, and was unsuccessfully trying to work out a way to erase it.

The other musicians began to drift back from their coffee break, including the Oakdean contingent. Naturally, they hadn't engaged anyone else in conversation but remained in a tight group to discuss the latest high-altitude weather reports for half term in Zermatt. Tarquin spotted Sir Marmaduke and flipped his fringe back in greeting.

'Ah, Tarquin, my boy,' said Sir Marmaduke, eager to divert attention and perhaps regain some ground.

'Marmaduke! Didn't know you were visiting.' They shook hands. 'Have you come to finalise my fanfare stuff?'

'Aye aye,' said Charlie, grinning. 'Here we go.'

'Don't tell me you've actually written a new piece?' said Ann. 'And for Tarquin here? How lovely.'

Tarquin looked around at Ann as if he couldn't quite square the caustic remark with the female in front of him.

'Sketches, my dear, sketches,' said Sir Marmaduke benignly. 'Waiting for the spark of this young prodigy to fan it into the mighty flame of orchestration.'

The small circle of people surrounding Tarquin and Sir Marmaduke digested this convoluted imagery in silence. If only Pearl had witnessed it, perhaps she could have translated the essence of truth hidden within the maze-like walls of its construction: she was, after all, an expert. But at that moment she was carefully untaping her plastic box from the table while darting frequent glances behind her in case anyone tried to half-inch her urn.

'Well, perhaps before the imminent conflagration, we could crack on with the rest of the rehearsal?' said Eliot, moving towards his stand. The others wandered over to their instrument cases.

David came into the hall with Rafael and spotted Sir Marmaduke at the same time Sir Marmaduke saw him.

'Ah. We may have to deal with our planned issue now rather than after the rehearsal,' he said to Rafael as they approached. 'Good evening, Sir Marmaduke. This is an unexpected pleasure.'

The rumble he got in response to this could have been a Harley-Davidson going past outside or Sir Marmaduke expressing either pleasure or disdain: it was impossible to tell.

'Came here to speak to Yarrow,' he barked, 'but been fobbed off with excuses about privilege and do-gooding. Look here, Irving has offered his hall. Now I've seen this place, I can't imagine you'd be fool enough to turn that down.'

Tarquin smirked. It was a smirk that had been handed down through many generations, honed at grouse shoots and fox hunts and unfortunate episodes at Henley when the waiting staff weren't up to scratch. A smirk that enjoyed watching prey being toyed with.

Rafael saw David's hand move to touch his eye, and smoothly stepped in.

'Pleasure to meet you, Sir Marmaduke. I'm Rafael, the treasurer, and am delighted to inform you that the orchestra committee plans to discuss this very issue tonight, after our rehearsal, and you can be assured we shall make it a priority to inform you and Dr Irving at the earliest possible moment thereafter.'

A further rumble from inside the green scarf indicated a possible cooling of the Blythe temper.

'So, if you will permit us to continue our music-making,' said Rafael, indicating the exit with one arm, 'we can reach our conclusion all the more swiftly.'

A couple of minutes later, Sir Marmaduke was gone. Tarquin, looking deflated, joined David in the horns. Eliot thanked Rafael as he went past to the bassoons, but Rafael waved away his thanks.

'Next time I come up with a brilliant idea like this,' whispered Eliot to Charlie and Erin, as Gwynneth played a sustained A for everyone to tune, 'tell me to shut up and have another pint.'

'Gotcha,' said Erin.

Charlie just laughed. 'I wouldn't have it any other way. Honestly, some people's orchestras just play the notes. This is far more interesting.'

What with the distraction of Sir Marmaduke's visit, none of them realised until later that the crime spree seemed to have stopped. Either Pearl's exhaustive taping or Erin's guard duty had worked, or a combination of the two. Pearl herself decided she would have to attempt a different method in future, as she tried and failed to unstick the seventeen layers of tape to retrieve her money box after the break. In the end, she had to use the tiny scissors in her travelling sewing kit to nibble through the tough webbing, and the whole thing left the table and her fingers very sticky. She found Mussorgsky's quavers much harder when her fingers kept attaching themselves to her viola.

Chapter 10

When Kayla got into school the next morning, she was waylaid by Rosalind in the staffroom. Rosalind had not been Deputy Head at Sunbridge long, but she knew if she needed an urgent word with anyone, the best tactic was to stand between them and the kettle to get their attention.

Rosalind planted her feet squarely, holding the full and steaming pint mug she had yet again won as a trophy in the cupboard scrum. Her rugby-playing youth was never wasted. She used the time before Kayla turned up to offer bon mots and bracing exclamation marks to her fellow colleagues as they swerved round her on their quests to or from caffeine.

'Good morning, Ayanna! SlimFast? Again? Good morning, Tony! I'll need those figures by lunchtime, thank you! Ah, Gerald, good morning! Have you completed those risk assessments? I'm sure the governors will be delighted with your fire-retardant ideas too. Good morning, Malik! Incoming memo regarding ties: looser could be sprucer! That's it. Right up! And the top button. We must present as the professional team we would like to see in the world! Ah – good morning, Kayla! May I have a word?'

Kayla stopped, trying not to let her line of sight slide behind Rosalind's head, where Malik was miming hanging himself from his newly spruced tie and Ayanna flicked V-signs at Rosalind's back while the kettle boiled again.

'Hi, Rosalind. Sure.'

'My office, two minutes?'

'OK – I'll grab a coffee.'

Rosalind left the staffroom, and Kayla was offered priority hot water from colleagues who knew her need was greater than theirs. The teamwork Rosalind was so desperate to engender flourished. It was just that she never witnessed it.

Across the foyer, Kayla knocked and went in.

'Ah, Kayla. Thank you. Do sit down.'

Rosalind tapped a few more laptop keys, then closed the screen. She picked up her mug and, with one push of her feet, wheeled herself along in her chair to the bulbous end of her new moulded desk: the end which pretended to be a small circular table with a couple of angular visitor chairs parked up like airliners round a gate hub. Kayla sat on the front edge of one of the chairs, but immediately slid back into the hammock-like embrace designed by body language specialists who understand submissive posture. She fought her way back up to the front of the chair, but couldn't balance on the narrow steel strut holding the mesh seat. Slowly, with resigned poise, she allowed herself to slide back again. At least she hadn't spilled her coffee.

'Won't keep you long, Kayla,' said Rosalind, opening a document folder to reveal a pad of lined yellow A4 paper inside. It was blank. She retrieved a ballpoint pen from its elasticated holder on the edge and clicked out the nib in readiness. 'As you know, at our last governors' meeting I posited the suggestion that Sunbridge Academy might host the forthcoming Stockwell Park Orchestra concert.'

Kayla took a gulp of coffee and nodded. She had had the dizzying experience of hearing Rosalind describe the imagined event to the governors in such hyperbolic terms she had difficulty in recognising her own music department, let alone the musical abilities of the pupils who were playing with the orchestra.

'I have since had sight of projected budgeting figures for the next financial year. The governors raised the possibility of utilising this cross-cultural community outreach programme to offset some of our ongoing fixed costs by attracting external market funding from the aspirational sector.'

Kayla sighed, and wished she had set her phone to record from her pocket. Nobody believed her when she tried to explain. 'What?'

Rosalind clicked her pen in and out a few times, as if shuffling her brain to get it to send another set of phrases out. 'In addition, if we can attract an uptick in attending units, we can benefit from the attendant per capita central funding achievable in a commensurate manner. Professional quality imagery has been demonstrated to influence the decision-making process in cognitive logical identification of pre-employment inculcation.'

Kayla thought about this for a moment, and attempted a translation. 'We're broke. You're printing yet another glossy school brochure, and you want to big up our links with the orchestra so we can get people to put adverts in it? And you reckon that'll bring in more kids and more funding?'

Some more frenzied clicking and a throat clearance. 'Yes.'

They looked at each other in silence.

'So what do you need from me?' asked Kayla.

Rosalind leaned forward and clicked eagerly. 'I understand you have recently undertaken to provide assistance to their ranks?'

'I'm playing bass with them this term, yes.'

'Perhaps, in view of your new-found camaraderie with your musical cohort, you might exert some influence over their decision as to their concert location?'

Kayla laughed. 'Well, from what I overheard last night, they were going to decide that after the rehearsal. I didn't go to the pub with them – they could have already made that decision. But I'll see what I can do.'

Rosalind sat back again, clicked her pen shut, replaced it in its elastic and closed her document folder cover over the still-blank yellow pad. 'Excellent. Thank you. Please keep me appraised.'

Kayla stood up and nodded. As she walked to the door she heard Rosalind's chair roll along to the computer-end of her desk, and she closed the door on determined keyboard clacking.

'Nutter,' she said to herself, and wandered to her own classroom for the first lesson.

The orchestra had indeed made their decision the night before, and quickly: it had taken the time between ordering a round of drinks and finding a table. Sir Marmaduke's visit had had the opposite effect than the one he intended. Eliot had apologised again for how his idea was panning out, but in fact David and Rafael – and the others – could see its possible advantages and were willing to submit to its unexpected difficulties. Plus they were rather enjoying their bonding against a common foe, which as any office behaviour specialist will say, is one of the most powerful forces shaping human society. It's not that Sir Marmaduke, Dr Irving and all the lanky posh boys were making Stockwell Park Orchestra play better and become closer friends, but it was a marvellous by-product of the situation.

David had even confided to Eliot (during his second glass of red) that, in the light of what he had learned over the last few weeks, he would not be letting his son continue into the Oakdean senior school.

They did spend some time discussing how best to communicate the orchestra's decision to Dr Irving and Sir Marmaduke. Ann suggested a carrier pigeon, given the news essentially had to travel back into the last century. Charlie said it should be a swan because pigeons were nowhere near classy enough and he wanted the option of some broken legs as collateral damage. Erin pointed out swans were (a) difficult to train and (b) almost impossible to get in Stockwell, whereas pigeons were all over the place. Eliot was all for setting up a trebuchet outside the rhododendron hedge and walloping a piece of paper over tied to a rock. While the friendly and mildly drunken bickering went on, David and Rafael drafted a short email together on David's phone, and sent it off before they lost their nerve. They forgot to copy in Rosalind Banks.

Chapter 11

Rosalind eventually learned that Sunbridge would host the concert after chasing Kayla, who asked Eliot, who checked with David, who confirmed he and Rafael had actually sent an email while they had all been in the pub, rather than locating and then training a flock of swans. Eliot agreed it would have been an ambitious plan. Kayla received the news all tangled up with the swans, but managed to unpick it and distil the essential facts for Rosalind.

Rosalind wasted no time over the next few days. When she greeted Eliot as he walked in for the following week's rehearsal, she was not alone. On one side she was flanked by a photographer festooned with straps, holding an array of variously sized black bags that shut with an excessive mileage of Velcro. A camera dangled below his waistband with a zoom lens that would have given the most flamboyant codpiece pause for thought. On Rosalind's other side, a small group of governors and parents gathered looking expectant. They had been invited to observe how Sunbridge Academy was reaching out and grasping the vines of cultural links in their community that would swing them all to a prosperous and luxuriant forest of opportunity. Thankfully, there wasn't a loincloth in sight.

Eliot saw them when he walked across the foyer and wondered what he had to deal with this time.

'Evening, Rosalind,' he said, trying not to slow his pace as he aimed for the doors to the hall.

Rosalind clicked with purpose towards him, making little flapping motions with her hands behind her to chivvy her entourage to follow, like a hen who wants her chicks to keep up and learn all there is to learn about running a photoshoot.

'Hello, Eliot! I'm delighted to hear you have decided to perform your concert here at Sunbridge! Absolutely delighted!' Even by Rosalind's standards, her voice vibrated dangerously close to glass-shattering frequencies. 'I hope you'll forgive my impetuousness, but I have taken the liberty of arranging for a few mementos of the hallowed rehearsal process to be captured for the benefit of our next Academy brochure.'

Eliot stopped walking. He stifled a sigh. 'That's lovely, but I guess we'll need to ask if everyone is OK with being in them? Plus there'll be other pupils there – not from here, but Oakdean – and I'm not sure—'

'I'm sure Doug here can do his little bits of blurry magic if there are any issues there, or perhaps just point the camera at our Sunbridge pupils, who are, of course, our focus here.' She turned to the photographer and smiled. 'Can't you, Doug? This is Doug, by the way. Photographer.'

'Alright?' said Doug, and nodded at Eliot. There was something about the droop of his anorak that implied he had worked on the previous brochure with Rosalind.

'Hello, Doug,' said Eliot. 'Now, if you'll excuse me, I must—'

'Yes, yes, of course! To work! Don't mind us. I've brought along a few – a happy few! – governors and representatives of the PTA, to observe our exciting community outreach programme in action!'

'Hello, everyone,' said Eliot. By this stage he was unclear about whose programme was reaching out to what community. It seemed to have taken on an alarming life of its own. 'Excuse me. I need to start the rehearsal.'

He walked into the hall, where most of the players were already setting up or doing warm-up twiddles on their instruments. Carl was playing a jazz riff on his trombone, and Kayla had picked it up and was improvising a bass line with him. The other two double bass players – each of stalwart classical orchestral stock who wouldn't know how to play without sheet music if their life depended on it – looked at each other with raised eyebrows and shared reserve.

Eliot unpacked his scores and baton, and took off his coat. Before too long, he was nodding along with Carl and Kayla's riffing, and looked over appreciatively. Kayla looked at him and smiled.

David appeared on his other side. 'Eliot, it appears we'll have some visitors during this rehearsal, including a photographer—'

'Yes, I met Doug just now. And his entourage.'

'Oh. Well then, we need to ask people if they're OK with their pictures being used.'

'Yes, you're right. Will do. God knows what the Oakdean lot will say.'

'Where are they?' said David, looking round at the doors. 'They're usually early.'

'Maybe they aren't allowed to come in until Carl plays "The Imperial March",' Eliot said, still enjoying the jazz vibe coming from behind the cello section.

'Maybe they're not coming any more now we're having the concert here.'

Eliot gave David his full attention. 'Do you think they'd do that?'

'It did occur to me.'

'Would be petty.'

David raised his eyebrows, shrugged, and wandered back to the horn section.

Just then, Eliot heard Carl switch into a laid-back, syncopated version of 'The Imperial March'. He caught Carl's eye and laughed.

Dr Irving had escorted his boys once more, but he didn't look happy about it. He turned his one eye onto Eliot and bore down on him, without any of the erstwhile dapper jauntiness Eliot had come to expect. The days of the Irving flamenco were long gone.

'We are continuing our support of your venture in spite of recent events,' he said to Eliot when he was within earshot. 'But I feel I should leave you in no doubt of *ira nostra*. However, once Oakdean men undertake a task, they follow through.' Eliot ignored Charlie's snort of laughter from the front desk of the cellos. 'I hope and trust that your faith in an establishment such as this is not... misplaced.'

Not waiting for Eliot's answer, Dr Irving turned on the spot (perhaps with a trace of his old flamenco fire) and stalked over to the side of the hall to sit incongruously on one of the brightly coloured plastic chairs. He looked as if a tear in space-time had allowed him to drop through from the eighteenth century, and the journey had not been a pleasant one.

His boys fanned out from the door to their respective sections. Tarquin (horn) and Hector (trumpet) were deep in urgent conversation until they had to part to go to opposite sides of the orchestra.

Eliot caught the sense they were out of sorts, but decided not to worry about it just then. There were other pressing matters. 'Hi, everyone,' he called over the hubbub of instrument twiddling and chat. 'Before we tune, can I just ask your permission for photos? Sunbridge want to include some pictures of us – well, probably mainly their pupils, to be honest – in a brochure or something. If anyone doesn't want to be included in that, I'd go and see Rosalind in the foyer now. She's with the photographer chap.'

'No,' said Dr Irving, immediately rising from his chair and striding to the door. 'No, no no. Absolutely not.'

'That'll be a no from Dr Irving,' said Charlie.

'I'm not surprised,' said Erin. 'It's not panning out the way he wanted it.'

'He'll get over it,' said Eliot. 'Gwynneth? Could we have an A, please?'

While the A was passed round the sections in turn, snatches of the conversation going on in the foyer could be heard, with Dr Irving's insistence that none of his boys would be in any image, and Rosalind's firm assurances that they wouldn't be. Eventually, Dr Irving returned to his seat on the edge of the hall, and as the first movement of Sibelius 2 began, Rosalind brought Doug and her other friends into the hall too. The pulse of the strings was soon joined by the peculiarly Finnish brass and wind chords Sibelius loved, conjuring the smell of birch forests and the feel of a hard frost underfoot.

The small chirrups of Sibeliusy birdsong began to be accompanied by intermittent rips of Velcro, as Doug sorted out what equipment he needed for the shoot from his myriad luggage. He had the air of a pack mule, with all his little foam-lined boxes carefully strapped to different bits of his body, leaving his hands free to take pictures.

Tracie, playing trombone next to Carl, was attentive and serious. She wasn't getting all the notes, but Carl was carefully putting her right when she needed a bit of help, showing her the way he wrapped each finger in turn into a fist when he was counting bars so that in the end she could count in fives and not get lost so easily. Then, when the trombones had finished a section together, he gave her a thumbs up and a grin.

The other Sunbridge kids over in the violins – Danilo, Marina and Reece – were also taking it very seriously and doing their best to keep up. Sometimes they floundered a bit in extended quaver passages, but with some help from violinists around them, who gave them a nod every now and then and pointed with the end of their bow which bar they'd got to, they managed to keep going. Caspar and Rufus accepted no help from anyone, even if they got it wrong. Rufus determinedly played a bar ahead of everyone else for almost a page, despite various people trying to signal his error. An Oakdean man, he was following through indeed.

Rosalind had parked her PTA lot on some chairs on the other side of the hall from Dr Irving, who continued to fire pointed looks in their direction. She then crept round the orchestra with Doug as if she were in front-line trenches under fire, almost crouching to indicate the shots she wished him to get. A camera is not the quietest machine.

Eliot and the orchestra were game for the most part, ignoring the clack-clack-clack as Doug took multiple frames per second. It didn't matter when the whole orchestra were going for it: nobody worried about a few clacks underneath massed triple trumpets, trombones and tuba, when the timpanist was rolling away. In the quiet bits, though, when Eliot was trying to convey subtlety and nuance, he would have preferred not to have his gestures augmented by what sounded like the red carpet at a film premiere.

When it got too insistent, Eliot lost patience. He brought the orchestra to a halt when they were trying to play a *piano* passage of the second movement.

'Um, Doug – I wonder if we could maybe take the pictures when we're all really loud? It's just that, well, it's a bit distracting for the players in the quiet bits?'

Doug sighed. Rosalind reacted by instructing him to take ever-more arty shots from weird angles, as if the noise of his camera would make less of a distraction if it came from ankle level. The trouble was, apparently this change of angle necessitated different bits of required equipment, out of different Velcroed boxes.

As they started work on the third movement, while all the strings were concentrating furiously on their terrifically fast triplets and hoping they weren't going to get flung off the merry-go-round, Rosalind made Doug slide among the players on his back to get shots of Reece and Marina looking partly terrified but determined, their tongues peeping out as they tried to keep up. Doug's progress through the upper strings could be observed by violinists being startled, lifting their legs out of the way, losing their place, cursing or giggling, finding their place again, putting their legs back where they wanted to and carrying on.

Once Doug had got his shots, he was effectively trapped in a forest of violinists' legs. He changed direction, and slid out of the back of the section through the horns like a mechanic wheeling himself out on a trolley from under a car. He stood up, his anorak showing just how much more improvement the cleaner could make on the lino with his new Truvox Orbis 400 rotary buffer (Rosalind took a mental note to raise it on his next 360-degree performance review).

The parents from the PTA started to get bored. Rehearsals are not for everyone. Sometimes, not even the orchestra wants to be there. But if the whole process is alien, it is difficult to appreciate why Eliot needed to start the same passage four times, stopping a few short bars in each time and explaining, in four different ways, why it wasn't quite what he was asking for and how he thought the players could get closer to his ideal. What the governors wanted was the bit of glorious tune they would recognise from the last movement, when the violins would soar in a lyrical romantic swoop like a broad-winged Finnish eagle over fjords and stunning scenery and hard-edged Scandinavian light. What they didn't understand was that to get there, they must plug away through the Finnish forest's tangled and scrubby undergrowth consisting of *pizzicato* strings plonking in the wrong places and a wind section whose chords needed some definite advice when it came to tuning or everyone started to feel nauseated.

They started to chat. Quietly at first, and only in the loud bits, when Hector was helping the trumpets blast out some insistent motif or Leroy puffed through his tuba so hard it vibrated the music on the trombone stands in front of him. Pretty soon, they had become emboldened by that camouflage, and carried on their discussions even when the music failed to hide them.

Eliot tried throwing them glances every now and then, but their attention had wandered so far they weren't even looking at him. When he next stopped the music to discuss a balance issue between the horns and oboe, he turned and made a request.

'Would you mind either taking your chat into the foyer, or keeping it down a bit in here? It's difficult to concentrate, that's all. Hope that's OK?' He thought he had phrased it in a suitably deferential way so as not to cause any offence, but saw at once that he had failed.

Doug took advantage of the pause in the music to snap a few more pictures of Irie in the percussion section. She jumped, having not seen him approach on his elbows and knees on the other side of the timps, and a stick fell from her hand with a smack on the skin of the drum. It bounced off, disappeared over the front of the timp and hit Doug on the head, where he was half-crouching, half-lying on the floor behind Carl. Doug recoiled and fell into Carl's trombone case lying open by

106

his chair, which slammed shut on him like a giant clam. The muffled cries of Doug's enveloped head were soon drowned out by an entire orchestra losing it.

Carl leaned down and opened his case. 'Alright, mate?'

'Yeah,' said Doug, sitting up and realising everyone was staring at him. He opened one of his many boxes with an exasperated rip of Velcro, took out a lens cloth and started to polish his zoom.

'Pearl? Perhaps now might be a good time to get the coffees ready,' said Eliot.

Pearl nodded and scuttled out, leaving her viola and bow in her case on a chair at the side of the hall.

'Great,' said Eliot, trying to wrestle any semblance of order from the sight of musicians weeping with laughter in front of him. 'Where were we?'

'Beyond help,' said Charlie, under his breath.

'Maybe we should let Doug out before we get going again?' said Ann, leaning her cello to one side to make a path.

Doug smiled at her. He climbed to his feet and squeezed through to the open space of the hall. He was immediately gesticulated at by Rosalind, who thought he might take some shots of the PTA group enjoying the rehearsal. The memo hadn't reached the PTA group, however, who were busy discussing a bullying incident in Year 11 and rumours about food poisoning after a cookery club bake sale.

'Bloody hell, they're worse than sopranos,' muttered Eliot to the first string desks within earshot, and then carried on, louder. 'Come on – let's get the last bit of the fourth movement done before the break.'

'At least the brass giving it some welly might drown that lot out,' said Erin.

Eliot nodded, and so for the final ten minutes of the first half he stood in front of an orchestra at optimal cruising altitude,

107

easily playing over any idle chat happening a few feet away. There is something solid and optimistic about the key of D major: it is one that brooks no obstacles and has your back. Sibelius knew it, but plays around with that subliminal knowledge near the end of the symphony. He takes the orchestra on a twisted, dark and obstructed path just in the final stages, across miles of barren and unfriendly territory, accompanied by relentless timpani and flute scales, and the trumpets and massed strings repeating a mournful – and, crucially, minor – phrase, until they emerge from the forest into the light and it transforms, suddenly, into the major key again. Sibelius was a clever bugger.

The final rolling chords built from Erin and Charlie in the cellos, Kayla providing most of the volume in the basses and Carl and Tracie on trombone, with Max helping Irie with her timpani rolls. The trumpets and horns cascaded over the top, and sent the violins up their fingerboards, scrubbing away on *tremolos*, showing the indefatigable nature of life and music. Eliot knew the end of this symphony left him somehow both aged and renewed every time he conducted it.

Chapter 12

The rush to coffee was its usual tsunami that broke around the rather surprised knot of PTA contingent still sitting between the orchestra and the doors to the foyer.

'Shouldn't one of us stay here again?' said Erin as she put her cello in her case.

'Nothing happened last week,' said Ann. 'Do you think they've stopped?'

'There are even more new people around than usual tonight,' said Charlie. 'Don't know if that makes it more or less likely.'

'Since we don't know who was nicking things, there's no way of knowing,' said Erin.

The Oakdean pupils had already gone to the foyer, accompanied by Dr Irving, who was taking the opportunity to remind Doug that if any of his pictures included his boys, he would be feeling the full force of a lawsuit at the earliest opportunity. He used more Latin words when he was explaining it to Doug, but that was the gist.

'I'll stay, if you like,' said Kayla. 'At least if it's any of my lot I'll know what they're up to. God, I hope not.'

'OK, thanks,' said Erin. 'I'll get you a drink – whaddya want?'

'Tea – white with two, please.'

They left Kayla in the hall and joined the queue. Rosalind had gathered her visitors on the far side of the foyer and was evidently wrapping proceedings up for the evening.

Charlie jerked his head over to Rosalind. 'Looks like our second half might be a bit quieter, at least,' he said. 'Unless she leaves Doug to finish off.'

'I feel sorry for Doug,' said Ann.

'Could have been worse,' said Carl, in front of them in the queue. 'He could have fallen into Leroy's tuba case and got lost altogether.'

'Do you think he has Velcro on his trousers' fly?' said Charlie. 'Imagine having your back to him in the gents and trying to work out what the hell was going on.'

Tarquin, Caspar and Rufus collected their drinks at the front of the queue. Caspar nudged the others then tried to pay Pearl with a contactless card, which flustered her and drew condescending smiles from the Oakdean boys. Pearl indicated her new-and-improved cash container: no longer the insulation tape art installation from the week before. This time she had cut a hole in the bottom of her ice cream carton and slotted it over the handle of a drain plunger, which she had then superglued and taped to the box. The handle rose proudly up through the centre of the box like an abstract art representation of some phallic deity, but there was ample room around it for people to drop their money in. The business end of the plunger was securely stuck to the tabletop, and remained immobile in its rubbery kiss throughout the break.

The queue shuffled forward and the Oakdean boys moved further over in the foyer. Carl dropped his change into Pearl's box and complimented her on its design. Pearl flushed pink with pleasure. Charlie reached the caffeine end of the queue.

'Should we go and congratulate Irie for stopping Doug sliding around on the floor like some weird photographic snake?' asked Ann.

'Or maybe check she's OK after startling him into a trombone case,' said Erin. 'Ooh, Pearl, may I have another one as well? Tea, please.'

'Nice plunger, Pearl,' said Charlie.

They moved out of the way of the rest of the queue and were turning back towards the hall with Kayla's tea when some raised voices on the far side of the foyer caught their attention. Tarquin's nasal saw of a voice cut through first.

'You don't look as if you've ever seen an orchestra, let alone played in one. Why don't you piss off to your grubby council estate and leave the real music to us?'

He was standing on one side of Tracie, while Caspar and Rufus were blocking her way on her other side. She had the wall at her back.

'Fuck off,' muttered Tracie.

'Ah, the dulcet, mellifluous tones of the working-class female,' said Caspar. 'She'll be breeding soon and won't bother the real world any more.'

'Who'd want to do that with her?' said Rufus. 'Ugly dyke.'

The boys congratulated themselves on their pithy social analysis by sharing a communal sneer.

Tracie laughed. 'You lot can fucking talk. You've only got four working eyes between you. Whaddya do at your pissing school – blind each other for fun?'

'I imagine our education eclipses yours,' said Tarquin.

'*Bona doctrina plurimi pretii est,*' agreed Rufus.

'Don't mean you can talk proper, though,' said Tracie. 'What an arse.'

Tarquin put his hand behind his ear in mock distress. 'Hark! Did she speak? I find it difficult to extract the meaning from her bewildering syntax.'

Rufus and Caspar laughed.

Tracie had had enough. 'This is what I meant,' she said, aiming a deft punch into Tarquin's stomach, doubling him over. She tried to push past him but was stopped by Rufus, who caught her with one arm around her neck and twisted her arm behind her so hard she screamed and promptly bit his hand before headbutting his nose with the back of her skull.

'Hold this,' said Carl, giving Charlie his coffee. He crossed the foyer in no time at all and grabbed Rufus by his hair, holding him at arm's length to keep Rufus's now profusely bleeding nose away from himself. Carl clamped his other hand around the back of Tarquin's collar while Tarquin was still bending over, winded. He eyeballed Caspar. 'You stay right where you are, mate, if you know what's good for you,' he said. Caspar nodded hurriedly and shrank against the wall.

Tracie staggered away from Rufus, rubbing her neck where he had squeezed it.

'You OK?' said Carl.

She nodded.

From her vantage point on one side of the foyer, Rosalind stared, open-mouthed, at the tableau. The assorted parents and governors behind her were equally stunned. Accustomed as they were to Sunbridge's sometimes feral nature, they were nevertheless taken aback by such violence erupting in the presence of visitors. Usually the kids managed to hold it together if they knew they were on show.

On the other side of the foyer, the musicians were equally mesmerised. It had all happened so quickly. Marco was holding on to the edge of Pearl's table, taking careful deep breaths and staring at the floor, trying not to have a panic attack.

'What's going on?' Kayla ran up to Carl. 'I heard Tracie scream. What happened?'

A sudden string of shutter clicks rang out, as Doug took advantage of the hiatus to indulge in some blood-soaked reportage.

'No!' croaked Dr Irving, leaping towards Doug and spilling half his coffee on the way. 'I thought I'd made myself abundantly clear there are to be no pictures of Oakdean College men!' He made a lunge for Doug's camera, which missed.

'Perhaps now is not the ideal time to add to our portfolio, Doug,' said Rosalind. She moved towards Carl and Kayla in what she hoped was a calm and purposeful way. It wasn't helped when her heel skidded in Dr Irving's coffee puddle and she ended up sitting on the floor. Kayla helped her to her feet.

'What do you suggest we do with these two?' Carl asked Kayla, still holding Tarquin and Rufus.

'You can let go of them or we'll be adding assault charges for you as well as that girl,' said Dr Irving.

'Hang on,' said Kayla. 'Let's get to the bottom of this.' She turned to Tracie. 'What happened?'

Tracie was looking her old-fashioned sullen self. 'These gits thought they could mouth off at me and get away with it.'

'Mouth off?' said Kayla.

'I did hear this one' – Carl shook Tarquin's collar to indicate who he was referring to – 'tell Tracie to leave. Something about pissing off to a grubby council estate – was that it?' He shook Tarquin again.

'I must insist you unhand my boys forthwith,' cried Dr Irving. 'I protest most strongly!'

Carl slowly relaxed his grip on Rufus and Tarquin. Rufus's hair remained in a Tintinesque homage to the imprint of Carl's fist.

'That's better,' said Dr Irving. 'And now,' – he turned to Rosalind – 'what is the disciplinary procedure against this child for assault?'

'I'm sure when we have investigated the facts of the matter, we can ensure a satisfactory outcome for all parties involved.'

Kayla had never been so thankful for Rosalind's obfuscatory nature. She looked at Rufus, whose nose was still oozing blood.

'Let's get you sorted first, shall we? Come with me. I know where the first aid box is.' She handed him a tissue and led the way to the admin office, calling back over her shoulder to Carl, 'Can you get some paper towels on those spills? I'll get some gloves on to clear up the blood in a minute. Don't touch it.'

Carl went to the gents for paper towels, and Rosalind turned to face her guests, clasping her hands in front of her like a member of the von Trapp family about to perform their final Vienna concert. Several governors looked uncomfortable. This was not the cultural beacon Rosalind had led them to believe had been ignited in Sunbridge Academy.

While Rosalind placated her governors, the rest of the orchestra slowly began to chat again, having been transfixed in silence since Carl's intervention.

'Never a dull moment,' remarked Charlie, biting half a digestive off in one go and pushing the corners into his mouth with a finger.

'Is Tracie alright?' said Ann.

'Yeah – she's over with Irie now,' said Erin, pointing to where they were both being given calming and fortifying hot beverages and extra biscuits by Pearl, who was fussing like a trouper. 'She looks fine.'

'Unlike them,' said Charlie, nodding over to where Dr Irving was having a muted but intense conversation with Tarquin and Caspar. 'What the fuck happened? Did you hear it start?'

'No,' said Erin. 'I turned round when you did, when Carl ran over.'

'Tell you what, though,' said Charlie. 'Tracie knows how to handle herself. She was like something out of *The Karate Kid*!'

'You pick that kind of thing up at Sunbridge,' said Marco, who was standing near enough to hear. 'It's either that or, well, get a bit squashed.' He swallowed his tea nervously.

'I'd forgotten you went here,' said Erin. 'Is this normal?'

Marco smiled. 'Yeah.'

'So underneath that mild-mannered exterior, you're really a deadly weapon, is that what you're saying?'

'Um, no.'

'Were you the one who got squashed?' asked Charlie, not unkindly.

Marco nodded. 'Would have been nice to have Carl around sometimes.'

'We could all do with a Carl now and then,' said Erin.

Charlie flicked her a quick look to see how serious she was being. In his as-yet undeclared, and indeed undecided, war to win Erin's heart, he didn't know if he had to watch out for rivals.

Rosalind ushered her governors and PTA parents out of the front doors, having calmed them with assurances it was merely a glitch in the pixels of the promised new brochure. She turned and advanced towards Doug, who, to his credit, had not attempted any more pictures since the fight, even though it looked as if he wanted to. He was hovering over the blood-soaked paper towels on the floor with a light meter. She intercepted him before the temptation overpowered him.

'Perhaps we could take a view on whether or not the brochure would require further aspects from the latter part of this evening's rehearsal?' she said, indicating Doug should follow her to the hall.

He trailed after her, putting his camera behind his back and firing off a few frames at the blood spatters without looking.

'Doug!' snapped Rosalind.

He sped to catch up.

Pearl started to clear her table and the players wandered back. Kayla and Rufus still hadn't reappeared. Carl walked through with Tracie, which kept Dr Irving, Caspar and Tarquin well away from her.

Eliot was waiting at his stand, smiling his calmest smile and fending off suggestions from David and Rafael, who were wondering if this outreach idea might not be worth it.

'Let me have one last chance at it,' he said. 'I've conducted youth orchestras. There have been incidents like this before, and with any luck it'll blow over and we can sort things from here. Kids are a bit volatile, that's all.'

He got a grudging go-ahead from two-thirds of the orchestra committee, and thanked them. He turned to the orchestra.

'Welcome back, everyone, from what has been a rather eventful coffee break.' There were snorts of laughter from various players. 'Um – I'd just like to say that we can't condone either violence' – jeers from the Oakdean pupils were directed at Tracie – 'or verbal abuse' – equally committed jeers came from Sunbridge kids at Tarquin and Caspar – 'so, anyway, after the rehearsal I'd like to speak to everyone who was involved in that fracas, to see how we can fix whatever went wrong. Does that sound OK?'

There was a general sound of agreement. Tarquin, Caspar and Tracie looked equally sullen.

'What's a frack arse?' Tracie whispered to Carl.

'A fight. Don't you worry – I'll stick up for you,' said Carl. He smiled. 'Not that you need me to, by the look of you.'

Tracie grinned.

'Good,' said Eliot. 'Now, if we could – er, can we put that away now, please?' He waved at Hector, the Oakdean trumpeter, who was standing near the door having a conversation on his phone. 'We're about to start again.'

Hector nodded and raised his hand, finished speaking and walked over to his chair. He nodded at Tarquin over in the horns.

Doug had already started clicking for the second half of his evening's work.

Gwynneth noticed Hector's nod, caught Carl's eye and asked him in sign language what was going on. He replied he had no idea.

'Could we have an A for the strings, please?' said Richard, the leader of the orchestra, and Gwynneth had to stop any further signing discussion to help all the violins approximate their open strings.

'Right, I'd like to work on the first bit of the fourth movement again, before where we left off for coffee,' said Eliot, turning back a few pages in his score. 'I know it's *attacca*, but let's pick it up right on the bar line – there's no great place round there to start it, so we'll just dive in. Leroy, I really need to hear those lead notes to kick us off. Give us some oomph. The tuba is working with the basses there – I'm sure Kayla will be back in a minute: do your best, you two, until then – while the cellos faff about playing the end of the lovely tune and pretending they are upper strings.'

'Oi!' said Erin.

'We're so versatile,' said Charlie.

'OK, then?' said Eliot. 'Let's go. Ready, Leroy?'

Leroy nodded, and settled his tuba on his lap.

'So, straight on the *allegro moderato*. In three – I'm beating minims.'

The basses scooped the upbeat and lurched nicely into the triple time. Leroy, who should have been playing the same notes as them, sounded as if he was playing through a curtain and possibly from another time zone. The trombones, who had off-beat chords that were supposed to fit into the bar just after Leroy landed on it each time, quickly fell apart. The cellos, who had rests, turned round to see what was going on. The basses carried on gamely, but after a few bars it was clear things were going hopelessly awry. The trumpets of course blasted their bit of tune over the top at the right time, but even they couldn't carry the whole orchestra with them. It fell apart.

'Um – hello?' said Eliot, looking over to the basses and tuba. 'Start of the fourth movement? Leroy, you have C sharp upbeats into Ds, like the basses, then the basses hold the D through the bar but you come off. Is that what you've got?'

'Yep,' said Leroy. 'Dunno what was going on there.'

'OK, let's go again,' said Eliot.

The second time was no better. Leroy's notes were flat and strangely muffled. Carl got the giggles. So did Ann, at the back of the cellos.

While the orchestra had stopped, Kayla came back into the hall with Rufus, whose face was now cleaned up and looking more normal, except for a bit of rolled tissue stuck up one nostril. He looked over to Hector in the trumpets before taking his seat near Caspar in the violins, who started whispering to him. Kayla returned to the basses to find most people near to her were giggling.

'What's up?' she asked Carl.

'Start of the fourth movement. Leroy's having a bit of a turn. You'll see.'

Leroy was checking his valves and emptying water from different sections, then sat back and shrugged.

'Third time lucky?' said Eliot.

'Pearl will be here in a minute,' said Kayla. 'She was having a bit of trouble de-plunging her money from the table.'

Eliot nodded, and started again.

At the sound of Leroy's first parp, which was wrong in exactly the way it had been wrong before, the entire trombone section and most of the lower strings dissolved into laughter.

'Fucking hell,' muttered Leroy, and stared at his tuba in disbelief.

'Sounds like you shoved a sock in it,' said Charlie.

'Several socks,' said Kayla. 'Or a pair of tights.'

'There are more convenient overnight bags,' said Carl.

Leroy stood up, rested the tuba on his chair and peered into the bell. 'Can't see anything,' he said.

'Need a torch?' said Ann.

'In your own time,' said Eliot, smiling.

'Hang on,' said Leroy, reaching one arm down into the bell as far as it would go. 'There's something.'

He was in almost up to his shoulder, feeling around blind.

'If you ever get a blockage, nothing better than getting a tuba player round to have a furtle in your U-bend,' said Carl, conversationally.

Leroy straightened up and pulled something out. It was a small, clear plastic bag with what looked like moss inside.

'What the fuck?' he said, turning it over in his hand.

'That's no sock,' said Charlie.

Leroy put the bag on his chair, and leaned back into his tuba. Three more identical bags appeared.

As Rosalind saw Leroy displaying what appeared to be a significant drug haul, she squeaked quietly.

'What the fuck?' said Leroy again.

A frisson spread through the orchestra, accompanied by whispers and murmurs.

'Not the greatest place to keep your stash,' said Carl.

'It's not mine!' said Leroy.

'Well, it is your tuba,' said Pete, who sat next to Pearl on the back desk of the violas. Pete liked things to be ordered and logical.

'Well, that at least explains what was going on in the Sibelius just now,' said Eliot. 'Although' – he frowned – 'perhaps not in the best way imaginable.'

'It's not mine!' repeated Leroy. 'What the fuck?' He seemed to be stuck on repeat.

At that moment there was a loud popping sound from the foyer, followed by a crash of what could have been many biscuit packets falling from a table and loose change rolling on the floor.

'Pearl's done it!' said Charlie. 'Maybe we should get her to plunge Leroy's tuba to see if there's any more in there.'

'Give it a blow, Leroy,' said Carl. 'See if you've cleared it.'

Leroy shot him a look that was part embarrassment and part amusement. He picked up the tuba and tried an experimental toot: it worked perfectly. A cheer went up from the orchestra.

'I must say, you all seem to be taking this far too frivolously,' said Dr Irving from his place at the side of the hall. 'One of your number appears to be in possession of a significant amount of drugs and you laugh.'

'Not *that* significant,' said Reece, one of the Sunbridge violinists. Kayla glared at him with enough urgency that he took the hint and shut up. Charlie and Erin exchanged looks.

'Well, I think the correct course of action,' continued Dr Irving, 'would be to—'

'*I* shall establish the correct course of action in my school, thank you,' called Rosalind tartly.

'It's not mine!' said Leroy, more out of habit now than with any hope he might be believed.

'I must insist that procedures—' started Dr Irving, but his oratory was interrupted by feet clattering in the foyer, a startled yelp from Pearl, some yelling and the crash of the hall doors being flung open.

The police had arrived.

Chapter 13

They spilled into the hall, shouting instructions and looking extremely matt black, stab-proof and crash-helmeted. The orchestra froze and did as it was told. Doug managed to get at least half a dozen pictures off before he was rugby tackled to the floor by the nearest police officer.

A keen springer spaniel skittered over the lino attached to a taut lead, tail wagging and tongue out. Her name, improbably, was Fang.

'Oh shit,' said Leroy.

'That was quick,' said Carl.

David attempted to get up and try to speak to the police officers, but was abruptly told to sit down, which he did.

'I am Deputy Head of Sunbridge Academy,' cried Rosalind. 'And that is my photographer, Doug. Please let go of him!'

The police officer who had tackled him slowly got off. Doug disentangled himself and stood up, looking wary. He un-Velcroed a bag to retrieve his lens-polishing cloth, which made the officer jumpy again. Fang wagged hopefully at Doug, imagining perhaps there might have been a biscuit in that bag, but was prevented from going over to check it out by her handler.

'Do you have a warrant?' said Rosalind. 'This is a school.'

'Don't need a warrant, madam,' said the officer who had told David to sit down. He appeared to be in charge. Although not of Fang, who continued to behave as if this was the most exciting thing she had been asked to do since chasing a ball on her walk earlier in the day, and she wanted to convey her utter commitment to any endeavour that might have a treat at the end of it.

The officer cleared his throat and continued. 'We have reasonable grounds for suspecting that a person has or has had an item on the premises that contravenes Section 139B of the 1988 Criminal Justice Act, and as such we have powers to search these premises and any person on them.'

Rosalind, although somewhat intimidated by the rapid expansion of a police state within her Sunbridge empire, was nevertheless impressed by the officer's clear grasp of precise definitions and appropriate vocab. She warmed to him as a kindred spirit.

'I see,' she said, although she didn't.

Kayla did, however. Over her Sunbridge career she had dealt with many incidents that had ended up with various pupils being arrested. She had heard that Criminal Justice section quoted before. 'You reckon someone's got a knife?'

'What, as well as the drugs?' asked Tarquin.

'Oh, for God's sake,' said Eliot.

There was a rattle of phlegm from the direction of Dr Irving, signalling his imminent wish to join the conversation.

'Hang on,' said Erin quietly. 'Keep your heads down.'

'If I might interject at this point—' said Dr Irving, rising to his feet.

'You may not,' barked the police officer. Dr Irving lowered himself again like a slow jack-in-a-box. 'You!' The police officer pointed at Tarquin. 'Repeat that, please.'

Tarquin shrugged and ran his fingers through his hair. 'The tuba player was hiding his stash – look.'

'It's not mine!' said Leroy, now looking properly panicky. He picked up the bags and waved them at the police officer. 'They were inside my tuba. Mucking up the Sibelius. But I didn't put them there.'

'It *is* your tuba,' said Pete again.

'Shut up, Pete,' said everyone within earshot.

The dog handler unclipped Fang's lead and let her dash into the orchestra, where she quartered the ground under the string section with huge enthusiasm. She accurately tracked the exact path Doug had slid along before emerging in the horns, then double-backed and zigzagged through the cellos and seemed to be on her way directly to Leroy. As she was passing through the trombone section, she stopped at Carl's case and started wagging at triple speed. She leapt over the case, sniffed Leroy's bags and jumped up at him, barking happily. Then she returned to Carl's case and barked at that too.

'What?' said Carl to the dog.

'Good girl!' said her handler, and then addressed Carl. 'Would you open your case, please, sir?'

'The only thing it's had in it during this rehearsal has been a photographer's head,' said Carl. 'But that's going to sound weird.'

He sighed, reached down and opened the lid. Fang let out an ecstatic yelp of triumph, wagging and barking and looking back to her handler. Carl leaned down and retrieved a plastic bag that looked identical to those Leroy had found in his tuba.

'What the fuck?' said Carl.

'Join the club,' said Leroy.

'Any more for any more?' said the officer in charge. He seemed to be enjoying himself.

Fang's handler sent her off again into the orchestra. After the first half of the rehearsal with Doug meandering around at floor level, having a waggy spaniel weaving in and out of the chairs would have been a welcome diversion were it not for the fact that she was a highly trained drug sniffer. There was an element of conflict in the dog-loving musicians, as they fought their natural urge to lean down to give her a scritch behind the ears, not wanting to tempt any kind of fate that seemed to be delivering packets of drugs on a whim to unsuspecting players.

Fang returned without finding anything else, but got a treat anyway from her handler. She sat on the floor polishing the semicircle of lino behind her bottom with a tail that put a Truvox Orbis 400 rotary buffer to shame.

'Right then,' said the officer. 'I am seizing these bags under Section 19 PACE. We appear to have mission creep.'

'That's new drug slang I hadn't heard,' whispered Charlie to Erin.

'PACE?' asked Rosalind.

'Police and Criminal Evidence Act, madam,' said the officer.

'So what happens now?' said Eliot, trying not to hope that he would ever get the second half of his Sibelius rehearsal underway.

'What happens now, sir, is that we search all of you in a systematic manner. In addition to which, the two gentlemen who were in possession will have to return to the station with us to answer a few more questions.'

'Hang on,' said Carl. 'We've been set up here. Someone's having a laugh.'

'I'm not finding it funny,' said the officer.

'That bag isn't mine. And Leroy definitely didn't have drugs in his tuba in the first half. He was playing it. You know, not brilliantly – this is Leroy we're talking about, let's face it – but there were definitely real notes there. And then suddenly after the break he was trying to fart out something that sounded like the morning after a pokey vindaloo, if you get me.'

'I think we all do, thank you,' said Eliot. 'And that's an image I won't be able to bleach out of my brain for a while, thanks.'

There was another attempt at an attention-seeking throat clearance from Dr Irving, but the police officer was too quick.

'Right. If everyone cooperates this shouldn't take too long.'

If there had been a narrator in the film of that evening, they would have cut in at that point, saying lugubriously, '*But it did take too long.*'

Hours later, long after any thoughts of rehearsing had evaporated, everyone had been searched and most had been given permission to leave. Even Pearl, who had come into the hall after the raid had started, clutching her plunger/box contraption and looking like the innocent middle-class, middle-aged woman she was. She refused to let go of her money box even when a police officer was patting her down.

The Oakdean pupils were hustled through the search system by Dr Irving like the fast-track queue at airport security they were used to. He then whisked them all out of the hall and back to Oakdean, informing David and Eliot that he would be in contact with them the following day. David and Eliot exchanged glances, each happy to postpone that delight for a few hours.

Rosalind, though continuing to be impressed by the efficient police officer, drew Eliot aside for a quiet word.

'In light of the unfortunate situation this evening, I regret I may have to rescind our offer of holding your concert on these premises.' She held her lanyard with sorrow as if it were a crucifix and she was drawing her strength from it. Which, knowing Rosalind, could well have been true. 'And, perhaps, your rehearsal facilities. I cannot in all good faith recommend to the governors and the PTA that we encourage Sunbridge's liaison with an entity which could bring disastrous publicity instead of the green shoots of high culture we were hoping to grow.'

Eliot sighed. 'I can see it from your point of view, of course,' he said. 'But I know Carl and Leroy. I'd bet anything they're telling the truth.'

'I shall discuss it with the Head tomorrow morning,' said Rosalind. 'A calm decision is a slept-on revision.'

And with that perplexing poetic maxim, she left.

Fang was without doubt the star of the police exercise that evening. Her duties complete, she spent the rest of her time in Sunbridge's hall dispensing cheer and friendly licks and offers to be a tummy rub recipient to bored musicians trapped in the queue.

Despite protestations from anyone who dared to voice their opinion, Carl and Leroy were taken with the police for questioning, after the mysterious plastic bags had been themselves bagged as evidence. Leroy pointed out that he had touched all of his bags when he retrieved them from his tuba, so they were bound to have his fingerprints all over them. Carl said the same. The police officers merely stared at them and said nothing.

Finally, it was over. Eliot, Charlie, Erin, Ann and Kayla looked at each other. Charlie mimed drinking a pint in the international sign language used by tired people everywhere who want to go to the pub. They trudged round the corner to try and make sense of the evening.

'That was… surreal,' said Charlie, when they finally sat at a table that had been remarkably easy to bag: the pub was not experiencing its usual post-rehearsal crush.

'Did that just happen?' said Eliot. 'I mean, actually happen? I've never been in a police raid before.'

'I have,' said Kayla. 'And that was the weirdest one I've ever seen.'

'There are a few things this evening that I want answers to,' said Ann, having drunk deeply from her pint. 'Things that don't add up.'

'Like what?' said Charlie.

'First things first,' said Erin. 'Does anyone have Carl or Leroy's number? Do we know what's going to happen to them? Can we help?'

'I've got Carl's,' said Kayla.

'Aye aye,' said Charlie. He raised his eyebrows and smiled.

'Not like that, shut up. It's just we were thinking of doing some playing together some time – you know, jazz stuff. And maybe some gigs.'

'That'd be great,' said Eliot. 'I enjoyed your noodling around before the rehearsal.'

'Nobody has Leroy's number, then?' asked Erin.

'David will have it on his database,' said Eliot. 'We'll be able to get in touch with him.'

'I'll text Carl now,' said Kayla.

'Go on, Ann,' said Charlie. 'You were about to decode the evening for us. I'm all ears.'

Ann chuckled. 'Well, look – apart from anything else, how come the rozzers manage to run in just as Leroy hoiked the stuff out of his tuba? I was going to try pointing that out at the time, but they weren't really taking questions from the floor.'

'Christ, that's a point,' said Eliot.

'And did they just happen to be passing, all kitted out like that? With a convenient dog?'

'Yeah – what was with that dog?' said Erin. 'Weren't they there looking for a knife or something? Wasn't that what he said?'

Kayla looked up from her phone. 'Yep. If they think people are carrying blades they can search where they like.' She carried on with her text to Carl.

'So why the dog?' said Ann. 'And it wasn't even a wolf clone with huge teeth that they send leaping over garden fences after idiots who try to run. It was a special sniffer.'

'A very lovely sniffer,' said Eliot, who had spent more time than anyone that evening giving Fang tummy rubs.

'Ann's right,' said Charlie. 'There's something about this whole thing that feels fishy. Did someone tip them off?'

'But we all know Leroy didn't have anything in his tuba in the first half,' said Eliot. 'We heard him.'

'So someone set him up?' said Erin.

'Obviously,' said Eliot. 'And it must have happened in the coffee break.'

'Oh God,' said Kayla, putting her phone away and looking aghast. 'That's it.'

'What?' said Erin. 'Has Carl replied?'

'No – I've just sent it. No. Listen. At the break. You went to get me tea, remember?' Erin nodded. 'And I stayed in the hall to be "on guard" in case anything went missing again?'

'Shit,' said Charlie.

'Tracie,' said Ann. 'Was that fight… a diversion?'

'I came running when I heard her scream,' said Kayla. 'God. Sorry. I should have stayed where I was.'

'Of course you came – nobody's blaming you,' said Eliot. 'We were all staring at it too. Well, except Carl.'

'Superhero Carl,' said Charlie, then noticed everyone staring at him. 'What? Oh, OK, that wasn't called for. He's just so bloody' – he fished around for the right word – '*capable*. And tall. And muscly. And talented.' He buried his face in his pint and they all laughed, happy to break the tension of a long evening.

'Don't worry, Charlie,' said Erin. 'I'm sure he'll take you to his gym if you ask nicely.'

'No chance,' said Charlie, wiping froth off his top lip with the back of a finger. 'Any gym that lets Carl in would ban me in a heartbeat. I'd be on those little tiny weights in the corner while people like Carl use normal-sized people like me as barbells.'

'Well, I'm glad he did get in there and break it up,' said Kayla. 'Tracie didn't need it, of course, but I wouldn't have wanted her to do any more damage.'

'She does look handy in a fight,' said Eliot admiringly.

'Hang on, back up,' said Ann. 'Are we seriously saying that those Oakdean boys picked a fight deliberately so someone could plant drugs in the hall without being seen?'

They stared at each other in silence.

'It sounds a bit far-fetched,' said Erin. 'We're not in an Agatha Christie plot.'

'Why would they want to do that?' said Eliot.

'That is a very good question,' said DCI Noel Osmar, who had just arrived and walked straight over to their table. 'Hello. Hoped I might find you in here.'

Chapter 14

'Jesus, Noel,' said Charlie, who had had his back to the room and hadn't seen Noel approach. 'Don't creep up on people.'

'Sorry. Gets to be a habit. Mind if I join you? Can I get another round in?'

'Drinking on duty?' said Erin, smiling.

'Just come off shift.'

'In that case,' said Ann, 'mine's a Pilsner Urquell, thanks.'

Noel took everyone's orders. 'And crisps?'

'I'll help carry,' said Erin, standing up.

While Noel and Erin were at the bar, the rest of them tried to work out how much information they could request about that evening's bizarre events.

'Do you think he has a "no shop talk" rule?' said Eliot.

'But he came here looking for us!' said Kayla. 'Surely that counts for something?'

'We don't know if he knows what happened tonight,' said Ann. 'He wouldn't necessarily know everything going on, would he?'

'Maybe he was just looking for Erin,' said Eliot, nodding over to the bar where Noel and Erin were laughing together while the pints were being poured.

'I prefer to imagine he is on professional business, no matter how many shifts he professes to have just come off,' said Charlie, with more edge to his voice than he wanted to betray.

'Relax, Charlie,' said Ann. 'Stop trying to pounce on her.'

'I wasn't—' said Charlie, but stopped as he saw Ann's face crease into a grin and heard her chuckle start to rev up.

'You're so easy,' she said.

'Cow.'

'Stop it, you two,' said Eliot. 'Do we think he can help us with Carl and Leroy?'

'No harm asking,' said Kayla.

When Noel returned to the table and all the new drinks were set down in front of their new owners, there was an air of hushed expectancy and salt and vinegar crisps. Noel took off his coat, took a deep swallow from his pint, and looked around.

'Evenin', all,' he said, smiling.

'Are you taking the piss?' said Ann.

'Yes.'

'Good.'

'I'm trying to fit in.'

'It's working,' said Erin. 'But, look, we've had a bit of an evening of it ourselves, and you said you were looking for us. I wonder if those two things are related?'

'They could very well be.'

'Oh God, don't go all enigmatic on us,' said Ann. 'Have you heard about what happened to us tonight?'

Noel smiled. 'Yes. And I wondered if talking to you – on an informal, off-duty sort of a basis, you understand – might throw some light on things.'

'We were trying to do what you suggested,' said Erin. 'You know, someone staying in the hall to check nobody was nicking stuff.'

'But then some of those Oakdean boys picked a fight with one of my pupils,' said Kayla. 'To be fair, they didn't know what they were getting themselves into. But she screamed, so I ran through to the foyer to check what was going on.'

'Leaving the hall empty?' asked Noel.

'Yeah,' said Kayla, and sighed. 'Rookie error, right? What an arse.'

'Don't worry about it,' said Ann. 'We would all have done the same.'

'No doubt,' said Noel. 'It's absolutely the natural reaction. It's just – fortuitous, shall we say, for whoever it was doing whatever they were doing, that we didn't have eyes and ears in the hall for a few minutes.'

'"We"?' said Charlie. 'Are we on a police team now? Excellent.'

Noel laughed. 'Consider it incremental training for being a Special. So, from what I've gathered, you all went back into the hall after your break and the tuba player discovered some bags in his instrument?'

'Yes,' said Eliot. 'They weren't exactly helping the Sibelius along.'

'Is Leroy going to be allowed home tonight?' said Erin. 'There's no way he knew about those drugs. Everyone who saw his face when he was fishing them out would tell you the same.'

'I may have some news about that a bit later,' said Noel. 'Meanwhile, tell me what happened next?'

He took another swallow of beer. His coat hung lopsidedly off the back of his chair, one pocket being pulled down by another book just as chunky as the one he had been reading in the pub a fortnight earlier. He had come prepared to wait.

'That's the odd thing,' said Ann. 'Just as Leroy had emptied out his tuba, your lot came crashing through the doors like they were flat out on the last furlong at Goodwood.'

'With a dog,' added Eliot.

'Yes, with a bloody dog!' said Ann. 'Which is another coincidence, don't you think?'

'Considering they were apparently looking for blades,' said Kayla.

Noel put his glass down again. 'They said that, did they?'

'Yeah. Quoted the right bit of spiel and everything,' said Kayla.

'I was impressed you knew that,' said Erin.

'Had to hear it quite a bit hanging around with Sunbridge kids over the years,' said Kayla.

'Hmm. And then?' said Noel.

'Then they sent the dog skittling into the orchestra, where she fetched up with Leroy—'

'She?' said Charlie.

'We had a lot of tummy rubs later,' said Eliot, rather defensively. 'There are no secrets during tummy rubs.' He turned back to Noel. 'And then she turned round to Carl, who apparently has been hiding weed in his trombone case. Which I also find hard to believe.'

Ann sighed. 'And then we were all searched for what seemed like weeks, and then we came here.'

'Apart from Leroy and Carl,' said Kayla. 'Who got taken away. Dunno if they were actually arrested or not. Do you?'

Noel pursed his mouth, wondering how much this new-found camaraderie might translate into friendship. Habit had made him a cautious man, trickling out bits of his life into appropriate, specified areas. He soaked up information like a thirsty plant, but rarely volunteered it. He brought books to pubs and kept his eyes and ears open. And he had not made it to the rank of Detective Chief Inspector by responding to many direct questions in pubs with equally direct answers. He raised his eyebrows and picked up his glass. 'You may be interested to know, Eliot, that everyone's favourite spaniel of the night rejoices in the name of Fang.'

133

Erin spluttered into her beer. 'What?'

'Oh now, that's just not right,' said Eliot. 'You're taking the piss.'

'I'm not,' said Noel. 'Honest. I think it was originally a mix-up on the puppy roster, but it stuck. She's a sweetie.'

Ann looked at Noel steadily. He met her gaze, and a flicker of what might have been an apology passed over his face.

'Do you think there's a slobbery killing machine of a German shepherd over in Balham that has to answer to Angelina?' said Charlie.

'Bureaucracy can be cruel,' agreed Noel.

Ann was still staring at him. 'Come on, Noel,' she said. 'Give us something. What the fuck is going on?'

Noel sighed. 'I know this is going to sound like an old cliché, but you're going to have to trust me. I can't, obviously, tell you everything I know. It isn't my case anyway. But – how can I put this?' He leaned back in his chair and gazed at the ceiling, where a fire alarm blipped its tiny red light occasionally and carried on saving lives without a fuss. 'There are certain aspects of this evening that interest me. And hearing your account of it has been very helpful.' He looked round the table at their faces, and wished he could say more. 'I know that sounds like bullshit. Sorry. It's not, though.'

Ann narrowed her eyes and took a mouthful of Pilsner from her bottle. 'I'm more inclined to trust someone who apologises for saying what sounds like bullshit, than someone who says the real stuff without thinking it needs an apology.'

Noel blinked.

'Christ, that was deep,' said Charlie.

'She gets like this,' said Erin. 'You should hear her sometimes in our cello lessons.'

Ann threw an empty crisp packet at them.

'But what about Carl?' said Kayla. 'And Leroy?'

'Ah, yes. Hang on a tick. Don't go away.' Noel walked towards the door, pulling his phone out of his pocket.

'This is sounding dodgier by the minute,' said Charlie. 'And now our friendly neighbourhood policeman has buggered off.'

'He's left his coat,' said Eliot. 'He won't be long. It's freezing outside.'

'He didn't disagree with anything we've been saying,' said Kayla.

'He didn't really say anything about it at all, did he?' said Erin.

'I don't think he can,' said Ann. 'This whole thing stinks.'

'Is this where I have to apologise again for having my brilliant idea?' asked Eliot, drooping towards the table and leaning his forehead next to his beer. 'What was I thinking?' He slowly raised his head and let it thump gently on the table a few times.

'You'll get sticky hair,' said Erin. 'This pub doesn't have the most diligent wipers.'

'And anyway,' said Kayla, 'I'm glad you did. I'm enjoying it.' She stopped. 'Mostly.'

Eliot raised his head and beamed at her. 'And we are enjoying you enjoying it. I must say, you make a huge difference to the bass section. Please don't leave just because we appear to be in the throes of organised crime.'

'Here he comes,' said Charlie, as the draught of icy air from the street shot around their ankles. 'Any news?'

'Carl and Leroy won't be held in custody tonight,' said Noel. 'As I thought.'

'Thank God for that,' said Kayla. 'It was crazy they were in there in the first place.'

'I must say, Carl's reputation in the station is now approaching legendary status,' said Noel, smiling. 'I don't think he took kindly to his evening's plans going awry.'

'I can imagine,' said Eliot. 'You should have seen him with the Oakdean lot. Textbook Brutus from Popeye manoeuvre.'

'Without any actual hitting,' Kayla added quickly. 'He was stopping the fight, not starting another one.'

Noel sat down. 'So, what music are you doing this time round? Not Elgar again, I guess?' He looked at Erin, who shook her head. 'Shame. I did enjoy that.'

'No – we had quite enough of that last term,' she said. 'Dunno the whole programme yet. We seem to keep getting distracted. Sibelius 2, which is gorgeous. And *Night on the Bare Mountain*. Mussorgsky. Do you know it?'

Noel looked politely blank.

'You'll recognise bits of it,' said Eliot.

'What else are we doing, Eliot?' said Erin. 'You mentioned something about a fanfare a couple of weeks ago – is that still happening?'

'Christ – two weeks in this orchestra can feel like a lifetime,' said Eliot. He looked round the table. 'Sorry, that came out wrong.'

'It's OK, we know what you mean,' said Charlie.

Eliot grinned. 'Yeah, well. I did want to do *Fanfare for the Common Man*, to use all the kids who play brass and show them something really punchy and exciting to play. But then Sir Marmaduke put his oar in, and—'

Noel put his beer down on the table and coughed for a moment. 'Who?'

'Ah. Welcome to the world of knowing who Sir Marmaduke Blythe is,' said Eliot. 'Though apparently none of us will ever know him as well as Ann does.' He giggled, and dodged Ann's kick at his shins under the table.

'Did,' she clarified. 'And one day, my dears, I shall tell you all the details. But I'm not up to it tonight.'

'Fair enough,' said Eliot. 'Anyway, he says he wants to write a fanfare for his horn-playing genius of a godson, but who knows

136

what will happen now.' Eliot's beer was kicking in. He looked positively maudlin.

'The posh horn player? Tarquin?' said Kayla.

'That shite who started the whole fight this evening and ended up dangling from Carl's arm?' said Erin.

Noel was following the conversation with quick eyes.

'Ah yes. The very same,' said Eliot. 'But since we may not be welcome to have our concert at Sunbridge any more—'

'Really?' said Kayla. 'Says who?'

'Says your officious boss, Rosalind. I don't think tonight was a good look for your governors. Oh God!' He turned to Noel. 'We haven't mentioned all this was witnessed tonight by a load of parents and governors, and Doug the photographer, who gamely kept snapping pics right up until he was rugby tackled by PC Plod.' He faced Kayla again. 'So anyway, we might end up at Oakdean to play at the end of term, and if that happens I don't fancy my chances of playing any kind of fanfare that isn't a Blythe fanfare.'

'Hang on,' said Noel. 'Don't you do your concerts at the Civic Hall? That's where I went last time. And the time before that, when you killed your conductor.'

They all exploded into laughter then. There was only so much tension one evening could take.

'Eliot keeps having good ideas,' said Erin, wiping her eyes. 'Keep up.'

'You lot can always bump him off later, in your usual way,' said Noel.

'Oi!' said Eliot. 'Don't be horrid.'

The bell rang for last orders, so they put aside their differences and got the final round in.

Chapter 15

The next morning, David was working from home and fielding telephone calls.

The first was from the Civic Hall administration office, returning his call enquiring if they could re-book the space for their concert, after having cancelled a few weeks previously. They regretted to say that all weekends were now fully booked for the rest of the term.

The second was from Rosalind, who informed him that the Head of Sunbridge Academy and its governors didn't feel hosting a concert on school premises was the most appropriate event, given the orchestra was under investigation for drug dealing. David tried to push back on her characterisation of Stockwell Park Orchestra, but when Rosalind icily pointed out that the governors were also going to debate whether Sunbridge should allow them to rehearse there at all in future, David decided to leave it. He bid her a good morning.

The third was from Dr Irving, who rang to express his intense displeasure about the previous evening's iniquities. David let him run on for a while on speakerphone without interrupting, during which he managed to draft an email about an entirely different subject for work. Eventually, he got a toe-hold in a crack in the Irving delivery, and diffidently wondered if the Oakdean hall was still available for a concert later that term. Dr Irving was entirely silent for a moment. David added another sentence to his email, and further wondered if Sir Marmaduke would be writing anything for the occasion. David could hear the fire in Dr Irving's office crackling away merrily, and wondered about the state of that tweed jacket. Eventually, Dr Irving suggested that Oakdean would indeed be an ideal venue, and that he would speak to Sir Marmaduke about any compositional ideas he might have, and disconnected.

David sent his email, and got up to make more coffee.

In his office in the police station, Noel Osmar was working on something that was not officially his enquiry. He was about four coffees ahead of David. He yawned and rubbed his eyes under his reading glasses, pushing the glasses back up his nose after they had slipped. An ordinary Tuesday morning was going about its grey business outside, but so dimly all the lights were on inside.

Noel was reading his colleagues' summaries from the previous evening's events at Sunbridge. He cross-checked times on call logs with the Short Descriptive Notes of the interviews with Carl and Leroy, and ran through the discs to check nothing had been left out. He looked at duty rosters and staff availability. He noted what evidence had been logged and stored, and what tests had been ordered. He searched online for local photographers called Douglas, and wrote down a telephone number.

There was a tap at the door.

'Coffee, boss?' asked Frank, leaning in. 'I'm just popping over the road for the good stuff.'

'Frank, you beauty,' said Noel. 'Yes please. How was – what were you learning this time?'

Frank sniffed. 'Data protection. Boring.'

'Oh dear. Never mind. It was probably essential.'

'Probably not. I'd rather do tourniquets or offensive driving or something.'

'Defensive. And yes, I remember you enjoying your last First Aid refresher. You kept wanting to be sent to riots.'

'Yeah. Anyway. Back in a tick.'

'Thanks.'

Noel smiled to himself. Frank was coming along nicely.

At lunchtime, Kayla walked into the Sunbridge staffroom to find Rosalind standing to attention by the kettle again. She swore under her breath and was about to decide to go for a walk before her Cup-a-Soup, but Rosalind sprang forward to intercept her.

'Might I have a few moments of your time, Kayla?'

'Well, I was just about to—'

'It won't take long. But it has the element of urgency, so if you wouldn't mind popping along with me to my office?'

'OK.'

'We can walk and talk. The conference call starts in five minutes.'

'Conference call?'

Kayla lengthened her stride to keep pace with Rosalind's clackity heels across the foyer. As they passed where Rufus had bled on the lino, Kayla noticed there was still a faint outline of the puddle. She skirted it silently.

'Yes,' said Rosalind, by now a pace and a half ahead as she rounded the corner of the admin office. In Boat Race terms, she had used up her Middlesex station advantage and was pressing ahead round the Surrey bend to see if she could get to clear water. 'We have a late-scheduled conference call with the Headmaster and Adrian, the chair of the governors. I'd like your input.'

'Input?' Kayla put on a spurt, aware she was merely repeating the key word in Rosalind's last sentence and that this put her at a disadvantage by any conversational measure. 'Into what?'

She had a feeling she could guess what the call was going to be about.

Rosalind had made it round to the far side of her desk by the time Kayla reached the office door. Sitting down and wheeling herself along to the rounded end, Rosalind beckoned Kayla to one of the hammock chairs. The yellow pad and pen were already out, lying next to the squat starfish of the conference phone.

'The Head thought it appropriate to have this call sooner rather than later,' she said, 'as several of the governors had expressed their strong opinions on the events of yesterday evening. I don't need to remind you of the crucial importance of Sunbridge's reputation and standing in the community at the current time and financial climate.'

'Yes. I mean, no.'

'I wanted to have your voice to represent the rank and file, as it were, of teaching input here.'

Kayla sank back a little in the chair.

'The governors are going to press for Sunbridge to sever its ties completely with Stockwell Park Orchestra.'

'Oh, no – surely not!' said Kayla. 'I mean, nothing's proved yet—'

'"Rumours fuel doomers",' said Rosalind, unpeeling a Post-it note with a telephone number written on it, moving it to a full arm's length from her eyes and squinting a bit. 'We can't take any chances at this stage of the financial cycle.'

She stabbed the numbers on the telephone with one finger and pressed green. The line clicked and asked for their conference call pin. Rosalind squinted again and entered four more numbers. Another click, and they were through to some white noise.

'Hello?' said Rosalind twice as loudly as required, leaning close to the phone. 'This is Rosalind Banks.'

'*YOU ARE THE FIRST CALLER ON THIS CONFER-ENCE,*' barked the computer that was apparently running things.

'Can the governors be persuaded to wait until the outcome of the police investigation, at least?' whispered Kayla.

Rosalind drew a few bullet points on her piece of yellow paper enigmatically, but didn't answer.

The phone crackled into life with a couple of loud clicks, a beep and some breathing.

'Hello?' said Rosalind. 'Has someone joined the call?'

'Hello?' said a male voice. 'Am I in?'

'Is that Adrian?' said Rosalind.

'Yes, hello?' said Adrian. 'I've got an echo here.'

'This is Rosalind,' said Rosalind. 'And I have Kayla, Head of Music, with me.'

'Hello, Kayla,' said Adrian.

'Hello, Adrian,' said Kayla.

'SECOND CALLER CONNECTED,' confirmed the computer.

'I've got an echo,' said Adrian.

'You *are* the echo,' murmured Kayla.

'We're just waiting for the Headmaster,' said Rosalind.

'That voice said I was the second caller,' said Adrian.

'Yes,' said Rosalind.

'But I thought you said Kayla was on the call too?'

'She is.'

'So I'm the third?'

'No, Kayla's here.'

Adrian's confusion was covered by more clicks and another beep.

'Hello?' said another voice.

'Headmaster?' said Rosalind. 'Good morning. Adrian and Kayla are already on the call.'

'Ah, good,' said the Headmaster, whose name was Henry but he couldn't ever persuade anyone to use it. 'Can't I pop down to your office, Rosalind? Wouldn't that be simpler?'

'Not at all,' snapped Rosalind. 'Modern technology builds an efficient team.'

'THIRD CALLER CONNECTED.'

'That machine has a delay,' explained Adrian. 'There are four of us, Headmaster.'

Kayla looked out of the window and tried to centre herself in some Zen way on a plastic bag caught in the fence.

'So, Headmaster,' said Rosalind. 'To business. I'm afraid the distressing events of last night indicate we should retract our offer of ongoing synergies with Stockwell Park Orchestra, don't you agree?'

'Well, we can certainly discuss—'

'I think we are beyond the stage of discussing, Headmaster,' said Rosalind. 'If you had witnessed the violence of yesterday's altercation and subsequent bringing of highly negative coverage of Sunbridge into the public domain, I think you might agree that action, and swift action, is essential.'

'Absolutely,' said Adrian. 'Absolutely. I was shocked. Shocked.' He was taking his role of echo quite seriously.

'Why don't we wait until the police have reported?' said Kayla. 'I mean, this could all be a mix-up.'

'This is another example of frankly poor judgement you have shown,' said Rosalind. 'I suggest you learn from it rather than digging in. The path to management is paved with the stones of bad decisions.'

Kayla stared at her. 'What?'

'Now, Rosalind, let's stick to the issue at hand, rather than *ad hominem* attacks,' said Henry.

An abrupt burst of crackling leapt out of the phone. It stopped for a moment, then came and went intermittently as they tried to continue their conversation.

'It cannot have escaped your notice, Headmaster,' said Rosalind, 'that Sunbridge's links with this orchestra have been facilitated and encouraged by Kayla from the start.'

'Well, yes, but you yourself—' began Kayla, but Rosalind was not to be diverted.

'And far be it from me to say I told you so, but I do think a little more high-level optics and analysis of potential outcomes might have worked in our favour here.' Rosalind was ticking off her blank bullet points with every word she emphasised, which was nearly all of them. She did not meet Kayla's eye.

The crackling reached persistent levels of distraction.

'I agree,' said Adrian, almost inaudibly, but sounding as if he were speaking with his mouth full.

'Adrian?' said Kayla.

The crackling stopped.

'Yeff?' said Adrian.

'Could you move your biscuit packet off your microphone please?'

There was one last burst of cellophane movement, and all was still.

'Forry,' said Adrian.

'I don't see we have any choice, Headmaster,' said Rosalind. 'We must be seen to sever any possible hint of ties with local drug culture and violence.'

'Give me strength,' muttered Kayla.

'She's right, Headmaster,' said Adrian, swallowing the last of his ginger nut. 'Shocking events last night.'

Henry's sigh rose out of the speaker and hung above Rosalind's desk like a heavy raincloud. 'Well, it doesn't sound as if I have much choice. Sorry, Kayla.'

'Thank you, Headmaster,' said Rosalind. 'Good day to you. Good day, Adrian.'

She reached forward and disconnected the call before either of them had time to respond.

'Thank you, Kayla,' she said. 'I'll implement the disconnection process immediately.' Life, in Rosalind's eyes, should be as easy to manipulate as telephone calls.

Kayla stood up and left the office without replying. When she had started as a music teacher fifteen years earlier, things had been very different. She sighed, and walked back to the staffroom. It was going to take more than a Cup-a-Soup to offset this development.

David's fourth telephone call that morning was from Rosalind, who regretted to inform him there had been a further development vis-à-vis their earlier communication, and that Sunbridge Academy felt it could no longer provide rehearsal premises for the orchestra. His fifth was to Dr Irving, enquiring if Oakdean could be persuaded to let the orchestra rehearse in their Old Hall for the rest of the term. Dr Irving was delighted to convey his pleasure and hospitality. In fact, Dr Irving's demeanour had performed such a reversal since their conversation earlier that day, David wondered what had happened in that carpeted office to produce such a change. Perhaps Mrs Batten had slipped something medicinal in his coffee.

He started to draft an email to the whole orchestra detailing a change of venue for the rest of term.

Chapter 16

Carl had offered to help Kayla get her bass and high stool over to Oakdean for the next rehearsal. It was only a couple of hundred yards across Stockwell, but a double bass is not the lightest of instruments. Without a car, two hundred yards began to look as daunting as the section of a Strong Man competition where they have to lie in a road and pull an articulated lorry along with their teeth.

Carl didn't have a car either (there really isn't much point in London unless you play timpani or the harp), but he did have muscle. A trombone case was as nothing to his biceps. He could probably have walked along with a timp under each arm and not break a sweat.

Kayla had a lightweight wheeled trolley she could strap her bass to, so she pulled that behind her and let Carl carry her stool along with his trombone case as they turned out of Sunbridge and made their way through the exhaust fumes to Oakdean. The February dusk had already fallen, and although it was still cold, there were early crocuses in Larkhall Park and chaffinches had just started to try out their courting voices.

'Thanks for helping with this,' said Kayla. 'I'm just sorry I couldn't stop Rosalind from chucking us out. I did try.'

'Not a problem. Glad she didn't see me, though. She might have tried to run me off the premises.'

'She's an officious cow, but she's not an idiot. She saw you with the Oakdean boys. There's no way she would have attempted anything.'

Carl laughed, but stopped as Oakdean's rhododendron hedge came into sight. 'Jesus. You ever been in here?'

'Nope.'

'Charlie wasn't impressed.'

'Yeah, I heard him and Erin talking about their visit,' said Kayla. 'Sounds dead weird.' She looked sideways at Carl. 'Heard any more from the police?'

'Not yet – it's all gone a bit quiet. My duty solicitor is on it, I think. She's good. I liked her. At least she believed me. Or said she did.'

'Did you know that other policeman – Noel somebody – met us in the pub last week?'

'No. What did he want?'

'He said it wasn't his case. But he wanted to talk about it. Well, get us to talk about it. I reckon there's something weird going on there 'n' all.'

'I reckon you're right.' They reached the gates, and looked up at the Latin motto. Carl snorted softly. 'For people who bang on about the English being better than anyone else, they're fond of a bit of the foreign when it suits them, aren't they?'

'Come on,' said Kayla, pulling her bass onto the gravel drive. 'We'd better not be the first ones here.'

They walked towards the door, around the enormous oak in the middle of the quad. Even in the gloom, the contrast between Oakdean and Sunbridge almost took Kayla's breath away. It wasn't just the raked gravel with no litter, or the little knee-level lights that subtly pointed out the path like the way to an enchanted grotto. The building itself had an air of permanence that Sunbridge's pre-fab panels simply couldn't replicate. Instead of shabby tarmac, there were cleanly edged kerbstones. Where Sunbridge had self-seeded couch grass and buddleia in its gutters, Oakdean had a gardener and a maintenance man and a budget that wasn't stretched as thin as the last scrape of marge.

'Jesus,' said Carl.

'Just thinking the same,' she said.

Mrs Batten had clearly been stationed behind the door, which swung open as soon as Carl pressed the buzzer. She did not look particularly welcoming, but then she was Mrs Batten. It probably didn't help that she had been asked to stay late. The hall still smelled of burnt coffee and lilies.

'Through that way,' said Mrs Batten, gesturing towards the other end of the hall. 'Follow the signs.'

There were about fifty laminated A4 sheets fixed to the walls at head height, leading the way like breadcrumbs through a forest, each displaying an identical arrow and, in case anyone was in doubt, 'STOCKWELL PARK ORCHESTRA' in 72-point capitals, to direct the musicians safely to the correct hall. For, in the words of Mr Collins, there were several.

As Carl and Kayla approached Old Hall it was clear they were not the first. Sounds of experimental oboe parps and violins starting to tune mixed with a growing hubbub of voices. Eliot was already there, talking to Charlie and Erin, in the centre of a hall easily twice the size of Sunbridge's. The walls were panelled with, naturally, oak, which gave off a scent that managed to evoke money and knowledge and a slight tendency to over-polish one's shoes.

'Imagine eating your dinner in here,' said Kayla.

'Oh, they'll have a dining hall,' said Charlie. 'Separate rooms for everything. Eating. Playing music. Fencing. Baiting the lower classes.'

'You weren't joking, mate,' said Carl. 'This place is mental.'

'Trying to look on the bright side,' said Eliot, with more hope than conviction, 'I bet the acoustics in here are good.'

Their attention was diverted by the sound of crockery rattling on a trolley being wheeled into one end of the hall. At its helm was Pearl, looking for all the world like someone taking their dream Ferrari out for a spin after looking at it in a showroom window for years. On the trolley was an urn, stacks of china cups and assorted cartons, and jars of coffee, tea, milk, sugar and biscuits. She carefully did a three-point turn, docked the trolley next to a power point in the wood panelling, plugged in the urn and switched it on. She reached underneath the urn to the lower shelf of the trolley to retrieve her viola.

'Pearl's got a trolley!' said Erin, with the appropriate level of awe in her voice.

'Sunbridge can't compete with trolleys,' said Kayla. 'There's no going back now.'

'Pearl!' called Eliot. 'Loving the new wheels! How did you swing that?'

Pearl smiled at them and came over. 'Isn't it marvellous? Dr Irving sorted me out with a catering liaison person, who was ever so lovely. They lent me one of their urns and all that crockery!'

'That was kind of them,' agreed Eliot. 'And I'll jolly well make sure we have an extra five minutes' coffee break, to make sure we make full use of the facilities.'

Pearl nodded, looking overjoyed, and bustled away to get her viola out of its case.

'So what's changed old Irving's mind then?' asked Charlie. 'Last time we saw him, he was spitting feathers and threatening to pull his boys out of the orchestra altogether.'

Eliot frowned. 'It's all a bit odd. David said he spoke to him twice on the same day last week: the day after the rehearsal.

Well, the half a rehearsal. Anyway, he seemed to have completely changed his attitude between those two calls. Which is just as well, since we didn't have anywhere to rehearse, let alone play our concert.'

'Yeah, sorry about that,' said Kayla. 'I'll tell you all about how *that* happened in the pub later.'

'Did it have something to do with Rosalind?' said Carl.

Kayla made a face at him and laughed.

'Come on, chaps. Time we were doing stuff,' said Eliot. 'Where are the Oakdean boys? It's not as if they have far to come this evening.'

'Here,' said Charlie. 'And don't they look pleased with themselves.'

Right on cue, Dr Irving marched his boys into the hall from one of the doors at the back, from where they immediately peeled off to put their instrument cases on chairs along the walls. They had an even more pronounced sense of entitlement on their home turf. Their strides were somehow longer, their hair more floppy, and their vowels even more stretched out without any hope of a consonant.

Dr Irving walked straight over to Eliot. He had entirely regained his original effervescence, and beamed at him as if the previous week had never happened.

'Delighted, delighted!' he cried. 'Welcome! I'm sure you'll find our Old Hall far superior to the other school.' He seemed to see Kayla for the first time, and smiled even more generously. 'Which of course is not their fault.'

'Easy, tiger,' whispered Carl to Kayla, as he turned to walk over to the trombone section.

Kayla said nothing, but wheeled her bass behind Carl, who was still carrying her stool.

'And I'm also delighted to confirm that Sir Marmaduke will be bringing copies of his new composition,' continued

Dr Irving. 'A fanfare, I believe. Featuring his godson, Tarquin. And, of course, Hector on the trumpet.'

'I hope Sir Marmaduke will have written some parts for other people too,' said Eliot mildly. 'Tracie, for instance, is a very promising trombone player. As well as our usual resident brass.'

At the mention of Tracie, Dr Irving's eye twitched a little, but he continued to smile. 'I'm sure everything will be most satisfactory. Ah! And here is the great man himself!'

He turned to the main door into the hall that the orchestra had used, which led from the front door. Sir Marmaduke was making his way towards them, leaning heavily on his cane. He had a briefcase in his other hand.

'Oh lord,' said Charlie in Eliot's ear. 'Good luck. Are we supposed to be sight-reading a Blythe handwritten scrawl, do you think?'

'You may not have to,' said Eliot. 'Rumour has it that this is just a short brass fanfare.'

'Let's hope the rumours are true,' said Erin. 'Come on, Charlie. Let's get set up.'

Sir Marmaduke arrived at the mid-point between the door and where Eliot was standing, and came to a breathless halt. Dr Irving sprang over to meet him, trying to ascertain which hand might be available for enthusiastic shaking, but since one of Sir Marmaduke's hands was holding his cane, and the other his briefcase, Dr Irving ended up bowing a few times instead.

Eliot wandered over at a more leisurely pace.

'Well, very good, very good, here we are!' said Dr Irving. 'And do we have the honour of being in the presence of a new work, Sir Marmaduke?'

'You do,' rumbled Sir Marmaduke, still wheezing. 'Ink's barely dry.'

Dr Irving clapped his hands above his head and looked around for an Oakdean man. Tarquin bounced up.

'Sir?'

'A chair for Sir Marmaduke, if you please, Tarquin.'

Once the Blythe buttocks were safely lowered, the briefcase could be opened. Eliot's heart sank as he saw Charlie had been right: there were pages and pages of handwritten manuscript paper. Sir Marmaduke favoured the fountain pen calligraphy nib. His notes splodged across the page like the aftermath of a particularly gruelling *Game of Thrones* battle between spiders.

'Wonderful!' he said, as brightly as he could muster. 'What's the orchestration?'

'Four horns, three trumpets, three trombones and tuba,' said Sir Marmaduke, handing over the sheaves of paper. 'And percussion, of course.'

'Let's hope the tuba can manage some notes this week,' said Hector, who was standing over by the trumpets.

All the Oakdean boys thought this was hilarious. The rest of the orchestra exchanged uncomfortable glances.

'Yeah, it was the best night of my week, banged up down the station,' said Carl quietly from just behind Hector. 'I'm sure Leroy feels the same. So you go on taking the piss, mate.'

Hector glanced round and saw who was talking. He flushed, and shut up.

Carl and Kayla looked at each other.

'Don't let your case out of your sight tonight,' she said.

'That goes for everybody,' said Carl.

Sir Marmaduke, who had not heard any of Carl's exchange with Hector, started to rumble in the direction of Dr Irving. He pointed to the music sheets in Eliot's hand.

'Yes, of course,' said Dr Irving. 'Might we hear how this sounds, do you think?' he asked Eliot. 'Since Sir Marmaduke is here now?'

'Well, it's not for full orchestra. It might make sense to do it at the end of the rehearsal, so I can let the others go,' said Eliot. The Marmaduke rumble grew more insistent, and Dr Irving hopped from one foot to another.

Charlie had an idea. 'We could always give Pearl's new trolley an early outing. Waddya reckon? Nobody will mind an early cuppa.'

Pearl perked up at the back of the violas, and half-stood, like a meercat about to start the hundred metres.

'Well, if people really don't mind…?' said Eliot. 'It shouldn't take long to read through.'

There was a murmur of agreement and general low-level expressions of delight that can be generated in Britain at any time by a surprise tea break. Pearl dashed over to her trolley and started fussing with urn dials and cups. Anyone who wasn't needed in the fanfare started to drift over towards her.

'OK,' called Eliot, leafing through the fanfare sheets. 'Could we have the horns, trumpets, trombones and tuba please, plus' – he looked over at the percussion section – 'do we have tamtam and bass drum as well as timps here?'

Max nodded. Irie, next to him, grinned.

'Great. Just play from where you're sitting for now, that's fine. Do you want to come and get a part?'

Carl came to get the trombone parts for the section, and had a quick look while he was standing next to Eliot. He frowned, and looked up. 'Anything look familiar?' he said quietly.

Eliot tried to smother a grin, and nodded. He showed Carl the title page of the full score. Individual parts merely had the single word 'Fanfare' scrawled across the top. Eliot's was distinguished by the full title: *Fanfare for the Oakdean Man*. It was dedicated 'to Tarquin'.

Sir Marmaduke saw him showing Carl the title page, and nodded appreciatively. 'My boy Tarquin will be playing first, of course,' he said.

Dr Irving almost bowed again. 'But of course. Of *course!*'

'Yes, I was thinking that all the kids should lead their sections,' said Eliot. 'I wanted to give them a space to have a go and see what it's all about.'

Sir Marmaduke and Dr Irving looked as though Eliot had just passed the port the wrong way.

'Great idea,' said Carl, before either of them could respond, and started walking off. 'I'll give the first part to Tracie.'

'There *will* be Hector on first trumpet, I suppose,' said Dr Irving to Sir Marmaduke. 'Oakdean will be in the ascendant.' Eliot wondered where the fulcrum of power was to necessitate such mollifying.

'Good luck,' said Ann to Eliot as she went past on her way to Pearl's trolley. 'I'm looking forward to this. The last time I heard anything original from Blythe was in the 1980s.'

'Don't hold your breath,' said Eliot.

Erin made a face as she walked past with Charlie. 'How are you going to read any of that?' she whispered, glimpsing the thick black notes all over Eliot's score.

Carl had put the first part in front of Tracie, and was going through it with her to see if there were any bits she needed pointers on. It all looked fairly straightforward, so Carl used the next couple of minutes furiously signing to Gwynneth what he thought she was about to hear. She had already got her tea, so was restricted to one-handed swearwords in response.

'Right, shall we give it a go?' said Eliot, walking forward to his stand. Dr Irving got himself a chair and sat next to Sir Marmaduke.

Eliot flattened out the rather creased papers and leaned down to peer at the orchestration. 'OK. *Fanfare for the Oakdean Man*, by Sir Marmaduke Blythe.' He shot a look at the rest of the orchestra before they got going.

'World premiere,' said Dr Irving, doing a little neck bow to his neighbour.

Eliot smiled. 'Right, all the percussion in right at the start. Fancy that. Ready to go?'

Max nodded at Irie.

The huge sound of timps, bass drum and tamtam playing in sync rang round the hall. Eliot smiled encouragingly at Irie, who bashed the tamtam with all her might. Then he turned to the trumpets, where Hector, for once, seemed to be genuinely concentrating. They managed most of their fanfare without a problem, except some of them had difficulty reading whether Sir Marmaduke had written a semiquaver or had merely dropped some ink in the wrong place.

The musicians who were drinking around Pearl's trolley started to look at each other. What had been obvious to Eliot as soon as he'd opened the score was quickly becoming apparent to any listener with half an ear.

Eliot pressed on, turning to bring the horns in with the trumpets. Tarquin split his first entry and ended up playing a third too low; an easy mistake to make on the horn. It is the most ridiculously curly bit of tubing, and is famously difficult to play, with its mouthpiece that is so much thinner than a trumpet's. All the natural harmonics are just waiting around one of those curls, ready to leap out at you as the vibrating air rushes round like a Formula One car but then has to round the Fairmont Hairpin at Monaco. Tarquin spent a few notes playing happily – some might almost say blithely – at his lower pitch, until he managed to leapfrog up to the right notes when he was aiming for a jump.

Eliot pressed on, despite the whispers that had started to build to at the side of the hall. He grinned at Irie as she again got her tamtam entry spot on.

There was a surprise middle section, given what Eliot had been expecting, which consisted of Tarquin playing an extended solo. It seemed incongruously like the *cadenza* of a concerto, when the rest of the orchestra shuts up and lets the soloist show off with the flashiest passages possible. The only difference was that the music had only been going a couple of minutes, and Tarquin's technical proficiency rather hampered any flash moves on his part. He stumbled through it in a dogged, four-square kind of way, and then it was over.

By the time Eliot brought in Tracie and the rest of the trombones, plus Leroy on his mercifully empty tuba, the giggles had started. Eliot glanced over but carried on gamely, concentrating on helping the schoolkids get to their right notes even when the parts had split and they were no longer playing the same as their neighbour. The whole thing finished, barely three minutes after it had started, with Tarquin turning an alarming shade of puce as he squeezed out a top note.

Eliot brought them off, and put his baton down on his stand. Max gave Irie a high five.

'Uh – that was brilliant, everybody.' He looked round and saw Ann's face, which was deciding whether it should be horrified or amused.

Dr Irving was already on his feet, delivering a solo round of applause and bowing to Sir Marmaduke while he did so. Sir Marmaduke nodded and acknowledged it graciously.

'Marvellous! Marvellous!' cried Dr Irving. 'Superb. A jewel in the Oakdean diadem!'

'But wasn't that just...' Erin trailed off.

'Basically, yeah,' said Charlie, next to her.

'And it's got to be still in copyright,' said Ann. 'It was only written in 1942.'

Someone had found the Emerson, Lake & Palmer version of Copland's *Fanfare for the Common Man* on their phone, and started playing it. The rock adaptation of something extraordinarily close to what they had all just heard was clear.

Eliot couldn't help a snort of laughter, and dropped his head to face the floor, looking out of the corner of his eye to try to see whose phone it was. He pressed his lips into a thin line to try to stop smiling. With his right hand in front of him, he indicated a *diminuendo* by bringing his thumb and fingers together until they touched. As if by magic, the tinny music ceased. Eliot mouthed the words 'Thank you'.

It had been Gwynneth, who had been forewarned.

Eliot turned around.

'Um… Sir Marmaduke?'

The chair rumbled in his direction.

'Perhaps we might have a word about the, um, orchestration of this later?'

'I'm sure Sir Marmaduke would be glad to discuss any aspect of his piece,' said Dr Irving. 'Meanwhile, shall we retire to my study? I had a rather fine cognac delivered this week…'

Sir Marmaduke lumbered to his feet and accompanied the sprightly Dr Irving out of the hall, wheezing as he went.

Eliot ran his hands through his hair and stretched both arms out wide, shaking his hands and fingers, as if to get rid of any trace of what he had just had to conduct.

'Thank you to Pearl, for her wonderful early break,' he said. There was warm applause. 'What the hell,' he continued. 'Shall the rest of us grab a cuppa now and carry on in a few minutes?'

As he walked past Ann, Charlie and Erin on his way to the urn, he said, 'I hope to God we're going to the pub after this? It's going to take some serious debriefing.'

Chapter 17

Of course they went to the pub.

'Did you notice, there wasn't anything nicked tonight?' said Charlie.

'Or fighting,' said Ann.

'Or drugs,' added Eliot. 'Which Carl and Leroy must have been glad about.'

'Where is Carl? He said he'd come for a drink.'

'He's giving Kayla a hand with her bass back to Sunbridge. I think they'll be here in a bit,' said Eliot.

'Mind you, they were running out of instruments to put them in – they'd already done the big ones,' said Erin. 'I was keeping an eye on the timps. You could fit a lot in a timp.'

'Wouldn't you have to undo all those twiddly tap things on the top first?' said Charlie. 'Too time consuming. Not worth it.'

'Hark at you, Mr Drugs Expert,' said Ann.

'Ooh – hang on,' said Erin, reaching into her back pocket for her phone. 'Text. From Noel.'

'Aye aye,' said Charlie.

'"Are you lot in your usual place?" Ha! Are we that predictable? Do we want to see him?'

'He might have a lead,' said Ann.

'Would he tell us if he had?' asked Eliot. 'Yeah, come on. Get him to come down.'

'OK.' Erin tapped out a text.

'Well, I think he'd be interested to hear how we were miraculously welcome at Oakdean this week,' said Ann. 'After the shenanigans last week. It's almost as if we've been... I dunno. Played.'

'Don't be going all Miss Marple on us,' said Charlie.

'Not forgetting what we had to end up playing tonight,' said Eliot. 'I still have to have that conversation with Sir Marmaduke about nicking someone else's music.'

'Shreddie hasn't written a note for decades,' said Ann. 'Nobody's heard a peep. And tonight's no different.'

'How much would we be liable for if we performed pretend Copland in public?' asked Eliot, of nobody in particular.

'Shreddie?' said Charlie to Ann.

'Shred. As in marmalade.'

'Ah.'

'But the point is,' she continued, 'why was he so keen to get a "new" piece out now, after all this time? Could be broke, I suppose. But surely a poxy fanfare in a school isn't going to get you to the Proms?'

'There was something weird about him and Dr Irving too,' said Eliot. 'I must ask David about that. He went to see Irving a few weeks back and Marmaduke was there.'

'Hang on, Ann,' said Erin. 'You're not seriously suggesting that Marmaduke somehow planted drugs to get us moved to Oakdean, to play a fanfare that isn't even his? It makes no sense.'

'Christ, what have we missed?' said Carl, overhearing the last bit. Kayla was with him.

'I ask myself that all the time,' said Noel, who had also just appeared, in his usual way.

'Perfect timing,' said Carl. 'What'll you have?'

'Thanks. Just a tonic water.'

'On duty?'

'Afraid so.'

'Are we now official business or are you skiving?' said Charlie.

Noel laughed. 'Possibly a bit of a combo. It's complicated. May I?' He sat in a spare chair next to Erin.

Carl went to the bar. Kayla sat between Eliot and Charlie.

'Bass safely stowed?' said Eliot.

'Yeah. Managed to get in and out of Sunbridge without Carl running into Rosalind, at least.'

'Rosalind?' said Noel.

'Deputy Head. Until last week huge supporter of the arts in general, and Stockwell Park Orchestra in particular. Since the drugs and the fights, not so much.'

'Have you heard, we've had to move?' said Eliot. 'Apparently we're too criminal even for Sunbridge.'

Noel laughed. 'That's a first. So where are you now?'

'Some parallel world in about 1894, I think,' said Charlie. 'Otherwise known as Oakdean.'

Noel looked interested. 'Really?'

'Can't you tell?' said Erin. 'Kayla's had to send Carl to the bar because our feminine brains can't cope with money and prices. I'm practically overheating just trying to talk to you.'

Carl returned from his alpha male quest for refreshment, put the drinks on the table and sat next to Kayla.

'So,' he said, 'what's this tonic water going to buy us? Inside information? News that I'm not going to be charged with drug dealing?'

Noel took a sip of his tonic. 'Cheers. Well, I've had an interesting week. I was hoping we could swap stories and maybe get a little closer to the answer to your little... difficulties.'

'Hardly little,' said Kayla. 'Not for Carl and Leroy.'

'No,' acknowledged Noel. 'But – how can I put this – I hope they may be short-lived.'

'Oh?' said Charlie.

'Spill,' said Ann. 'Come on.'

'What if, hypothetically, there were anomalies in this case that gave me pause?' said Noel. 'I have a young PC back at the station – name of Frank. Now, Frank is diligent. Dedicated. Loves a bit of riot control, but he'll grow out of that. He's a nice lad. Likes to learn.'

'He sounds lovely,' said Kayla. 'Why are we talking about Frank?'

'Frank's learning all the time, and to do that he asks a lot of questions. To be honest, sometimes I wish he'd keep a bit more inside and a bit less directed at me, but there you are. A police officer should never stop asking questions. We should all remember to be a bit more like Frank.'

There was a pause while everyone round the table digested this nugget of wisdom. Somehow it didn't seem enough of a reason to compel Noel to make a special trip to see them.

Noel smiled. 'So, I wondered how I might get my hands on a bit more information about what went on last week. I mean, I've had a look at the call logs, and the staffing roster which apparently put some staff unexpectedly and fortuitously close to Sunbridge the very evening a raid was called in. Which then coincidentally turned into a drug seizure. I give you full marks for making it feature a tuba, by the way. We don't get many incidents involving a tuba in our paperwork.'

They laughed, but he had their rapt attention.

'And so then I wondered if there was any angle I hadn't covered. To complete the picture, as it were.'

He reached into an inside pocket of his jacket and pulled out a large brown envelope. He opened the unsealed end, and took out a couple of dozen six-by-four-inch photographs, which he spread out over the table.

'That's us!' said Erin.

'Some of you,' agreed Noel. 'I'd be grateful if you could identify anyone in these pictures who isn't here now.'

They leaned over the photographs, which were assorted pictures of their rehearsal the previous week. Some were taken from very artistic angles.

'These are Doug's,' said Ann.

'I did manage to locate a local photographer who was happy to help with my enquiries, yes,' said Noel.

'Christ, he took Rosalind's directions to heart, didn't he?' said Charlie.

'You should have seen the last brochure she did,' said Kayla. 'Black and white, very moody. You'd think she was going for an exhibition or something. Think her strapline for that one was "Our process is our pupils" or something wanky like that.'

'So,' said Noel. 'Who's here?' He produced a couple of pens from his pocket and put them on the table too. 'Maybe you could write some names on the back of the prints, if you know them?'

'A lot of these are from Oakdean,' said Erin. 'There's the trumpeter – what's his name?'

'Hector,' said Eliot. 'I think. And there's the golden boy of the moment, according to Sir Marmaduke. Tarquin.'

Doug had snapped Hector a few times, as he had walked past him on his phone just after the break, and then there was a fine portrait of him looking intently across the orchestra. The picture of Tarquin showed him similarly looking out over the heads of the orchestra, over to the other side. As a photograph, it was intriguing. There was clearly something kinetic happening.

'Doug's wasted on school brochures,' said Erin. 'These are really good.'

'Oh – there's Leroy, just after he found the bags in his tuba,' said Ann. 'Now look – if that doesn't show an innocent man horrified with what he's just found, I don't know what will.'

'And that's Dr Irving,' said Eliot, reaching for a couple of pictures showing him sitting on his chair at the side of the hall. 'Looking quite pleased, which in my experience is rare.'

'He won't be for much longer if he knows Doug's still got all these pics of Oakdean boys,' said Charlie. 'Remember he went off on one about it?'

They sorted through all the photos in the end, passing them round and confirming to each other the names of the more unfamiliar people from Oakdean. Noel watched them quietly, sipping his tonic. Just ordinary mates having an ordinary drink in a pub, sorting through photographs of their friends. Noel looked round the room over the rim of his glass. Nobody was taking any notice of them at all.

Eventually, the pictures were gathered together again, and Noel tapped them into an orderly bundle like a newsreader at the end of a bulletin. He slid them away into his envelope again, and stowed it safely in his jacket.

'Thank you,' he said. 'That was extremely helpful.'

'How is that going to help me?' said Carl. 'We already knew all these people were there last week.'

'Ah,' said Noel. He felt as if he was in the centre of a Venn diagram showing unofficial detective work, official policing and making friends. He wasn't yet sure which of the segments would have the greatest influence. In his experience, one usually started to take over and push the others out. He drained the last of his tonic water. 'I'm afraid I'm going to have to ask you to trust me. Again, I know. Sorry. But it's the best I can do at the moment.'

'And just when we thought we were getting to be the plucky amateur sidekick team,' said Eliot.

'Christ, you make us sound like *Scooby-Doo*,' said Charlie.

'Well, we've got plenty of pesky kids,' said Ann. She looked at Noel, who was smiling in a crinkly-eyed way. 'Sorry. We're just trying to help. In our own way.'

'Believe me, you are helping,' he said. 'I have to get back now. Thanks for the drink, Carl.'

Carl nodded. 'Let us know if you need anything else. I'm quite keen to get this sorted.'

'You and me both,' said Noel, and stood up. 'I'll be in touch.'

Chapter 18

On Friday morning, Sir Marmaduke collected Tarquin from Oakdean in a taxi. Dr Irving had waved through the permission to miss lessons until lunchtime, and indeed had seen them off personally from the front door.

Their black cab drove north, over Vauxhall Bridge. It was one of those rare, crisp London mornings when spring threatened to vanquish winter and anything seems possible. As they skirted Green Park and made a slingshot around Hyde Park Corner to head into Mayfair, the cabbie didn't interrupt his passengers with any pleasant remark about the fine weather or how great the old Thames looked with the low sun glinting off its swell, and they ignored him. The cabbie had already accurately inferred that Sir Marmaduke was not the type of man to squander good money on tips for the working classes. You could always tell.

Sir Marmaduke was concentrating on briefing Tarquin.

'Excellent suit, my boy. Good choice. D'you have the same tailor as your father – Jermyn Street?'

'Yah. Drapes well, doesn't it?'

The cabbie rolled his eyes.

'Now, a word about Henrietta. She's easy on the eye, I grant you, but we're here to get her to sign. So, by all means sugar the compliments, but let's play softly, softly, catchee Hennie.'

Tarquin raised his chin and looked out of the window, as if he were on top of the battlements of an unexpected windfall of a castle, measuring by eye just how profitable the fields he had inherited would be.

The cab pulled up outside a substantial Mayfair terrace. Tarquin got out and looked up at the brass plaque by the door, which announced the building to be home to Popplewell Sounds, a family firm which had been recording and distributing brass-specific classical music to its niche market since the 1960s. Sir Marmaduke paid the driver and waited for his exact change, which by then was also no surprise to the cabbie. As he drove off into the gorgeous morning, a faint cry of 'wanker' floated back out of the open cab window, but Sir Marmaduke didn't catch it and Tarquin was concentrating on other things.

The few steps up to the door were slow for Sir Marmaduke and his cane, so he was quite breathless by the time they were buzzed into a plush hallway. A vast bunch of yellow roses in a pink vase was placed in the exact centre of a circular table in the exact centre of the hall which stood at the exact centre of a circular rug. It was like stepping inside a kaleidoscope. The effect was enhanced by salmon pink and teal candy-stripe wallpaper above the dado, with different colours below. The heavy scent of rose petals vibrated in the air.

A door opened on the far side of the hall. Neither Sir Marmaduke nor Tarquin could see the person who emerged because she was entirely hidden behind the roses. Tarquin leant down to one side just as she walked round the other, and for a few moments they went back and forth like the couple who take turns to come out into the garden in one of those novelty weather predictor barometers.

Meanwhile, Sir Marmaduke was shuffling round the table at his own pace, and before long caught up with Henrietta, for it was she.

'Sir Marmaduke!' she cried. 'How lovely. Do come in. And this must be Tarquin?'

Tarquin took her hand and made a small bow, stopping short of kissing her fingers. 'Delighted to meet you, madam.'

She giggled. 'Oh! Please call me Hennie. This way.'

Once through the door to her office, it was clear that whoever was in charge of interior decoration had firm views on tying a space together to create flow. There was a general assault of peach and duck-egg blue tones. If fabrics were not frilled, they were furbelowed.

Sir Marmaduke sat firmly in the first chair he came to. Henrietta walked behind her desk and indicated that Tarquin should take any of the others. He attempted to sit without disturbing the five cushions that had been casually arranged against the seat back.

'Won't take up much of yer time, Hennie,' said Sir Marmaduke. 'Know yer busy.'

'We always have time for you, Sir Marmaduke,' said Henrietta, beaming at him. 'What can we do for you? We were rather hoping this visit may herald a new era of Blythe creativity! A renaissance, if you will.'

'Ah now – took the words out of my mouth, young lady. Want you to meet my godson, Tarquin.'

Tarquin began to stand again, in case he was needed to be at attention, but was waved down by Sir Marmaduke's stick.

'He's a fine boy – a fine talent,' Sir Marmaduke continued. 'French horn. Great future ahead of him. I'm writing a whole new repertoire for him. He's going to be bigger than Dennis Brain.'

Henrietta leaned forward, her elbows on her lace-covered desk. 'I'm listening.'

Tarquin leaned back on his cushions and crossed one leg over the other, making sure the drape of his trousers remained optimal for Henrietta's sightline. He smiled at her. It would have been impossible to tell if he winked or merely blinked, on account of his eyepatch, but he was adept at implying that he might have done.

'Little concert planned at his school at the end of term,' said Sir Marmaduke. 'Got a local orchestra in. Think of it as a showcase. I've written a fanfare for him – you know, with some other brass in the background, but essentially spotlighting Tarquin's talent. Want you and your father to come along to our rehearsal next week and hear the potential. This boy can sell records – you can put his face on one of those television programmes – anything. He could knock what we did for that trumpet quintet into a cocked hat.'

Henrietta's eyebrows raised as she remembered anecdotes told by her father, the founding Popplewell, about a racy world tour undertaken by the ensemble that made their name and fortune in the eighties. The quintet, Valvelicious, had enjoyed a stellar rise to fame and toured to sell-out venues across four continents and crossed the classical/pop divide with dazzling success. Popplewell Sounds, and Sir Marmaduke himself, had lived comfortably off the proceeds of that tour well into the nineties.

'We would be delighted,' said Henrietta, upping the wattage of her smile in Tarquin's direction. She was visualising his cover art already. 'I'll draft the contract, as per all the usuals. I'm sure the concert will merely be a formality. After all, Sir Marmaduke, we go back a long way.'

Sir Marmaduke rumbled to indicate his deep pleasure, and the meeting drew to a close with promises from Henrietta to send over the draft text of their contract within a week.

Chapter 19

That same Friday morning, Noel was in his office, frowning at Doug's photos spread out over his desk. One of the tabs on his laptop showed the timeline from the night of the raid. On another tab was the original file that Doug had emailed to Noel.

He matched each print on his desk with a picture from the file, and then clicked through to the metadata behind the image to find the timestamp carved into its digital DNA. On his unofficial social call round to Doug (who had been very helpful and generous with the biscuits and coffee), Noel had checked Doug's camera was showing the correct time and date. Any timestamp is only as useful as its internal clock.

He wrote the date and time in the corner of each print with a fine-point Sharpie. Then he arranged them in order. There were a few of Hector talking on his phone, walking into the hall – three timed at 20:46 and one at 20:47. The one of him looking across the orchestra was at 20:48, as was the picture of Tarquin looking across the orchestra the other way.

Noel tried to remember how Stockwell Park Orchestra arranged its sections, and looked up online plans to confirm. The trumpets and the horns were indeed on opposite sides.

He looked at the timeline. The raid on Sunbridge had started at 20:56. Noel already knew it hadn't come in as a 999 call: it had been a tip-off direct to Walter Price, the police officer in charge. He clicked through a few more pages on the report file, but couldn't find any reference to the time of the initial incoming call.

He sighed, and rubbed his eyes under his glasses. Desk work made his eyes ache but there was no substitute for being methodical. There were call logs and lab results of the drug analysis that he should request. There was a whole line of enquiry about why Fang and her handler had happened to be so close to Walter Price when he got a call about a possible knife that he decided he should take Fang along anyway. There were a number of issues about this case that made Noel frown. And it wasn't even his case. Was he some kind of private detective for a whole orchestra now?

He looked over at Frank's empty desk on the other side of the office, took his glasses off and walked to the door. He needed Frank and his dogged, thorough ways. And maybe a coffee first.

Chapter 20

On Saturday morning, Carl and Kayla met at Carl's flat. He had given her a call asking her if she wanted to try out some more jazz improvisation, since their impromptu noodling around before the rehearsals had gone so well. It had been Eliot mentioning it that made Carl call: hearing someone else appreciate what he thought was OK but hadn't been concentrating on crystallised a vague intention.

He buzzed her up, and leaned out into the hallway to check she was alright lugging her bass up the stairs.

'It's only one flight. Put your back into it.'

'No lift, then?'

'Nah.'

She reached the top and turned into his doorway, putting her bass down in the space in front of the sofa. 'Decent size room. D'ya rehearse other stuff here too? Don't your neighbours complain?'

Carl grinned. 'Ah – you missed the genius reason I got this flat. Furniture showroom downstairs, so nobody's there in the evenings. And nobody above. Honestly feels like I've got the block to myself sometimes.'

'Maybe you've just driven everyone else away?'

'Oi!' He laughed. 'Coffee?'

'Can I have tea? White with two. Please.'

He wandered into the small kitchen while Kayla looked down onto the street below. It was busy with Saturday-morning shoppers huddled into their coats against the cold, with the usual London buses rumbling past and making the windows shake if they stopped outside with the revs at just the right sympathetic resonance.

The sounds of teaspoons in mugs came out of the kitchen.

'Did you say two sugars?' he called.

'Yep, thanks.'

'Your teeth will drop out.'

'There are worse vices to have.'

He emerged from the kitchen carrying two mugs, and handed one to Kayla.

'Thanks,' she said, and took a sip. 'So – what kind of stuff did you have in mind this morning?'

'Dunno really. Thought we could try some stuff out – you know, like we were doing before the last rehearsal. It sounded OK.'

'Before you abandoned me to play the *Star Wars* stuff for the Oakdean boys.'

Carl laughed. 'Yeah. Sorry. Those wankers didn't notice, though.'

'Everyone else did.'

'Yeah.'

'It was funny. You did the same when you came to play to the kids in my music class. Got them really listening and loving it.'

'Even Tracie,' said Carl, smiling.

'Even bloody Tracie Scott, who'd done bugger all work all term and missed a load of school. You turn up and it's like the Pied Piper and off to orchestra they all go.' Kayla took another gulp of tea. 'Not that I'm complaining. Now I sound ungrateful.'

'That's a trombone for you,' said Carl. 'You don't mess.'

'So – do you, like, gig and stuff?'

'Yeah, now and then. Me and some mates are on the list at a few pubs and clubs. You know, depends who's around and what they want. We've got a trumpeter, drummer, pianist. Couple of saxophones. You know, mix'n'match.'

'Nice,' said Kayla, with a grin.

'What we don't have, of course, is a bass player.'

'Christ, is this an audition?'

Carl laughed. 'Nah. You passed that already.'

They got their instruments out of their cases and tuned.

'D'ya want something to sit on?' said Carl. 'I've got a high stool in the kitchen if you like?'

'No, don't worry. I'll stand for this,' said Kayla. 'Somehow it's different playing this stuff than classical with a bow. Maybe all classical bass players are lazy or something.'

Carl started playing a riff, wandering round his living room slowly while he felt his way through where he wanted the tune to go. Kayla plucked a few experimental notes to get a feel for the key Carl was playing in, then she hooked onto his riff and started laying down a rhythmical bass line that gave the whole thing a structure, like suddenly it had something to sit on. It didn't box in what Carl was doing; rather, it gave him something to bounce off, to try new ideas against.

Every now and then they looked at each other and smiled, and maybe one of them led the music in another direction. They would settle on a repeat pattern for a while, with one then the other exploring possibilities and returning to the repeat, and then they went down another road together, each listening to what the other was playing and responding to it all the time. Improvisation makes you listen. Sometimes having a piece of paper telling you what to do lets you pretend you are playing in a vacuum. Music that isn't written down is a completely

173

different animal, and improvisation is the untamed version of that animal.

They played for maybe a couple of hours, with more tea needed at the end. While Carl was boiling the kettle again, Kayla checked her phone, and called out to him.

'Hey – what are you doing later?'

'Was going to ask you the same. Got a gig and hoped you might be free?'

'No, not *that* much later. After lunch. Just got a text from Erin. Apparently Noel wants to call in his amateur gang for a meeting.'

Carl walked through with mugs. 'Sounds promising.'

'Do you think he's found anything else out?'

'Hope so. He's not a man to waste time.'

'Maybe he's cleared your name.'

'And Leroy's.'

'OK – shall I say yes for us both?'

'Wait – did I get one too?' Carl dug in his pocket and looked at his phone. 'Yep. You might as well then. Get the gossip started.'

Kayla laughed. 'What, that we're about to start a cutting-edge jazz combo and leave the orchestra?'

'Huh. The trombone section wouldn't last a week without me,' said Carl, laughing. 'At least, until I've trained Tracie up.'

'Right – I've said we can do it. Dunno where yet. I'd better get my bass back to school and nip home to make sure the teen eats something that isn't Pringles.'

Carl raised his eyebrows. 'Teen, as in child?'

'Yeah. They're not good at vitamins at that age.'

'Fair enough. Some of us aren't any better now. Especially after a gig when it's either a kebab or an old crinkly apple you know you've got on the side in the kitchen.'

Both their phones beeped at once.

'Right,' said Carl. 'Ann's house it is. Not far – other side of the Oval. You OK to get there or shall I…?'

Kayla laughed. 'This from the man who told me it was only one flight and to put my back into it? I think I'll manage. But thanks. We'd better not turn up together or they'll think we had a rehearsal *and* lunch together and there'd be no stopping the gossip machine.'

At half past three, Noel knocked on the door of Ann's house, while admiring her quiet, tree-lined street. Erin opened it and stepped back, motioning him in.

'Hi. Ann's got the kettle on. Most of us are here already – just waiting for Kayla.'

They walked through to the kitchen, where Eliot, Carl and Charlie were already sitting at the table. Ann poured steaming water into a cafetière and then a large brown teapot. She then plonked their respective warmer and cosy on, and turned round.

'Ah – Noel! Hello. We're mostly here – except Leroy 'cos he's working. And bloody impatient to know what's going on. All a bit cloak-and-dagger.'

'Hello,' said Noel, taking his coat off and hanging it over the back of a chair. 'I know. Sorry. I didn't want to have this at the station, that's all. You'll see why in a minute.'

The door knocker sounded again, and Erin disappeared to answer it, in her new role as butler.

Ann put mugs on the table, then dug around in a drawer for some teaspoons. She found sugar in an open bag and put that in the middle of the table too, along with a two-litre milk carton, which she opened and sniffed before slamming it down. Teapot and cafetière followed, then a biscuit tin. 'That's your lot,' she said, smiling. 'Help yourselves.'

'Oh, don't be putting on airs and graces for Noel, Ann,' said Charlie. 'He wants to see how you really live.'

175

Ann stuck her tongue out at him. Noel laughed. It seemed the camaraderie of the pub had been transplanted in space and time but was intact. He liked it. He almost felt he was among friends, and he was wary of liking that too much.

Erin returned with Kayla. 'That's everyone,' she said.

'Sorry I'm late,' said Kayla. 'Complications. A disagreement about how many vitamins a lunch should contain.'

'Come in,' said Ann. 'Help yourself to whatever you want from this lot on the table.'

'You're not late,' said Eliot. 'We were all early.'

'Couldn't wait to hear what Noel's going to say,' said Carl. 'Which I hope is something like "you was framed, sunshine, and we've nicked them wot dun it" so Leroy and I can get back to normal and stop having meetings with our solicitor.'

He looked expectantly at Noel, who smiled and said, 'Well… something like that. Maybe.'

'Oh for God's sake, sit down everybody and, Noel, tell us,' said Ann. 'Now. Please.'

'You're doing it again, Ann,' said Charlie.

'I'll do you in a minute,' she said. 'Noel. Go.'

'Thanks,' said Noel. 'And thanks for coming, everybody. I know it's all a bit Agatha Christie drawing room vibe—'

'Christ, did one of *us* do something?' said Charlie.

Noel laughed. 'No. But this isn't my case, as you know. And the more I dug about in it, the more things didn't add up. And, well, you remember when I found the Stradivari?'

There were nods all round the table.

'Of course,' said Erin. 'Without you, I wouldn't have played the Elgar.'

'Well,' said Noel, 'that raid wasn't exactly by the book either. I took Frank, my young colleague, along with me, and we happened to have some bolt cutters and, well, it all turned out alright.'

Noel glanced round at the five people looking at him intently. He hoped he was doing the right thing.

'I like the sound of a policeman who "just happens" to have bolt cutters with him,' said Eliot. 'How can we help?'

'OK. The timings on that evening don't add up. Someone (and I can guess who) called it in, but didn't go via 999. The call came directly to the officer in charge of the raid: Walter Price. They went in on the pretext of searching for a blade, but just happened to have a drug sniffer dog with them, and what do you know? They didn't find a knife, but they *did* find some drugs. More of which in a minute.'

'One man's bolt cutter is another man's sniffer dog,' said Ann.

They laughed.

'Quite,' said Noel. 'But one man and his sniffer dog were hanging around close enough to Sunbridge when the call came in to make it through the doors ten minutes later. I know we're all for making our response targets look good in the stats, but I reckon the chances of scrambling a team from the station and running down there in that time is small.'

'So they were expecting the call?' said Kayla.

Noel nodded. 'And knew what they were looking for when they got there.'

'Hey – that's one thing we forgot to tell you in the pub,' said Eliot. 'We reckon that Oakdean kid started the fight in the foyer to get our attention.'

'Don't rub it in,' said Kayla. 'If I hadn't moved from the hall...'

'We all moved, don't worry,' said Erin.

'Yeah – so someone could plant whatever it was in my case,' said Carl. 'And in Leroy's tuba. Which, in spite of obviously being a wanky thing to do, *is* an inspired place to hide it.'

'It did make Sibelius sound a bit woofy,' said Eliot. 'I'm not sure it's quite what he had in mind for the fourth movement.'

'And that brings me to what was actually in the bags,' said Noel. 'You've got to hand it to Fang: she's brilliant.'

'I can't get over her name,' said Ann.

Noel smiled. 'She managed to locate five bags of bits of assorted leaves, moss and grass that had a tiny amount of cannabis mixed in. I've seen the lab report. The percentage was miniscule.'

'Go Fang,' said Carl, not completely enthusiastically.

'She was just doing her job,' said Eliot.

'Yeah, we know you fell in love,' said Erin.

'So, hang on,' said Carl. 'You're saying that not only were these drugs planted, but there was piss-all drug in the bag anyway?'

'Yep,' said Noel. 'Which leaves a few outstanding questions.'

'Who planted the gear?' said Kayla.

'Someone who was either too broke or too tight to use the real stuff,' said Carl.

'Why would anyone do that anyway?' said Charlie.

A thoughtful silence fell, and Ann reached across the table and opened the biscuit tin. She dug around to find a chocolate Hobnob and passed the tin round.

'The thing we've got to ask ourselves,' said Noel, swallowing the last of his digestive, 'is what was the result of this raid? And who benefits from that?'

Kayla took a deep breath. 'I don't want to sound as if it's all about Sunbridge, and God knows Rosalind is a piss-poor manager and deserves all she gets, but surely the main result was that this concert – and in fact the whole Stockwell Park Orchestra shebang – has been kicked out of our school and ended up at Oakdean?'

'If I were being paranoid,' said Eliot, 'I could read all this as a warning never to interfere in the perfect working order of an orchestra I've only just joined. Honestly, and I thought being a choral conductor was as complicated-with-strings-attached as you could get.'

'Never work with kids or animals,' said Ann, laughing. 'Remember?'

'Now don't blame Fang,' said Eliot.

'Kayla's right,' said Noel. 'The orchestra has moved. So who benefits?'

'I guess… Oakdean?' said Kayla. 'I mean, Rosalind was going to milk all the stuff about the school's links to the community to raise our profile and get more funding and kids. So I suppose the same could be true for Oakdean. If they care about that.'

'Pearl did end up with her trolley, remember,' remarked Carl. 'But I can't see her masterminding a full drugs raid and arranging for her own petty cash to go missing just for that.'

Charlie broke into song: '…and she drove the fastest tea-tray in the south.'

They laughed. The idea of Pearl as head of a criminal gang was as bizarre as one of her metaphors.

Noel looked around the table and wondered how far he could either push or trust them. There was only one way to find out.

'So, will you help me find out what's going on?' he asked. 'Is there any way I could come along to the next rehearsal without marching in with my size whatevers and a blue light flashing?'

'A sting?' said Charlie. 'Fantastic. I'm in.'

'If only we could disguise you as a woman,' said Erin. 'Nobody would take any notice of you in Oakdean then.'

Carl grinned. 'Easy. Come and sit in the trombones. I've got a spare tenor you can carry, and we get so many rests it won't matter that you never play. Nobody notices who's playing what anyway. Chas & Dave used to get into loads of other people's gigs for free by carrying their guitars in.'

'Nobody will notice if you join in either, given what usually comes out of the trombone section,' said Ann. Carl threw a V-sign up at her.

'Aaaaaand we're back to normal,' said Eliot. 'But what do you want to observe, Noel? How are we going to sting anyone into doing anything?'

Noel smiled. 'Right then. Here's what we're going to do.'

It took another round of tea and coffee for him to explain his plan, after which he went back to Carl's flat to collect a trombone. Which was another aspect of his police career that he hadn't predicted as a young trainee.

Chapter 21

Mrs Batten was back on door duty the following Monday evening, opening it to a stream of orchestral players and directing them once more along the overly signed and laminated corridor to the Old Hall. Noel walked in carrying Carl's second trombone, trying to impersonate a man who had played it all his life. 'Just put your shoulders back and look like you mean business,' was the only advice Carl had given him. It seemed to work.

Even though he was early, as he approached the hall he could hear some chat and instruments twiddling about. As he opened the door, he saw Carl was already there and warming up his trombone – this time with Joplin's 'The Entertainer'. He walked over to Carl and put the trombone case down.

'Like a natural,' said Kayla, who was taking the cover off her bass. 'Now we just need to get you drinking three pints to everyone else's one and you'll be away.'

The meandering ragtime next to them stopped. 'Oi!'

'Am I wrong?' said Kayla.

Carl considered. 'No. As you were.' Joplin started up again.

Eliot walked into the hall and nodded at them. Carl put a bit of a flourish on his closing bars of 'The Entertainer' in response, then stopped playing.

'Come on, let's get this trombone out,' he said to Noel. 'You can sit down and put some cream on the slide. Background busyness. All brass players learn that.'

While they sat together and Carl tried to show him how to spread cream on a trombone slide without making it look as if it was Noel's first ever attempt, the hall filled with players. The Oakdean boys began to wander in through the doors at the back. Tracie and Irie came in and walked over to the trombones and percussion together. Tracie saw Noel sitting next to Carl and opened her mouth, but before she could say anything, Carl was there.

'Hi, Tracie. This is Noel. Bit of a novice, so I'm showing him the ropes. If he comes in wrong, you can hit him.'

'I won't,' said Noel.

Tracie laughed, and sat down on Carl's free side. 'You'd better not.'

'You really hadn't,' said Carl. 'Tracie doesn't take prisoners. Unlike some.'

Noel's lips twitched, but he said nothing.

David walked in and nodded at Eliot, but then spotted Noel. Eliot strode towards him and quietly intercepted anything David had been about to say.

'Isn't that…?'

'Yes. The policeman. Noel. Haven't time to explain everything right now, but will you trust me? With any luck, everything will be straightened out by the end of the rehearsal.'

David took another look at Noel, who was by then spraying fine mist from a water bottle onto his slide with the air of a seasoned professional. 'Didn't know he played trombone.'

'He's a talented man. So – are we good?'

'Well, yes. I suppose so.'

'Thanks.'

David went to sit down with the other horns. Eliot nodded at Noel, and returned to his stand.

'Evening, everyone,' he said, arranging pages in front of him. 'I'd like to start with a quick run-through of the Blythe *Fanfare*, if that's OK?' Sniggers erupted around the orchestra. Eliot glanced round, and saw Dr Irving and Sir Marmaduke walking into the hall.

Kayla leaned towards Carl and Noel and said under her breath, 'Right on time. Here we go.'

Sir Marmaduke was leaning on his cane and moving slowly, while Dr Irving bounced along beside him, shorting out his frustration about lack of forward linear motion by letting it escape in little bursts in other directions. They reached a small archipelago of chairs in the middle of the hall, where Sir Marmaduke sank down with a wheeze. He waved his cane at Eliot as if to give permission for him to continue.

Eliot turned back to the orchestra and raised his eyebrows, smiling. He checked Irie and the other percussionists were ready to play, and brought them in with confidence. Irie smashed the tamtam with all the force her small arms could muster, making an excellent stab at the *fortissimo*.

As Hector led the trumpets into their first part of the fanfare, there was a flurry of movement at the back of the hall. Mrs Batten clicked her way towards Dr Irving and Sir Marmaduke, followed by Henrietta Popplewell and her father. Henrietta's clothes appeared to have been designed by the same person who had frilled and pastelled her office. She moved as if she were an underwater anemone: tendrils of scarf and bias-cut frill wobbled around her like a living fabric aura. Her father marched next to her in an altogether more soberly cut suit under the regulation wool coat one apparently wore at Oakdean. Sir Marmaduke levered himself up out of his chair and shook the elder Popplewell's hand enthusiastically, kissed

Henrietta's, eventually gesturing that they should all be seated for the remainder of the *Fanfare*.

By this time, the music had reached Tarquin's few bars of solo glory, which he again failed to deliver to quite the dizzying heights of raspberry-blowing athleticism that Dennis Brain had made sound so effortless in the fifties. Sir Marmaduke seemed oblivious of any musical failing, and beamed at both Popplewells with godfatherly pride.

Noel sat back in his chair with his arms folded throughout, Carl's extra trombone resting bell-down on a stand by his chair. Carl had schooled him in the standard body language of a Trombone Player Sitting Through A Rest.

Eliot continued manfully, bringing the piece to a close with Tarquin turning his usual puce as he strained for his final top note. He brought them off and smiled.

Sir Marmaduke and Dr Irving were still sitting with peaceful smiles on their faces, gazing at the orchestra in general and, in Sir Marmaduke's case, Tarquin in particular. The Popplewells had turned to each other with quizzical frowns.

'Great. Well done,' said Eliot. Carl raised his hand, and Eliot looked over at him. 'Hello?'

'Yeah. Eliot. Here's the thing about this *Fanfare*. Don't know if anyone else has had that nagging thing in the back of their mind that it reminds them of something else?'

There was a huge peal of laughter from the players.

'Well, now you mention it,' said Eliot. 'There is something about it.'

'Listen to this,' said Carl, putting his trombone to his lips and playing the first phrase of the Blythe *Fanfare*, which was an arpeggio going down, followed by a string of notes all from somewhere on the arpeggio, ending up high in the trombone register. There was a small shuffle of feet on the floor from other players as he finished, in the habitual response of an orchestra to one of their own playing a note-perfect solo.

'And now this,' said Carl, lifting his trombone again.

This time, he played the opening trombone phrase of Copland's *Fanfare for the Common Man*, which again started with an arpeggio, but this time an ascending one. The rhythm was identical. It was in the same key. The notes were upside down. It was like hearing an echo through a horizontal mirror. Carl finished, and again generated a foot shuffle, which sounded like a spontaneous rearranging of leaves on a forest floor.

Eliot stood cradling his right elbow in his left hand, chewing the end of his baton. 'Do you know, you might have something there?' he said. 'What was that second one?'

'Copland,' said half the orchestra all together.

'Hmm,' said Eliot, turning to Sir Marmaduke, whose face had darkened from beatific smile to what could only be described as a glower. Dr Irving was looking at him too. The Popplewells had turned from each other and were also looking at him. An air of expectation hung over the hall.

'I mean, as an exercise, it really is terribly good,' said Eliot. 'To invert harmonies that accurately takes no small skill.'

The Marmaduke rumble started to rev up.

'But one can take homage too far,' said Ann from the back of the cellos. 'Especially when the piece is still in copyright.'

At the mention of copyright, Henrietta Popplewell jerked her head towards Ann, which set all her clothes waving like tentacles around her body to their own independent rhythms. Popplewell Sounds knew how to make money, which involved learning copyright law off by heart.

'I wonder if perhaps we should revisit this endeavour, Sir Marmaduke,' murmured Mr Popplewell. 'One doesn't want to attract accusations of…'

'Plagiarism,' called Charlie.

'I say!' shouted Tarquin at Charlie. 'Watch what you're saying. Libelling someone isn't very bright.'

'I wasn't thinking of putting it in writing,' said Charlie.

Sir Marmaduke's rumbling had reached tipping point. 'Outrageous!' he spluttered. 'Wrote the *Fanfare* for Tarquin here. Anyone can hear it is an original work.'

'The way Tarquin plays it is original,' said Carl.

'Fuck off,' said Tarquin.

Dr Irving stood up and raised his hands. 'Now, Tarquin, there is no call for such vulgarity. Despite provocation.' He stared at Carl.

'What?' said Carl. 'He can't play. We've got Neema there, one of the finest horn players in London, sitting as an understudy to your boy, who splits every other note and can't pitch.'

There were muted cheers from the rest of the orchestra's brass players.

'Perhaps I did promote some of the young players beyond their ability,' said Eliot. 'I just thought, you know, to give them an opportunity—'

'And all credit to you for that,' said Erin.

'It's not your fault some of them are rubbish,' said Carl.

'Or that they're playing some illegal knock-off piece,' said Charlie.

Hector, the Oakdean trumpet player, was watching this exchange with widening eyes. He was younger than Tarquin, and clearly in awe. One day he hoped to have an eyepatch just like his, but now he looked worried.

'In fact,' said Carl, 'I wouldn't be surprised if that whole bloody drug raid nightmare a couple of weeks ago was a set-up to get the whole shebang relocated here, and me and Leroy being hauled off by the police was just an amusing sideline.'

'How dare you!' shouted Tarquin.

'What?' said Leroy, turning to Carl. 'You serious?'

'How dare he what?' asked Ann to Tarquin's general direction.

Hector licked his lips and went pale. Noel unfolded his arms and looked at him steadily.

Sir Marmaduke rose to his feet and clutched the back of another chair so he could gesticulate with his cane from a position of stability. 'Nobody insults my godson!' he said. 'This piece will launch his career.'

Dr Irving started to clear his throat in his accustomed manner, heralding an oration. Carl didn't let him get started.

'Yeah. I reckon those drugs were planted by this guy' – he pointed at Hector – 'who, now I come to think about it, was hanging round in the hall before the police arrived. I'm sure they'd love to take your prints to see if they match what was on the bags.'

'Oh my lord,' whispered Pearl, from her seat at the back of the violas. The rehearsal was not going at all as planned. She glanced over to her urn on the trolley at the side of the hall, as if hoping to draw fortitude from a brief meditation on beverages.

Hector's face whitened even more as he stared at Carl. 'How did you—' he whispered.

Mr Popplewell leaned towards Henrietta. 'What are they talking about now? Did someone mention drugs?'

She shrugged. Dr Irving's phlegm was beginning to shift alarmingly.

'So it *was* you!' said Carl to Hector. 'I knew it.'

'Hector, shut up,' shouted Tarquin, also getting to his feet and moving round the front of the orchestra, between Eliot and the group of Popplewells, Dr Irving and Sir Marmaduke.

'He made me,' said Hector, looking miserable and terrified but, despite that, he started to attempt a full confession before Tarquin reached him. 'He said he'd get me expelled if I didn't do it.'

'Shut *up*!' yelled Tarquin, speeding up behind Eliot, who spun around and caught him by the arm as he went past. Tarquin turned and threw a badly aimed punch which by chance hit Eliot in the face, but he hung on.

Hector spoke more urgently. 'He said Sir Marmaduke got him the stuff, and—'

'Unhand my godson!' shouted Sir Marmaduke at Eliot. 'Immediately!'

'Your godson is a thug, Shreddie,' said Ann.

Charlie balanced his cello on its side on the floor and stepped out of the orchestra to hold Tarquin's other arm. 'You alright, mate?' he said to Eliot, who nodded. Tarquin kicked Charlie's shin. 'Ow! You little bugger,' said Charlie.

Caspar and Rufus left their violins on their seats and came out to help Tarquin try to get away from Eliot and Charlie. Not to miss out on a good fight, Danilo, Marina and Reece followed them from their places in the violins, to show the Oakdean boys how it was done at Sunbridge. Eliot and Charlie were suddenly surrounded by three tall Oakdean boys being systematically taken apart by three scrawny Sunbridge kids who knew how to fight dirty. Tarquin broke loose and the fight drifted away from them and expanded into the hall.

Dr Irving finally got his voice working, only to wail ineffectually at the writhing mass of flailing limbs in front of him, imploring them to stop it at once.

Hector lost his nerve and bolted out of his seat, still holding his trumpet, and sprinted for the back door of the hall. Tracie put her trombone on her own seat and shot after him, felling him with a rugby tackle when he was only halfway to the door.

Carl whooped his delight and gave her a round of applause as he too rose to his feet, leaving his trombone on his chair. He walked over to the scrum still going on next to Eliot and Charlie and leaned in to collect Tarquin, who was swinging wildly at anyone within reach. Given Carl's wingspan, he could happily hold Tarquin at arm's length and remain entirely safe. Any punches Tarquin did manage to land on Carl's arm were as effective as a very cross flea on an elephant.

'Right,' he said, putting his other hand in between Caspar's face and the flurry of fists coming from Reece and Marina. 'Time to stop.' Rufus knew better than to carry on, despite not actually being restrained by Carl this time. Once had been enough.

Tracie returned holding Hector, who was in turn holding his slightly dented trumpet.

'Nice one,' said Carl.

'Thanks,' said Tracie. 'Orchestras are fun.'

Kayla groaned, but looked proud nonetheless. Noel got to his feet and picked his way out of the orchestra and along to Eliot.

'Hello,' said Eliot. 'How was that? Not quite according to plan but, all in all, OK?'

'Very much so,' said Noel, smiling. 'How's your eye?'

Eliot put a hand up to feel. 'It'll be a shiner tomorrow, but hey.'

Dr Irving cantilevered up to them. 'I demand you release Tarquin,' he barked at Carl. 'How dare you, as invited guests to Oakdean, then *rampage*—'

'You'll do no such thing at present,' said Noel to Carl.

'Since when did trombone players decide they were in charge of everything?' said Dr Irving, with a sneer in his voice. 'Eliot, I demand that you—'

'I think you'd better be quiet,' said Eliot. 'Firstly, as far as I'm concerned, Carl can be in charge of anything I'm near, and anyone who disagrees with that is a fool. Secondly, well, I'll allow my newest trombone player to introduce himself.'

Noel smiled. 'Thank you. I'm Detective Chief Inspector Noel Osmar, and I've had a very interesting evening so far.'

He pulled a radio out of his pocket and spoke into it. 'Frank? Come on in, and bring some backup.'

'Oh shit,' said Tarquin from somewhere under Carl's armpit.

'Henrietta,' said Mr Popplewell, 'I think we've seen all we need to see tonight. Shall we?'

Henrietta nodded. 'I think so, Daddy.'

They both stared coldly at Sir Marmaduke, who was looking as if his brain was trying to process recent information but not quite catching up. He opened his mouth and closed it a few times, which only added to the underwater imagery that Henrietta's wardrobe conjured up. The Popplewells turned and walked towards the door.

Dr Irving scuttled after them, calling, 'But what about the piece in your *Sounds Magazine*? The profile of Oakdean? The sponsorship…?'

'Goodbye, Dr Irving,' said Mr Popplewell, without turning or stopping.

Sir Marmaduke seemed to snap out of his reverie at that moment, and turned for the door himself. His getaway dash was rather more slow-motion three-legged tortoise than an Aston Martin tyre-squealer, and it took Tracie only a few strides to catch up with him and plant a chair in his path. Sir Marmaduke glanced back, saw everyone looking at him and sank into it, looking defeated.

Noel looked at her admiringly. 'If the trombone thing doesn't work out, have you ever thought about a career in the police?'

Tracie yelped with laughter, as did Kayla. 'I hadn't, no.'

'Reckon you could do anything,' said Carl, smiling.

Voices from the doorway caught their attention, as Frank (coming in) tried to stop the Popplewells (going out).

'It's OK, Frank,' called Noel. 'They can go.'

Frank stepped to one side to allow Henrietta's frills to pass, and came over to Noel, followed by a rather flustered looking Mrs Batten.

'Right,' said Noel. 'This is Frank. He's with me.'

'The uniform kind of gave it away,' said Eliot.

Mrs Batten skirted Sir Marmaduke on his chair, and approached Dr Irving. 'This gentleman' – she gestured to Frank – 'insisted on making his own way to the hall, sir. He informs me there will be a number of police vehicles arriving. I wonder, should I request that they refrain from lights and/or sirens, if applicable? I'm concerned about' – she lowered her voice – 'the look of the thing.' She cut the volume entirely and merely mouthed the next bit. '*The newspapers.*'

Dr Irving sighed. 'Thank you, Mrs Batten. You can certainly try. I imagine there will be a number of enquiries from parents before all this is over.'

She nodded, and clicked over the parquet towards her office.

'Frank,' said Noel. 'We'll need to invite a few of these good people down to the station. This one that Carl's holding,' – he pointed to Tarquin – 'that gentleman sitting over there,' – he indicated Sir Marmaduke – 'this little chap with the dented trumpet' – he nodded at Hector, not unkindly – 'and probably some of this lot,' he added, pointing at the now sullen group of Caspar, Rufus, Danilo, Marina and Reece. 'Let's have words with them here and see if we can sort a few things out before we go, and decide if we need all of them.' He looked at Dr Irving. 'And maybe him.'

Dr Irving bristled. 'I cannot leave Oakdean College. I am the Headmaster, and as such I must insist—'

'You'll do what I tell you,' said Noel, straightening up and suddenly appearing more solid. Less camouflaged. As if he'd stepped into a closer dimension. 'Despite what you clearly believe, this school does not exist in a moral vacuum in the

191

middle of south London.' He pointed out of the window. 'That rhododendron hedge does not constitute an international border. Your rules bend to *my* rules.'

Dr Irving, for once, remained silent.

The orchestra shifted restlessly.

'Are we going to rehearse or what?' called Gwynneth from her seat in the oboes. 'Or can we at least get a brew on while you're fannying about?'

The musicians laughed and looked to Eliot, who smiled. 'What do you think, Pearl?' he said. 'Is your urn up to yet another impromptu break?'

Pearl beamed. 'Of course. Give me a moment.'

Chapter 22

Noel and Frank had a late night at the office. They had ended up taking statements from all the Sunbridge kids involved in the fight, but decided not to haul them into the station. They knew where to find them if they needed to later.

Even so, there were a number of people who found themselves in police interview rooms that evening: Sir Marmaduke, Dr Irving, Tarquin and Hector. Noel established that Hector's role had indeed been coerced, and explained that to Hector's parents, who turned up to collect him. Noel even felt sorry for him as they left, with Hector being harangued with force from one side about his dented trumpet and the other about being caught up in a drug deal. He could see that being the only child of rich, ambitious parents was no picnic, especially if you were sent to boarding school at seven and left to achieve your potential with parental input by correspondence course.

It was nearly midnight when Frank brought Noel a coffee in their office, and they tried to piece together what they had learned from the interview rooms downstairs.

'Who'd have thought posh musicians would get up to this kind of stuff?' said Frank, gulping his heavily sugared latte.

Noel smiled. 'Being posh is no indicator of anything. People are people.'

Frank didn't look convinced, and sniffed. 'Never had three people with only one eye each all in together, though. *That's* a bit weird.'

'Yeah. I might have a word with the schools inspector. Suggest they might want to pop in. Right: what have we got?'

Frank opened a file and pointed to a bullet-point list. 'These are the things Tarquin reckons Blythe made him do. So we've got two of them – Hector and Tarquin – trying to shove blame up the chain of command.'

'Hmm,' said Noel, pulling the file towards him and reading. 'Create a diversion. Plant the drugs.'

'Except we know he made Hector do that.'

'Yeah. And Irving here' – Noel opened another file – 'says Blythe promised that the Popplewells would run a big splash about Oakdean when they covered the concert and then produced Tarquin's album, and basically fame and fortune would drop into their laps. They're all trying to pin it on Blythe.'

'Maybe we should've got them Popplewells down here and all,' said Frank.

'They're easy to find. I'll pay them a visit tomorrow.' Noel rubbed his eyes under his reading glasses and sighed. 'The thing I want to know, though, is which of them had the link to Walter Price. You don't just phone up for a police raid on a whim. What have they got on him? We've got until he comes in tomorrow morning to work that out, as he'll kick up a right old stink and I'll have to boot it upstairs. Like to get my facts straight before I do.'

'We know the call was from Hector's phone,' said Frank. 'I cross-checked the call log.'

'Tell you what,' said Noel, picking up one file and his coffee before standing up, 'you have another go at Irving, and I'll

194

take Blythe. Ask about Walter Price. There must be something there.'

They went back downstairs and split off into separate interview rooms. Sir Marmaduke looked up as Noel opened the door.

'This is an outrage,' he said. 'How much longer is this going to go on for?'

'Just a few more questions, Mr Blythe,' said Noel, timing his ostentatious check of the file to just before Sir Marmaduke was about to correct him. 'Sorry. Sir Marmaduke. My apologies. Or is it Sir Blythe? I can never get the hang of these feudal things. Must be my peasant heritage.'

Sir Marmaduke grumbled to himself in his lower register without resorting to actual words.

'Did you want to call your solicitor?' asked Noel. 'Or I can get the duty solicitor along if you like?'

Sir Marmaduke shook his head.

'As you wish,' said Noel, sitting down, switching on the recorder and giving details to restart the interview. 'Now, tell me how you know Walter Price.' He clicked his ballpoint pen to ready it for writing, crossed one leg over the other and arranged himself into a position to take notes, looking brightly at Sir Marmaduke as if he were an amanuensis about to capture dictation of apercus from a fine mind.

Sir Marmaduke stared. Noel waited. After twenty seconds, during which the only sound in the room was the second hand ticking round the electric clock on the wall, Noel picked up his coffee and took a relaxed drink. He put it back on the table. The clock ticked. Sir Marmaduke had not moved.

'Well,' said Noel, 'our tech team is, as I speak, going through your mobile comms, and I'm sure they'll pick up whenever you two last had a chat. It would just save time if you could tell me about it now. You know.'

Sir Marmaduke said something under his breath that was inaudible beyond the first strained button of his waistcoat.

Noel leaned forward. 'I didn't catch that?' Another pause drifted across the table, fell lightly to the floor and settled in the corner of the room. 'My colleague, Frank – I think you met Frank earlier? – is currently in with Dr Irving. He had to come out for a break earlier because his hand was getting cramp. A lot of writing. A *lot* of writing. Dr Irving is a chatty guy. And do you know what Dr Irving thinks is the most important thing in the world?'

Sir Marmaduke narrowed his visible eye at Noel and looked as if he wished him very ill indeed.

Noel smiled. 'Oakdean College. The glorious past, the terrific present and, of course, the great future of an institution that relies on parents voluntarily sending their kids there to be educated. Parents who are famously skittish when it comes to a whiff of scandal in an educational establishment. Now, if it is within Dr Irving's power to – shall we say, divert? – attention from Oakdean as a whole to, say, one named individual who can then neatly shoulder all the blame and be packed off, then Dr Irving, the dedicated headmaster, will take that course of action.'

Sir Marmaduke straightened in his chair, which creaked under his weight. 'It was Irving who offered to give Price's son a place. The boy has no talent, apparently. Couldn't get in. Didn't have the grades.'

Noel blinked, but wrote nothing.

'I was against it, of course,' Sir Marmaduke continued. 'Bringing down standards. Letting riff-raff in. It's not Oakdean.'

'I see. So you planted the drugs and Irving sorted the raid. Neat.' Noel nodded. 'But, one other thing.' He leaned further forward, smiling. 'Where did you get all the greenery you mixed up with your cannabis? I mean, there was such a tiny amount in there, you were lucky we had such a great sniffer dog. I'm not even sure there's enough there to charge you with dealing.'

Sir Marmaduke allowed himself a wry smile. 'I occasionally indulge in an after-dinner... smoke. Helps with my asthma. Had it lying around and thought, why not?'

'Why not indeed.'

'The rest of it was from my garden. You know – rockery moss, last year's teasel stems, what have you.'

'And who doesn't have last year's teasel stems to hand to pad out one's stash?' said Noel quietly.

He and Frank reconvened in their office upstairs to compare notes, after which Noel sent Frank home for some kip while he drafted an email to the Headmaster of Sunbridge Academy.

Chapter 23

The following morning, Kayla was again intercepted by Rosalind as she was on her way to the kettle. She could tell by the number of furious faces and top shirt buttons done up around the room that Rosalind had been standing there for quite some time. That, and the way everyone behind Rosalind cheered silently as they saw her come in.

'Ah, Kayla!' Rosalind began, but before she could get any further into her speech, Kayla put her hand out towards her.

'Rosalind. Hi. Yeah – I'll get you those GCSE figures at break time. Right now, though, I need a large coffee. Had a bit of a late – and weird – night.'

'I know,' said Rosalind. 'That is indeed the subject of my meeting request.'

The teachers behind Rosalind started to mime stern tickings off, wagging their fingers and shaking their heads at Kayla.

Kayla tried to ignore them. 'What?'

'I need to speak with you. My office. Five minutes.'

A few 'ooOOoooh's escaped from the miming crowd. Rosalind turned round quickly, but all she saw was a bunch of teachers busily looking at each other's diaries and digging in their bags for something urgent.

'Er – right,' said Kayla.

Rosalind nodded and left the staffroom, holding her usual enormous cup of coffee.

'Bye bye, Rosalind!' several people intoned, once the door had safely shut behind her.

'Shit,' said Kayla. 'Just when I thought everything had been sorted out.'

She made it to Rosalind's office with thirty seconds to spare, and was waved over to her now usual sling-seat at the end of the desk. Rosalind scooted her way towards her and prepared to dial into what Kayla assumed was yet another conference call.

'What's this about?' she asked. 'I've got 9C first lesson. Last time I left them unsupervised they put a couple of the science gerbils in a bongo and I didn't know anything about it until we had a surprise gerbil colony several generations later behind the maraca drawer.'

Rosalind smiled. 'This won't take long. The Headmaster requested you were on this call, since it concerns the orchestra.'

'Ah, yeah – about that,' said Kayla, but was shushed by Rosalind, who was mid-dial-in.

The computer delivered them onto the conference call, where they assumed Adrian, head of the school governors, was already there, judging by the cellophane crinkling. It stopped abruptly as the artificial voice announced their arrival.

'Hello?' said Adrian. 'Who's that?'

'Hello, Adrian,' said Rosalind. 'Rosalind and Kayla here. Good morning.'

'But it said there were two of us,' said Adrian.

'Give me strength,' muttered Kayla, and then louder, 'Morning, Adrian.'

The computer tried to announce another caller, but seemed to get cut off twice.

'Is anyone still here?' said Adrian.

'Rosalind and Kayla,' said Rosalind. She waited. 'Anyone else?'

The digital equivalent of tumbleweed rolled down the line.

'Who else are we expecting?' asked Kayla.

'The Headmaster,' said Rosalind, looking at her watch. 'It's not like him to—'

The door of her office opened and the Headmaster popped his head round.

'May I come in? Tried to get on the call but the blasted thing wasn't having any of it. So I thought I'd pop down. Seemed easier all round. Hello, Kayla.'

'Hello, Headmaster,' said Kayla, moving her chair round so he could sit next to her.

'Oh, please call me Henry,' he said. 'It would make a lovely change.'

Rosalind was staring at this exchange as if it were happening in a foreign language.

'Hello?' said Adrian, out of the phone.

'Ah, Adrian! There you are. Good morning,' said Henry.

'The Headmaster called this… call,' said Rosalind, 'to apprise us of the updated situation with regard to Stockwell Park Orchestra. Headmaster.' She gestured that he had the floor, or at least, a segment of her desk end.

'Well, yes,' said Henry, smiling. 'I received a rather interesting email this morning.' He reached into his inner jacket pocket and drew out a piece of paper, which he unfolded and flattened to read. 'From the police. Who,' – he squinted at the email header small print at the top of the page – 'judging by the time this email was sent, work far too hard. Anyway – there has been a rather extraordinary development on the whole drugs thing with the orchestra. Kayla, you must know more about this than I do, since I imagine you were there last night?'

Kayla nodded.

Adrian, who couldn't see what was going on, felt left out. 'What?'

'So you still play in the orchestra, do you?' said Rosalind. Her tone implied disapproval on a job-promotion-limiting level.

'Ah, but it has all been sorted out,' said Henry. 'There was some "incident", the police call it, last night at the rehearsal at Oakdean. Several people being questioned. What does it say here?… da-da-da… all lines of enquiry leading to certain persons of interest, and indeed one of our number, a Miss Tracie Scott, is singled out for particular praise for her conduct. Well, look at that!' He beamed at Kayla. 'Isn't she one of your musical people?'

Kayla smiled. 'She is indeed.'

'What's this?' asked Adrian. 'I thought we'd sent them packing. Violence, wasn't it?'

'All a misunderstanding,' said Henry. 'I must say, it sounds very exciting. Can you tell us all about it, Kayla?'

'I'm not sure if I know any more than you do, Henry,' she said. 'I haven't seen this email.'

'From a DCI Noel Osmar,' said Henry.

'Well, if Noel sent it, it's certainly true. He was there last night. There were a few, um, loose ends that got cleared up, yes. And it appears, as some of the musicians have been saying all along, that they were framed. None of this was any of their fault.'

'Exactly,' said Henry. 'And so, in light of this new information, I wonder if we should reconsider our decision not to let them rehearse or perform their concert here at Sunbridge. It doesn't seem fair now.'

Adrian ate another quick biscuit to help him think.

Kayla drank some more of her coffee, and thought perhaps some more detail might aid Rosalind and Adrian's decision. 'I agree. And we discovered last night that not only was any of this situation nothing to do with the orchestra players, they had been set up by some people at Oakdean.'

'Really?' said Rosalind, clicking her pen into readiness should she be required to make urgent notes. 'Were these "persons of interest" from Oakdean itself?' Ever alive to the possibility of a state-funded academy getting one up on a private school with over a century of history behind it, she was already recalibrating her pitch to the governors.

'Well, yes,' said Kayla. 'They carted off Dr Irving, their Headmaster, and a couple of the boys, plus that composer, Marmaduke Blythe, who I think is godfather to one of the Oakdean boys. It's all a bit complicated.'

'So the orchestra is blameless?' asked Adrian.

'Yes,' said Kayla.

'I suggest, now we have a fuller picture,' said Henry, 'that we perhaps ask the orchestra to return to Sunbridge? Rosalind here can carry on with producing her wonderful brochure, highlighting cultural links in the community and what have you, and our children can carry on benefitting from having a real live orchestra right on their doorstep. What do you say?'

'I say yes,' said Kayla.

'Absolutely,' said Adrian.

Rosalind nodded. 'I concur, Headmaster. It is a sign of a strong management team that it can be flexible when information changes.'

'Er, quite,' said Henry. 'So, can I leave it with you, Rosalind and Kayla, to convey our renewed invitation to the orchestra?'

'Yes, of course,' said Kayla. 'I'll find out David's email for you, Rosalind. I guess we should write to the chairman.'

'Right then,' said Henry. 'Good to talk to you, Adrian.'

'Yes indeed,' said Adrian. 'Bye.' And with that, he disconnected.

Henry grinned at Rosalind and Kayla. 'Well, I must say, it's nice to start the morning with a bit of good news. And one day, Kayla, perhaps you can tell me all about last night. It does sound tremendously exciting, even by our Sunbridge standards. I suppose it's the novelty of not having *our* pupils in the police sights.'

'Early days, Headmaster!' said Rosalind automatically.

Henry looked at Kayla and tried not to laugh. 'Indeed, Rosalind. Indeed.'

Chapter 24

The next Monday's rehearsal, back at Sunbridge, had a definite party air about it. Both Henry and Rosalind had stayed late to welcome the orchestra back. They formed a short guard of honour on either side of the hall doors, greeting players like old friends as they went in. It gave the whole evening a celebratory feel of the Netherfield Ball.

David was speaking to them both by the doors when Eliot arrived.

'Ah, Eliot!' he said. 'I was just saying to Rosalind here how happy and relieved we all are to be back.' He turned to Henry. 'This is Eliot Yarrow, our conductor.'

'Delighted to meet you,' said Henry, shaking Eliot's hand. 'I'm Henry, the headmaster here at Sunbridge. And I'm ashamed to say I've not heard Stockwell Park play before, so if you have no objections, I'd like to listen to some of your rehearsal?'

'Of course,' said Eliot. 'I can't promise surprises like police raids this time, though. It might just have to be music tonight.'

Rosalind tried to giggle girlishly and join in, but didn't quite make it. 'I'm sure music will be just fine, thank you. We've all had our fill of that kind of surprise lately.'

'Amen to that,' said David. 'Well, we must get on. See you later.'

Kayla was already there getting her bass ready when Carl walked in. He grinned, went straight up to her and gave her a hug. Carl's hugs being what they were, she disappeared from view briefly, but emerged a moment later grinning herself.

'Back where we belong,' he said. 'As if the last few weeks never happened.'

'Are you now officially no longer a felon?' she asked.

'All expunged. Noel has made it all go away, for me and for Leroy. Thank Christ.'

The hall filled up with players, some of whom didn't quite know what to make of the Henry/Rosalind gateway but enjoyed the slight feeling of celebrity nonetheless. Tracie and Irie thought it was hilarious when their headmaster insisted on shaking Tracie's hand as they went past, in honour of her mention in dispatches. Reece, Marina and Danilo grinned as they went in. In Sunbridge, seeing the Headmaster usually meant you were in trouble. They enjoyed the novelty.

Just as the noise level had reached its peak in its usual pre-rehearsal chat and instrument warm-ups, it suddenly ceased as three boys from Oakdean appeared at the door and stopped.

'What the fuck?' said Carl.

Eliot turned from sorting his scores on his stand, and smiled. 'Ah, good. Hello. Come in.'

The boys looked at the wall of musicians' faces staring at them in hostility, and didn't move. Behind them, Rosalind and Henry were looking alarmed.

Eliot walked towards the door, and spoke to the orchestra over his shoulder. 'I meant to say earlier, and strictly we should probably put it to a vote or something, but I reckon assuming all the Oakdean boys are as bad as each other is very unfair. Come in, boys.'

The three took a few tentative steps into the hall.

'You want to run this by us first, Eliot?' said Carl. There was an edge to his voice.

'Yes. Sorry. I should have. But these three either had nothing to do with it, or, well, deserve a second chance. Look: Sebastian and Rupert didn't get involved. I mean, Sebastian plays viola, for heaven's sake. Since when did any viola player have a criminal mind?'

There were a few laughs around the orchestra, and the entire viola section nodded in complete agreement.

'Rupert has been sitting in the cellos minding his own business,' said Eliot.

'True,' said Erin.

'And making a half-decent fist of it, actually,' said Ann.

Eliot gestured to the third boy. 'And Hector, here. Well, if you look on it in a certain light, he's as much of a victim as any of us were.'

'He shoved drugs into my tuba!' cried Leroy.

There were some 'yeah's from the heavy brass.

'I'm not sure about this,' said Carl.

'I'm really sorry,' said Hector, in a small voice, and turned to Eliot. 'Maybe I should go.'

Tracie looked at Carl, then at Hector. She swallowed. 'I reckon he's had a shit enough time.' Carl stared at her. 'Well, I did make him dent his trumpet. And he knows if he tries anything again he'll basically be dead.'

The orchestra laughed, and even Hector managed a smile.

'Well, then,' said Eliot. 'How about that? You lot can come back, but if you mess up, we'll set Tracie on you. Does that sound fair?'

The Oakdean boys smiled and nodded, then went to find their places.

'I promise,' said Eliot to the orchestra in general, 'that Caspar, Rufus and Tarquin will never set foot in this orchestra again.'

There were cheers.

'And we don't have to play the sodding Blythe *Fartfare*?' said Carl.

'Absolutely not,' said Eliot. 'I thought we'd do the Copland, as originally planned. You've basically rehearsed it already. Upside down, anyway.'

The brass players laughed.

'Right then,' said Eliot. 'What with all the recent excitements, we're a bit short on rehearsal time. If we're to get anything up to standard in time for our concert we'll all have to pull our socks up.'

'Maybe don't invite strange kids in again, then,' said Charlie.

'Oi!' called Tracie.

Eliot grinned. 'Sibelius. Come on. Let's get cracking.'

As they started the first movement, it was clear the ensemble benefited hugely from the lack of Caspar, Rufus and Tarquin. Caspar and Rufus, with their twin handicaps of an eyepatch each and unshakable confidence in their own pitch and rhythm, despite any hard evidence from around them, had never been the easiest of desk partners in the violins. And without their constant low-level sledging, Danilo, Marina and Reece managed to concentrate properly and ended up playing very decently halfway down the violins. Marco turned round to them several times during the rehearsal to grin and give them a thumbs up. Sometimes all people need is encouragement and they can achieve surprising things.

Neema, David and the rest of the horn section settled happily back into their original line-up. Even before being singled out by Sir Marmaduke, it had been clear that Tarquin's talent was unequal to the rigours of being a horn player. Confidence is essential on any brass instrument if you are to sit through hundreds of bars' rest and then blast a bit right over the orchestra before going back to count more bars. It is a binary existence that switches between terror and boredom, and it takes a certain unflappable character to flourish in that kind of environment. Tarquin had the confidence but not the technique. He would probably make a career as a minor City trader.

Henry and Rosalind sat next to each other at the back of the hall, Henry with a blissful smile on his face, and even Rosalind seemed to have relaxed enough to be enjoying the Sibelius.

Henry leaned towards Rosalind's ear. 'Are you going to invite the governors to the concert? I think you should. This is really jolly good.'

'That was the original plan, yes,' whispered Rosalind. 'And I can see no reason not to revert to it now.'

'Well done,' said Henry. 'A very good idea of yours.'

Rosalind flushed with pleasure. Henry noticed out of the corner of his eye, and smiled to himself. Perhaps the management team of Sunbridge Academy was worth persevering with after all.

Pearl nipped out ten minutes early before the break, as usual, to ready her urn. Her plastic wicker money basket was back on the table, unsecured by plunger or gaffer tape. She spooned coffee granules into plastic cups with an air of carefree happiness. Her world had returned to its rightful axis.

As the rest of the orchestra streamed into the foyer for their coffee and biscuits, Rupert sidled up to Ann at the back of the cellos. He looked sheepish and more than a little worried.

'Could I have a quick word with you, please?'

Ann turned from strapping the neck of her cello into its open case, and frowned when she saw his expression. 'Of course. Rupert, isn't it?'

'Yes.' He didn't look as if he was ready to speak to anyone, and indeed would have rather been elsewhere.

'I'm Ann.' She softened, and smiled at him. 'I promise I won't bite. We leave that to Tracie now.'

Rupert exhaled a small laugh through his nose. 'I – er – wanted to tell you something. Well, to give you something.' He looked excruciatingly embarrassed, took a deep breath and glanced towards the door to check nobody was looking. He reached into an inside pocket of his jacket and produced four thick, square paper envelopes, and offered them to Ann.

'Well, well,' she said. 'Those look familiar.'

'I'm really sorry.'

'Do you know how much a full set of cello strings cost?'

He looked even more embarrassed. 'Um, no.'

'Well, your parents will. Or maybe they don't – are you terrifically rich?'

Rupert laughed, surprised at Ann's direct lunge through everyday politeness. 'Not compared to some boys at school.'

'Ah yes,' said Ann, not unkindly. 'Relativity is what it's all about, isn't it? Put it this way, these strings are worth a big chunk of my monthly income these days.'

'Sorry,' Rupert mumbled, looking at his shoes.

'Well, luckily for you, I am also the kind of person who is rubbish about getting round to claim on insurance for stuff, so I don't have any awkward paperwork to deal with now they've mysteriously turned up in my cello case.'

She took the strings from him and tucked them back in the inside pocket in the top of her case, beside the cello scroll.

'Thank you. That can't have been easy for you, so – without wanting to sound like a condescending older person – well done. Just one other thing, though – do you happen to know where Pearl's cash got to?'

Rupert renewed his look of awkward terror. 'That really wasn't me – I think it was Caspar or Rufus. I'm not sure. Tarquin was kind of sharing out the jobs he said we had to do.'

'Huh. I suppose there's no way of getting it back off them now,' said Ann. 'But we might try approaching Oakdean for reimbursement of funds. Don't worry,' she said hurriedly as Rupert's face grew increasingly worried, 'I'll keep your name out of it.'

He gave a small smile. 'Do you have to tell Eliot now?' he said. 'Because he said we hadn't done anything, but I have, and—'

'Do you want to play in this orchestra?' said Ann.

He looked at her seriously. 'Yes.'

'Then I think we can leave it at that.' She smiled. 'Come on. Shall we get a coffee?'

They walked together into the foyer and joined the queue for Pearl's fig rolls.

Chapter 25

The pub was busy later. What seemed like most of the players of the orchestra were crowded up to the bar, trying to get their rounds in. Carl, of course, had got to the front first and handed pints over the heads of people waiting, to the outstretched arms of Kayla and Charlie, who passed them back to Erin, Ann and Eliot, who had bagged a table. The cello cases were shoved against the wall, as usual.

'Cheers, mate,' said Charlie to Carl, as they sat down.

Carl took a long swallow, and a third of his pint disappeared.

'Anyone heard from Noel?' asked Ann. 'Do we know what's happened to Irving and Shreddie?'

'Not since he sent that email to our school explaining things. Up to a point,' said Kayla.

'Bloody glad he did,' said Eliot. 'We'd have been up shit creek without a rehearsal room if he hadn't persuaded your lot to let us back in. And, let's face it, I'd have been in more trouble with the committee than I probably am.'

'We should've asked the Oakdean guys about it this evening,' said Charlie.

'Bit of a difficult conversation to start,' said Erin. '"Hi, I couldn't help noticing your headmaster was arrested last week – any news?"'

'Were they actually arrested?' said Carl. 'Or did Noel just put the frighteners on them?'

'Dunno,' said Erin.

'I resent the implication that I'd put the frighteners on anyone,' said Noel, who had arrived in his usual cat-like manner.

'Bloody hell, man!' said Ann. 'It's like being haunted. Can you actually walk through walls?'

Noel laughed. 'Even you have to admit that your routine is easy to clock. I found myself at a loose end and decided to wander down.' He looked round the table at the level of the drinks. 'Anyone need a top-up, apart from Carl?'

'Crisps,' said Erin. 'I'm starving. Carl got the first round in and he's rubbish at the extras.'

'Right you are,' said Noel, and went to the bar.

'Is he going to keep doing this?' said Charlie. 'It's a bit unnerving.'

'I like it,' said Erin. 'Makes me feel safe. Like a guardian angel.'

'Steady on,' said Ann.

'Guardian angel who brings crisps,' said Kayla.

'It's like having a tame poltergeist,' said Charlie. 'You never know when he's going to turn up next.'

'Probably why he's good at his job,' said Carl.

They shifted round and got another chair for Noel when he returned with drinks. He dumped the promised crisps on the table in a heap. 'One of everything. Don't argue.'

'Yes, sir, thank you, sir,' said Erin, giggling. She dived in for the salt and vinegar.

'So, come on,' said Carl. 'We're dying to know what's been going on. I know the stuff against me and Leroy has been dropped – we got that from our solicitor. How much of the other stuff are you prepared to spill?'

Noel raised his glass to them. 'Here's to my amateur sleuthing gang. I think it's safe to say we knocked it out of the park last week. Several aspects of life round here are going to be significantly better now. So thank you.'

'Theveral?' said Erin, round a crisp.

'What our young friend here means,' said Charlie, 'is please go on. Erin, we can't take you anywhere.'

'Thorry.'

Noel smiled. 'Yes, several. Well, the immediate stuff you know: Sir Marmaduke (is that really his name?) seems to have embraced a roguish criminality in semi-retirement that hasn't quite worked out for him.'

'I suppose the writing was on the wall on that one when we heard his *Fanfare*,' said Ann. 'But why? Is he broke or something? Or harking back to his glory days?'

'Both, from what I can gather,' said Noel. 'Whether it'll go any further – well, I don't know. Things would need to trundle through the CPS and probably Sunbridge.' He looked at Kayla. 'Do you think any of your lot will want to prosecute? Since it all seems to have settled down? I'm not sure.'

Kayla frowned. 'Well, Rosalind seemed very happy the orchestra was back on site and has proved not to be a den of violent thieves. Doubt she'll want any more adverse publicity she'd have to explain to the governors.'

'And your headmaster?' asked Eliot.

'Henry? Lovely Henry. He does what Rosalind says. Within reason.'

'And what about Dr Irving?' said Charlie. 'What did Blythe offer him so he'd get involved? Was he involved? Difficult to tell, with him, what's normal and what's… just odd.'

'He was probably still in shock from discovering that a girl could play a Strad,' said Erin. 'That kind of information is likely to throw any self-respecting sexist off track.'

'I believe Dr Irving was hoping for a hugely complimentary article about Oakdean (and himself, of course) in *Sounds*

Magazine, and therefore a rise in demand for Oakdean places and pats on the back,' said Noel. He looked around at the blank faces. 'No, me neither. Apparently it's an august publication from Popplewell Sounds, a recording company that had highly profitable links with Blythe years ago.'

'Oh God, yes,' said Ann. 'I remember them from the eighties. Hang on – weren't there a couple of people from there at the rehearsal last week?'

'That girl with the twangly clothes?' said Charlie.

'Indeed yes,' said Noel. 'They left when it all – ah – kicked off, understandably. But I managed to track them down to corroborate Irving's story. There was talk of some sponsorship of a music prize or something. Dr Irving was keen to drive up Oakdean's profile.'

'He and Rosalind basically want the same things for their schools,' said Kayla. 'Why does it all have to be such a minefield? Why isn't it: here are some kids. Teach 'em.'

'I'd vote for you,' said Ann, smiling.

They drank their pints and ate crisps in the British way of sorting out the world's problems in a pub without a fuss.

Noel put his glass on the table and twisted it on top of the condensation ring. 'There was one other thing about Oakdean,' he said.

'You look as if you're working out if you can trust us,' said Carl. 'I think, after last week, you know you can.'

'Unless a bad guy offers us a shitload of money to snitch,' said Charlie.

Noel laughed. 'Yes. I know. Well then, in the course of my enquiries—'

'Oh hello – Dixon of Dock Green rides again,' said Ann. 'Come on, man. Loosen up.'

'Let him speak!' said Erin.

'Right,' said Noel. 'While I was talking to the Oakdean guys – the pupils, and Dr Irving, and Blythe – I couldn't help noticing the eye thing.'

They laughed.

'Oh – you spotted that too,' said Carl.

'We call them Cyclopses,' said Charlie.

'*He* calls them Cyclopses,' said Erin to Noel.

'I know,' said Noel. 'Anyway, tradition is one thing, but maiming kids is another. So I thought I'd have a word with the schools inspector and maybe they can pop in and have a little bit of a chat.'

'That's a *very* good idea,' said Kayla. 'Let's hope it will be unannounced. They're always the fun ones.'

'Knowing them, they'll probably march the inspector to whatever has been doing the damage and proudly point at it, saying it's the making of an Oakdean Man,' said Eliot. 'Mind you, it would be the making of the Oakdean orchestras if they didn't all have *literal* blind spots so they couldn't see the conductor.'

'It's not all about you, Eliot,' said Carl.

'Yes it is. I'm a conductor.'

The conductor was then hit with empty crisp packets which had been expertly folded into little triangles: a skill learned by most orchestral players from long hours spent in pubs. Eliot discovered the pointy corners were deceptively sharp when attached to a missile. Noel drank his pint and looked bemused, but fond.

Ann looked at Noel. 'There's something else, isn't there? What have we missed? And are you allowed to tell us?'

The others stopped throwing things at Eliot and tried to compose themselves, with varying degrees of success.

'Yes. It's not so much on your side of things, but on ours. The police, I mean.' He had all their attention now. 'Remember the night of the raid? The one with Fang?' Nods all round.

'Lovely Fang,' said Eliot, smiling.

Noel glanced at him, and carried on. 'You know how we were wondering why there just happened to be a team right outside Sunbridge at the very convenient time they were called in to look for a possible blade. But in fact, found drugs. With their equally convenient sniffer dog they just happened to have handy.'

'Yeah?' said Ann. 'And?'

'And... it wasn't a coincidence at all. Surprise surprise.'

'Do you need me to pay anyone a visit?' said Carl.

'Christ,' Eliot said, spluttering into his pint.

Noel looked at Carl with appreciation. 'Tempting though that offer is – and don't think I'm not grateful – I think I'd better stick to the usual channels with this one.'

'So what happened?' said Ann. 'You've got a bent copper, yeah?'

'But why would they get involved with a poxy orchestra?' said Charlie. 'Sorry, Eliot,' he added, as Eliot was about to get defensive about his poxy orchestra. 'But, I mean, come on. We're a bit niche.'

Noel glanced round the pub and lowered his voice. 'I happened to glean, during my informative discussion with Blythe, the nature of his relationship with Walter Price. Our bent copper.'

'You "happened" to glean?' said Ann, smiling. 'God, you're good. Shreddie doesn't give anything away unless you've already got something on him. So you must have done some first-class sleuthing to break him.'

Noel laughed. 'I have my moments. So, anyway, Walter has a son who, I understand, is too thick to get a scholarship to Oakdean. Walter would dearly love him to attend the local posh school, but can't afford the full fees. We have demand, and we have a potential supply.'

'And you're not even talking drugs now,' said Charlie. 'This is getting complicated.'

'But hang on,' said Kayla. 'Marmaduke doesn't give out Oakdean places, does he?'

Carl, down at the business end of his second pint, tapped his nose and pointed at Kayla, then turned to Noel and indicated he was ready to receive answers.

'Right,' said Noel to Kayla. 'You ready for this?' he asked Carl. Carl nodded. Noel took a deep breath. 'Blythe needed the concert to be at Oakdean to tempt the Popplewells to come and be impressed and write a glowing article about the school and sign his godson up to a record deal to make them lots of money, so he got Tarquin and his mates to make the orchestra look so bad you got chucked out of Sunbridge. Which, given Sunbridge's reputation, was no small ask.'

Kayla nodded. 'Fair point.'

'Irving desperately wanted the Popplewells to visit Oakdean, for all the previously mentioned puff pieces and kudos and commensurate attention which might well translate into more bums on seats for them. Irving knew of Walter Price's delicate situation because Walter's kid had already failed the scholarship exam. Didn't take long for everyone to come to a mutually satisfactory arrangement.'

Noel took a long swallow of beer. The others just stared at him, processing.

'I think I'm going to need some sort of diagram for this,' said Charlie.

Carl frowned. 'So I nearly got nicked for being a drug dealer because some snobby dick of a policeman wanted his son to go to a school to get his eye poked out?' He failed to suppress a burp. 'At.'

'Uh-oh,' said Erin. 'They've riled Carl now. You don't want to do that.'

'Steady on, big fella,' said Kayla.

'Carl,' said Noel, leaning over and putting his hand on Carl's arm. 'Walter's in big trouble. Leave him to me.'

'Will you shaft him good and proper?'

'Good and proper.'

Erin was smiling at Noel.

'What?' he said.

'Oh – just thinking about the Strad. They didn't stand a chance, did they? Are you part Mountie or something? "Always get your man"?'

Noel considered. 'No horse. But, yeah, I try.'

Eliot jerked upright and nearly spilled his beer, making everyone else jump. 'The Popplewells!' His eyes were bright and excited.

'Eliot,' said Ann. 'Are you having one of your ideas again?'

There were groans around the table.

'Oh fuck, no,' said Charlie. 'Remember you said, you *told* me, if you ever have one of these again, I was to stamp on it straight away? Have you learned *nothing*?'

'No, no, no, hear me out. The Popplewells, right? They were up for doing an article and what have you about Oakdean and how marvellous Tarquin was and yada yada yada?' Grudging nods round the table. 'What magazine worth their salt would not *also* be up for writing a similar article about, say, a plucky inner-city comprehensive that everybody's written off because of drugs and thugs and bad behaviour generally, until a music teacher took some of her star pupils to play in an orchestra that just happens to rehearse in their hall? An orchestra that's going to be playing a concert in a few weeks featuring *those very kids*?' Eliot was almost trembling with excitement.

They all looked at each other.

'Blimey,' said Erin. 'I can't actually fault that, as an idea.'

'There must be something horribly wrong with it,' said Carl. 'He's got form.'

'I'll tell you what's wrong with it,' said Kayla, sounding harsh. They looked at her, Eliot worrying that he had overstepped the mark and was about to be thoroughly told off for cultural snobbishness or just bad conducting.

Kayla pointed a stern finger at Eliot. 'We're an academy now. If you call Sunbridge a comprehensive, you'll have a hell of a time explaining yourself to Rosalind.'

Chapter 26

Since it was Eliot's idea, he offered to go. There was also the small matter of his not having a nine-to-five job he had to be at, so he could factor in a jaunt to Mayfair at short notice. He wanted to take Kayla, as representative of the relevant downtrodden inner-city former comprehensive, but her timetable wouldn't allow it. In the end, Carl said he could wangle a couple of hours' flexitime, and so, later that week, they made their way to Popplewell Sounds. Unlike Sir Marmaduke and Tarquin, they got the Victoria line up from Stockwell to Green Park and then walked the rest of the way.

'This one, I think,' said Eliot, as they neared the Popplewell steps. 'Yep. Here we are. Few minutes early, but within the "polite" window.'

'Not exactly plate glass and skyscraper country, is it?' said Carl.

'From what I gather, Popplewell Sounds is more your traditional, family outfit.'

'What – you reckon they started it from here because it was their third house and they weren't needing it during the week?'

'Something like that.'

'Fucking hell. Different world.'

'Come on. Let's be persuasive. For Kayla's sake, OK?'

'Yes, boss.'

Eliot pressed the bell, and they were buzzed through the front door into the sensory assault chamber that passed for an entrance hall. The roses had been replaced by a stook of multi-coloured gladioli stems in the pink vase on the table.

'Whoa,' said Carl, taking in the candy-stripe wallpaper and dado ensemble effect. 'I've had hangovers easier to deal with than this.'

'Shh.'

Henrietta's office door opened before Carl could say anything else, and they watched her feet walk round the table until the rest of her appeared from behind the gladioli. She smiled and held out her hand to them both. 'Good morning! I'm Henrietta Popplewell; how lovely to meet you. Eliot, is it?'

'Yes, I'm Eliot,' he said, shaking her hand. 'And this is my tame trombone player, Carl.'

Carl smiled and shook Henrietta's hand too, taking care to dial down his usual hand-crushing ability in view of the pastel shades and alarming vision of her many-layered clothes. It was like shaking hands with a kelp frond.

Henrietta giggled. 'Not too tame, I hope! For what would a trombone section be worth if populated by timid underlings?'

Carl raised his eyebrows and laughed. He was willing to overlook a large deficiency of interior decoration and personal style if it was accompanied by an absolute acceptance that the trombones were the finest orchestral section. 'Girl after my own heart!' he said, rather more gallantly than he would have put money on himself being five minutes earlier.

'Now I feel outnumbered,' said Eliot.

Henrietta laughed and led the way to her office where, to their credit, Carl and Eliot successfully hid their reaction to the ramping up of the ruffle and pelmet index.

'Thank you for finding time for this meeting,' said Eliot, after he had rearranged some of the cushions on his chaise longue to give him enough space to sit down. 'I know I didn't give you many details.'

'My pleasure. How can I help?' said Henrietta. 'Are you alright there?' This last was to Carl, who was trying to fold his large frame into an overstuffed tub armchair which was already quite full of scatter cushions. He grinned at her and nodded, ending up perched higher than he had perhaps intended but styling it out.

'Well, I didn't manage to introduce myself properly the last time we met – understandably,' said Eliot. 'But I did hear some intriguing rumours about the reasons you were there. I wondered if I – we – could talk to you a bit about the project we're trying to develop with Stockwell Park Orchestra.'

'Yes, it was a most distressing evening. My father and I had made the effort to travel south of the river for Sir Marmaduke and I don't think it's any betrayal of confidence to tell you that we feel he let us down. Quite shamefully.'

Carl caught Eliot's eye at the mention of travelling south. Eliot managed to convey his hope that Carl wouldn't say anything stupid about it.

'What if I were to tell you that the reason Tarquin was playing with the orchestra this term in the first place was because I invited some musical pupils from a couple of schools?'

'You?' Henrietta was confused. 'But Sir Marmaduke said he had got your orchestra on board for his little venture?'

'Other way round,' said Carl. 'Eliot here had one of his bright ideas, and we visited Oakdean and the local comp, Sunbridge, to see if there were any kids who wanted to come along and try us out.'

'Sunbridge is where we normally rehearse,' said Eliot. 'And, although it does face quite a few challenges on its patch, I believe its recent transition to academy status is trying to help with those.' He stared at Carl, who did look slightly guilty.

Henrietta was still frowning.

'We've got a few Sunbridge kids along,' said Carl. 'One of them – Tracie – plays trombone and is coming along very nicely. Real potential there.'

'I'm sure you can appreciate that Carl doesn't put up with passengers in his trombone section,' said Eliot. 'If he says Tracie is good, she's good. She certainly looks as if she's doing all the right things from where I stand on the podium. And we've got some others too: there's a kid who's taken to percussion like it's her native language. Won't stop grinning. And three decent violinists too.'

'Certainly decent little fighters,' said Carl.

'Pardon?' said Henrietta.

'And we still have some boys from Oakdean, who had nothing to do with Sir Marmaduke's scheme,' said Eliot hurriedly. 'Anyway, to cut to the chase, I understand you were planning to cover our concert for Sir Marmaduke. We wondered if you might want to write an article about what we're trying to do instead?'

Carl leaned forward on his cushions, swaying a bit, but his trombonist's core strength held firm. 'There's a music teacher at Sunbridge who has encouraged her kids to try us out. These are kids who don't have much money for posh instrumental lessons. I reckon your readers would love a feel-good story like this.'

Henrietta folded her hands together on her desk and looked at them both.

'And we're not even *thinking* of recording contracts or any of that malarkey,' said Carl. 'Britain never really recovered from St Winifred's School Choir singing "There's No One Quite Like Grandma" in the eighties – we're not going to go anywhere near that amateur kids' stuff. Don't worry.'

Eliot, who had looked alarmed at the start of Carl's speech, burst out laughing. Henrietta joined in.

'Very well,' she said. 'You've sold it to me. Give me the details of that music teacher and the date of your concert and I'll see what I can do.'

Chapter 27

Shortly before nine o'clock the following Saturday night, Carl and Kayla were walking down the cramped staircase to the basement of Night Blues, a jazz club in Shoreditch. Clouds of vape and other chemicals drifted down after them from street level. Kayla tried to protect her bass as she rounded the corner at the bottom of the stairs.

'Fuck. Hope I haven't gouged out a bit of the bass there.'

'Oh, yeah — sorry. Forgot to tell you that stair always takes a piece of first-timers as a sacrifice. It won't touch you again.'

'I'm not sure this is a good idea.'

Carl smiled at her as he waited at the bottom. 'Course it is. We'll smash it. Now, the other two should be around somewhere…'

He wandered off into the low-lit room, weaving past small tables that filled most of the space, towards the back corner where the jumbled outlines of a piano and mics and wires and a drum kit were dimly visible. A few people were already sitting drinking, but the place had yet to hit its night-owl stride. The club smelled of warm dust inside a spotlight and a faint electric tang, like something almost alive itself. There was a long bar along the side wall, where a couple of staff were re-stocking ready for the night ahead.

Kayla followed him to the back of the room and parked her bass in a corner. Carl was talking to a man with a short beard and a wide hat. Another man with almost no hair at all was standing next to them.

'Here she is. Kayla – this is Neep and Sticks. I make no apology for their ridiculous names.'

'Hi,' she said. 'Let me guess, Neep's the drummer?'

Sticks (no hair) laughed. 'Yeah, no, sorry about that. It just stuck from school.'

'Good to meet you,' said Neep, shaking her hand and making a gesture that might have been tipping his hat.

'Piano, yeah?' said Kayla.

'Yeah.'

'It's just four of us tonight,' said Carl. 'It's great here – they don't mind what we play. Very relaxed.'

'Suppose it's too late to worry we should have rehearsed properly before now?' said Kayla.

'Don't be daft,' said Carl. 'We've gone through the stuff. These guys can do it in their sleep. You're brilliant. *I'm* brilliant. We'll be fine.'

Neep and Sticks nodded, smiling.

'Well, you all seem very relaxed,' she said. 'I'll take that as a vote of confidence. Thanks.'

She turned to get her bass out of its case while Neep went to sit at the piano and Sticks behind the drums, taking his namesake tools out of his satchel as he went. Carl bent to get his trombone out and decide which mutes he needed.

'Maybe you should have got Henrietta along here too, to get more diverse material for her magazine profile,' he said.

'Don't you start. I've already got half the staffroom on my back as it is.'

'What – they envious?'

'No. Don't think so. It's more – every time Henrietta turns up they think they've got to be on their best behaviour or they'll be letting me – or the school – down. It's probably a bit of a strain. Mostly all you want, when you get five minutes between lessons, is to flop in the staffroom and have a brew without worrying about sitting on an extra piece of flappy jumper that's escaped.'

Carl laughed. 'Tell them they should be grateful they didn't have to visit her office. I still get cushion nightmares. And how many times has she visited anyway? It's only one sodding article.'

'Couple. She's very thorough.'

'Let's hope she writes you to the skies.'

'Tell you something, though. Rosalind is lapping it up. It's like all her Christmases came at once. She's got Doug back to do more photos, and she's lined up all the governors to come to the concert and everything.'

'Maybe next time somebody gets pulverised on the outside of the staffroom door she might scrape up the mess herself, then, instead of leaving it to you.'

Kayla smiled. 'Those winged pigs again. I've warned you.'

They got themselves into position with Sticks and Neep. Kayla and Carl tuned to Neep's soft piano chords, then Carl nodded to Sticks, who counted them in, and they were off into something late-night and mellow, which was as far away from Mussorgsky as anyone was likely to get. Improvisation is such a different skill from the usual sight-reading required in an orchestra that not many players can do both, even if they play the sort of instrument that lends itself to jazz – double-reeded instruments like oboes and bassoons are simply too perky and strict. They can't bend a note out of shape when it's needed.

Carl could persuade his trombone to play anything. In the orchestra, he was fearless and reliable, counting hundreds of bars' rest as required and then coming in at the right time with conviction before going back to the next chapter of his book. With his jazz friends, he was a different beast altogether. With its slide, a trombone is one of the brass instruments capable of bending a note into the interleaving microtones we don't usually hear. Any decent *embouchure* can push a note up or down, and a horn player will use their right hand in the bell to adjust tuning, but a 'bone can flatten out all the bumps in the ride.

They played their first set at Night Blues as if it were their hundredth. Kayla had done improv like this before, but never as part of a band who were going to get paid at the end of the evening. Pretty soon, though, she forgot to be nervous, and the four musicians melded with a conviction and simplicity that disguised the musical intelligence underpinning it.

The night grew old and the room filled with Shoreditch hipsters with their beards and vegan manbuns. Neither Carl nor Kayla saw Ann and Erin come through the door and quietly sit at a table near the bar, which was exactly how Ann and Erin wanted it to be. They drank beer and nodded along to their friends' inventive musical lines, and only revealed themselves after both sets had finished. Being truly musical often means knowing when to fade into the background.

Chapter 28

Spring terms are short, and the day of the concert arrived almost by surprise. There was the usual scheduled afternoon rehearsal, but Eliot knew that by that time all he could do was some cosmetic topping and tailing – the heavy lifting had already been done, successfully or not, and most amateur concerts, being slightly under-rehearsed, are the result of luck and terrified concentration rather than finely tuned conducting management. This was Eliot's second concert with Stockwell Park Orchestra: his first had been as an emergency stand-in conductor for Erin's Elgar concerto, and he hadn't been in charge of most of those rehearsals. He was relieved this one wasn't *quite* as seat-of-his-pants as that had been. Even so, he couldn't shake a vague feeling of being on edge as he wondered if he would have to rely on Carl to head off a drunk and belligerent former conductor turning up to usurp him.

Rosalind was, somewhat predictably, in the foyer at Sunbridge as Eliot arrived at two-thirty for the rehearsal, despite it being a Saturday and already having committed herself to being at the evening concert. Her hair was vibrating even more enthusiastically than usual, which was quite a feat. She had Doug at her side once again.

'Afternoon, Rosalind!' called Eliot as he strode past them. 'Lovely to see you. And Doug? Again? Marvellous.'

Rosalind tapped towards him with glee. 'I've been given the headmaster's green light to design a bespoke brochure around this event! This musical endeavour could shape the very direction of Sunbridge's future!' Doug's eyes met Eliot's over Rosalind's shoulder. Doug's were curiously devoid of discernible emotion. He was a man who appreciated a paid job as much as the next professional, and threw himself into them to the best of his ability, but preferred to keep any actual passion separate from his photographic contractual requirements. His heart belonged to Sheba, his nine-foot python who lived in a custom-built tank in his spare bedroom.

'Jolly good,' said Eliot, as vaguely as he hoped might be possible and still within the bounds of politeness. He carried on walking into the hall and decided to try to ignore Rosalind and whatever she made Doug do. There were gym ropes looped against the walls of the hall. He prayed there would be no Tarzan re-enactment.

A lot of the orchestra were already there, tootling and squawking to warm up. Pete was already in his seat at the back of the violas practising an especially fiddly bit of the Sibelius, very quietly and about half the speed it was destined to go. This meant that Pete could feel virtuous about having practised and anticipate being able to play it, but in fact would yet again be defeated by the tempo and general technical skills that were above his pay grade and desk position, and he would end the movement blinking rapidly, sawing his viola along his bow rather than the other way round.

The harpist was setting herself up between the first and second violins and squidging the horns over a bit. She was extremely glamorous, and wore her jet-black hair scraped tightly into a bun on the very top of her head, into which she had pushed her orchestral pencil. Even though it was an ordinary Saturday afternoon in a rundown school in south London, she wore full and professional-level flawless make-up and radiated a perfume that made her nearest neighbours' throats itch. Her name was Bożenka.

The Sunbridge kids arrived, self-consciously in home clothes rather than school uniform and feeling rather out of place in their school hall on a Saturday. The Oakdean pupils were also there, but had made no concessions to the weekend: all were in their usual jacket, tie, definitely non-jean trousers and highly polished Oxfords. Eliot did spot Hector, the Oakdean trumpeter, talking to Tracie next to him in the trombones, without either of them looking aghast at each other's attire or accent. He supposed this was progress, and that perhaps some understanding could travel back and forth if he could keep this kind of communication channel open. Then he told himself off for rampant social engineering aspirations and concentrated on what they had to play that afternoon.

David introduced him to Bożenka before they started playing.

'Lovely to meet you,' said Eliot, shaking a hand which clasped his in an icy ratchet grip. 'Thank you for coming along for your few bars of Mussorgsky. We very much appreciate it.'

'It is the way of the harp, to deliver perfection in tiny pockets,' said Bożenka in a heavily accented low voice. 'But what else can we do before death?'

Eliot met David's eyes briefly. 'What else indeed?'

Walking back to his podium, he looked at his right hand, which still had white marks where Bożenka had gripped it. He wriggled his fingers and tried to shake the feeling that death could be summoned by a harpist.

'Just think happy thoughts,' said Charlie as he returned. 'She doesn't like it when we do that.'

Eliot laughed, and tried. He kept more than his usual half an eye on the clock, as he was aware that brass players' lips are liable to 'go' if overused and not allowed enough rest. Seasoned adults are one thing, but kids who are not used to playing for hours don't have the muscles hardened for it. Even the best brass player on earth won't get that top note if their embouchure is exhausted. Once a lip has gone, only rest will return it. Eliot couldn't afford to do that to his kids. Not in front of Rosalind and the army of governors and other influential people she had no doubt arranged to be there.

'Just take it easy, brass, OK?' he said before they had even played a note of the rehearsal. 'My old guys – the grown-ups, I mean – I'm relying on you to pass on all your top tips to the kids for saving your lip. They may not have done this before. We need them to be able to play at seven o'clock.'

Carl immediately began to show Tracie how to blow the loosest, wobbliest raspberry imaginable, without any mouthpiece, to relax her face. Hector turned round and, after a moment, joined in. It was like suddenly being transported to a *Scooby-Doo* convention.

'That's it!' said Eliot. 'Brilliant. Just drop out if you feel you're getting tired in the rehearsal. Tonight's the important bit. So: could we have an A, please, Gwynneth?'

They rehearsed the programme in the same order that they would play it later: Copland's *Fanfare for the Common Man*, then Mussorgsky's *Night on the Bare Mountain* followed by Sibelius 2. Throughout the rehearsal, Rosalind and Doug darted about in the hall clicking off shots, but Doug at least restricted himself to doing that during the *forte* passages. He attempted a few of Bożenka, but she fixed him with such a glare he melted back and kept a very observant distance thereafter.

During the break, when Pearl had broken out her usual lucky dip Concert Day Special (this time: chocolate-dipped ginger thins), the players were ambushed in the foyer by an enormous banner being erected by Rosalind. It was one of those that rolled itself up into a base on the floor like a window blind. She was trying to add more sections to the carbon fibre support rod as she lifted the banner up to its appropriate height, rather like an old-fashioned sweep's brush. At its halfway stage, a greater-than-life-size picture of Eliot with raised baton was emerging from the base. It looked as if he were a billowing genie in the process of being summoned.

'Christ, Eliot,' said Charlie when he saw it. 'Fame at last.'

Erin and Ann turned to look.

'That's... quite alarming,' said Erin.

'I wonder what's being unrolled next,' said Ann. 'It's only got down to his waist.'

'Do we all get one?' said Carl.

'Need a hand, Rosalind?' said Kayla.

Rosalind beamed at them. 'No, I'm quite alright thank you. These marketing tools are the absolute business for the roving manager. Many's the conference when I—'

The banner took the opportunity of her attention being diverted to snake out of her grasp and roll itself up again with a snap. She fell forward as it retracted, ending up on her hands and knees.

'God – are you OK?' said Kayla, running to her.

'My lanyard,' Rosalind said, in an only slightly strangulated voice. 'It's got caught.'

While Kayla was sorting her out, the rest of the musicians drank their coffees and bickered good-naturedly over the ginger thins.

'Well, Eliot, despite some significant hairy moments,' said Ann, 'I have to admit that your idea seems to have worked. We have a few really decent young musicians who seem to like us.'

'Don't know if Carl would agree it was worth the trouble,' said Charlie, 'but, yeah, if we're ends-justify-the-means-ing it, then yep.'

Carl smiled. 'Oh, nothing I couldn't handle. And there have been some great upsides.'

He was looking over at Kayla as he spoke, which they couldn't help noticing.

'She's very nice,' said Ann.

'Damn good musician too,' agreed Erin.

Eliot leaned a bit closer to Carl. 'Are you blushing?'

'Fuck off,' said Carl.

'Oh, he's smitten,' said Charlie.

'I'll smite you in a minute,' said Carl.

They turned to give a small round of applause to Kayla and Rosalind, who had managed to get the banner to its full height and secured it in position. Giant Eliot conducted them, looking out over their heads to somewhere beyond the admin office.

'When was that taken?' said Erin. 'Did you have to pose specially?'

'Oh no,' said Eliot. 'I reckon that's a Doug special. Don't remember him taking it. I was probably trying to get the trombones' attention or something.'

Carl elbowed Eliot in the stomach, which only left him breathless for a minute or so.

The drift back to the hall for the second half started. As Sebastian, Rupert and Hector wandered past, Eliot said to all three in general, 'Everything alright, boys? You set for this evening? Are any of your parents coming along… or teachers?' He didn't like to be too specific, but wanted to be prepared.

'Oh, yah,' said Sebastian. 'My parents said they'd drive down and stay over in the flat.'

'Oh? Good,' said Eliot. 'Do they come far?'

'Yorkshire.'

'Crikey.'

'They'll have to stop on the way otherwise the chauffeur is out of hours, but they said they didn't mind.'

'Ah.'

'Did you mean Dr Irving?' asked Rupert. 'I doubt it. He's not been in school all week. Apparently the governors were having, like, a big meeting about him or something?'

Eliot raised his eyebrows at the others behind him. 'Well, I'm sure it'll all get sorted out.'

'My parents are coming too,' said Hector. 'I told them about the *Fanfare* and they sounded really keen.'

'So they should be,' said Eliot. 'Hang on – do they know we're doing a real one, not the Blythe knock-off?'

Hector laughed and nodded, and they carried on into the hall.

'I wonder if any of the Sunbridge parents are coming,' said Eliot.

'Hope so,' said Kayla, who was just wandering over with her coffee. 'I sent a note home with the kids who are involved. Some families you get more support from than others.'

'So, just to recap,' said Eliot, preparing to count on his fingers, 'tonight we could have Oakdean parents, Sunbridge parents, Sunbridge PTA and governors, Sunbridge management, a classical music magazine researching an article, a photographer and quite possibly a policeman turning up? And that's before our usual audience of friends 'n' family and Gwynneth's mother from Merthyr.'

'Blimey, you learn quick,' said Ann. 'And probably Mr and Mrs Ford-Hughes too. Let's not forget them.'

'How could we?' said Eliot. 'Just when I think tonight's performance could be quite fraught. I should look to my blessings.'

'If Daniel Barenboim can try to sort the Arab–Israeli conflict with a cross-border orchestra,' said Charlie, 'this will be a piece of piss.'

Chapter 29

By half past six, the orchestra were already back at Sunbridge. They had been allocated a couple of classrooms for changing, and there was the usual milling around of musicians in varying states of undress. Eliot had asked the kids to wear dark trousers or skirts and a white shirt, since he'd seen that was basically the Sunbridge uniform and wouldn't cause them any hassle. The Oakdean boys, he had assumed, would be able to cope.

Rosalind had spared no effort to make the foyer and hall look welcoming. She had rigged up home-made bunting over the main doors. Along with the Giant Eliot banner, there were now two others at strategic positions in the foyer, to herd audience members into the hall in a natural eddying motion. One showed Giant Irie smashing the tamtam while grinning, and the third was a group picture of Giant Danilo, Reece and Marina playing their violins in what was clearly a passage requiring great concentration.

Irie's mum and older brother had brought her to the concert, and stood in the foyer when Irie had gone off to find the rest of the musicians. Her brother was transfixed by her picture on the banner.

'Oh my days! Mum – *Mum*! Have you seen this? Irie on the poster, yeah? Oh my days.'

Her mum stood next to him, looking up at the picture of her tiny daughter that was now twice as tall as her. Her eyes filled with tears, and she hugged her son tightly. 'That's your sister. That's my girl.'

'Hey, Mum. Can I learn an instrument too, yeah? It looks wicked.'

She nodded, and they walked hand in hand into the hall to find a seat.

Doug, who had folded himself into the corner of the foyer, took several pictures of this exchange, which would later feature prominently in Rosalind's brochure. She may have been accused of having a cynical money-chasing management ethic, but when a project can be distilled into such direct and powerful results, even her detractors gave her grudging support.

Rosalind was on the other side of the foyer by the main doors, greeting everyone who arrived with the affable confidence of a woman who knows she has her best lanyard on and is not afraid to wield its power. Even the snooty looks from the first lot of Oakdean parents could not dampen her enthusiasm for the evening. Sebastian's parents had endured a fraught journey from Yorkshire, having been forced to alight briefly in the outskirts of Leicester while their chauffeur had a rest stop.

Sebastian's mother saw Rosalind and immediately fired a question at her. 'Where do you want us to put our driver?'

Their driver, George, was at that moment parking their Mercedes in the Sunbridge playground and awaiting orders.

Rosalind widened her already preternaturally wide eyes, and smiled helpfully. 'I'm sorry?'

'Our driver? Where should he go? To wait. At Glyndebourne they have a hut for the chauffeurs.'

'Well, I don't know. He could come in and listen to the concert if he likes?'

'No. I don't think that would be appropriate. Darling' – she turned to her husband – 'tell George to wait in the car. He can drive us on to Pimlico later.'

Sebastian's father offered his arm to his wife as they walked into the hall, and with his other hand he dialled George to deliver the good news.

Knots of people in twos and threes arrived, chatting and smiling. Mr and Mrs Ford-Hughes swept through the doors, all graciousness and chiffon and perfume (her) and supportive smiles (him). Hector's parents walked in looking almost as apprehensive about entering a state school as they had when they'd collected him from the police station. However, they were thawed by Rosalind's genuine welcome, and walked through to the hall admiring the banners.

Henry wandered in, looking delighted his school was playing host to such a cultural event. He shook Rosalind's hand warmly as he went past and congratulated her on the evening. She basked in her headmaster's praise like a flower in sunshine.

Noel Osmar walked in quietly on his own. He allowed his hand to be shaken by Rosalind, and smiled to himself as he saw Giant Eliot in the foyer. He could spot a Doug frame with the best of them.

The Sunbridge governors arrived en masse, led by Adrian. They had been at a pre-arranged early supper round the corner, and several of them had taken advantage of the large glass of wine that came with the all-inclusive buffet option. There was some giggling from the stragglers.

Henrietta and Mr Popplewell arrived arm in arm, looking eagerly around with great interest. Henrietta held a small notepad in her free hand, which had a pen with an integral light clipped to it in readiness for a mid-music muse strike.

Behind them was a small group of unexpected audience members. Sir Marmaduke was at its centre, and around him oscillated Dr Irving, Tarquin, Caspar and Rufus. Because of Sir Marmaduke's slow progress, Rosalind had plenty of time to see them approach the doors. She looked around anxiously for assistance. Doug saw her discomfort and came to see if she needed help.

'Doug! Can you find Eliot and get him here, right away please? Quick as you can. Tell him we have Oakdean visitors.' Doug nodded and melted away.

She straightened her shoulders, patted her lanyard and inhaled through her nose, held it for three counts and exhaled as a flat stream of air through her mouth. Thus primed, there was almost nothing she felt she could not achieve.

'Good evening, Dr Irving,' she said as they crossed the threshold. 'And your Oakdean boys. What a surprise. You are very welcome.'

Dr Irving had dark shadows under his eyes that had not been there a week earlier, but otherwise seemed in his usual spirited good mood. 'Good evening, Rosalind. Delightful to see you again. Yes, as you see, we have conveyed our metaphorical olive branch from behind our rhododendron, as it were. I don't believe you have met Sir Marmaduke Blythe, esteemed composer and Old Acornian?'

Rosalind let the ridiculous term break gently over her like a caressing wave in the southern seas, and held out her hand politely. 'Good evening, Sir Marmaduke.'

'Everything alright?' said Eliot, who had appeared behind her in a manner Noel would have endorsed.

'Fear not!' said Dr Irving. 'We come in peace. Hatchet buried, and all that.'

Sir Marmaduke began rumbling in what appeared to be agreement.

'I'm not sure if Carl and Leroy would agree to any hatchet burial without an apology from you,' said Eliot. 'And I'm not sure, if they see you, they won't say that to you in person. Quite forcefully.'

'My dear Eliot,' said Dr Irving, 'I am convinced that, as civilised men, we can all agree to letting some water pass under this particular bridge.'

There were so many metaphors flying around that Eliot got the distinct feeling Pearl was involved somehow. But he was ten minutes away from the start of a concert and he didn't have time to dwell on that. 'Well, fine. But, if you want some advice, sit on the left. Away from the trombones.'

'Thank you, Eliot,' said Rosalind.

He nodded and returned to the musicians.

And so the hall filled, and Doug took pictures, and Rosalind finally closed the outside doors with one minute to go and went into the hall herself. The orchestra was already seated, except for the leader, Richard. He walked to his place, prompting a round of applause, and nodded at Gwynneth to play an A for the final tuning. As the strings played their fifths, and some of them even adjusted their pegs, Carl scanned the audience.

Eliot had caught him before he had gone to sit down, so he knew the Oakdean contingent was there. Even so, he wanted to pinpoint exactly where they were sitting. He noted, instead of sitting in one group, they were scattered across the available seating. Sir Marmaduke and Dr Irving had indeed taken Eliot's advice and were on the far side of the hall from Carl, but a couple of the boys were sitting, separately, quite close. Carl assumed they had come in too late to find seats all together. He decided not to let them bother him, and joined in with the brass tuning when Gwynneth played their A.

Eliot bounded up to his stand to huge applause, which he acknowledged with outstretched arms and a grin.

'Thank you. Thank you very much.' The clapping died down. 'And welcome to tonight's concert by Stockwell Park Orchestra in a place very familiar to us, since we rehearse here every week: Sunbridge Academy!' Another short burst of applause. 'Now, the orchestra has been very indulgent with me this term' – he smiled at a few conspicuous groans behind him – 'because I had the idea that it would be great to encourage some kids along to play in the orchestra. So tonight's concert is very special, featuring as it does pupils from both Sunbridge Academy and Oakdean College.'

Eliot pointed out where they were sitting, to whoops from the audience. The kids themselves looked proud and embarrassed in equal parts.

'So, with them in mind, the programme tonight will give these youngsters a chance to show you what they can do. Our first piece, a very short one, is just for brass and percussion. It only lasts about three minutes, but if you haven't heard it before, it'll blow your socks off. With any luck, it'll still blow your socks off if you have. Copland's *Fanfare for the Common Man*.'

He turned and raised his baton, checking everyone was ready. Irie copied Max and stood with her sticks up, feet planted in her signature stance, her eyes bright. Eliot nodded, smiling.

He brought them in, and Irie's tamtam shivered through the hall, the sound decaying like the fronds of a firework succumbing to gravity after the first burst of light. She and the other percussionists controlled the *diminuendo* beautifully over four bars, from *fortissimo* to *mezzo forte*. Those four bars of nuclear strength concentration laid foundations that Irie felt she could carry into anything else she tried to do. Her mother sat with silent tears running down her face. Her brother watched open-mouthed.

Eliot wrinkled his nose at Irie in affirmation as he turned his attention to the trumpets. Hector played perfectly in sync with the others, as they ripped up the arpeggios and down again, evoking the vast American Great Plains as any Copland will to those brought up on old movies. After more percussion punctuation, the horns joined in, swelling the volume in the hall. Without Tarquin's fluffs, Neema led her section in glory, bells up and confident. Even the violins, who spend their playing lives sitting directly in front of the horns, were turning round in their chairs in admiration at the sight and sound of a horn section in full cry.

Then it was Irie's turn again, before Carl, Tracie and the other trombones, together with Leroy on tuba, kicked off the final section for everyone to join in. The bass drop had been invented by Copland long before twenty-first century pop. Carl (playing bass trombone in this) and Leroy together pumped out low hertz at enough volume to buzz loose sheets of paper against music stands. It was a physical energy the audience could feel in their skeletons as it passed through them in the unknowable way of transient music: it left them somehow changed but at the same time took away their vocabulary to describe how.

As the *Fanfare* approached its apogee, which had some string players in front of the trombones and trumpets flinching with fingers in their ears, and Eliot thanking Kayla's health and safety knowhow that had suggested small ear plugs for the kids, a sharp metallic *ping* entered the soundscape. Leroy, his puffed-out cheeks showing how much he was putting into his *fortissimo* accents, looked simultaneously surprised and alarmed. The onslaught of brass noise carried on like an unstoppable force, but the *pings* grew more frequent. Leroy's eyes flicked from Eliot to the audience and back again. He had four bars' rest while the mighty brass machine roared on, and quickly tipped his tuba upside down and shook it. Several acorns fell out and rolled away under Carl's seat in front of him.

Carl, whose bass trombone part had only two bars' rest at the beginning of Leroy's four, sensed some of this unfold behind him before he made his next entry. He saw the acorns roll past on the lino out of the corner of his eye, just before another acorn struck the bell of his trombone.

By the time Neema hit a top G sharp, slicing through the texture like sudden sunlight bouncing off a drenched slate roof after a storm, tiny acorn missiles were regularly flying into the orchestra and pinging off various instruments. Several went into Leroy's tuba again, spiralling down his bell like acorny water down a plughole.

As Irie played her final *crescendo* roll on the tamtam, one hit her on the forehead. She blinked, but carried on, concentrating wholly on Eliot until he brought them off the final chord and the hall erupted in a wall of applause that if anything was louder than the music that had just stopped. Irie put her hand up to her head, where a trickle of blood started to ooze over her eyebrow.

None of the audience was aware of the acorn missiles. The music had been too loud for them to register any other unusual effects. The musicians, in their ingrained Show Goes On mentality, had valiantly carried on. Even Eliot, who had noticed the puzzled glances and of course Leroy upending his tuba, wasn't quite sure what had just happened.

But now the music was over, and a small child was bleeding. And that made Carl slip his leash.

Before the applause had even started to diminish, he had put his trombone on its stand and lunged through the cellos in front of Ann, who wisely shifted round in her seat to give him a clear run.

Tarquin was sitting on the end of a row near the front of the audience, and Caspar a couple of rows behind, also on the end. These positions gave their right arms free movement: not something one would ordinarily factor in when choosing a seat for a concert. But these boys carried slings. A fair amount of free time at Oakdean was spent learning how to make slings out of wool, braiding the cradle to fit an acorn exactly. It was no accident that the rhododendron perimeter enclosed an almost entirely squirrel-free zone. Target practice must be had.

Tarquin, Caspar and, on the other side of the hall for the left-handed Rufus, had arrived at the concert with pockets bulging with acorns. Most of those acorns were now on the floor under the orchestra, having dented an instrument or a head on their way there.

Carl roared and bore down on Tarquin and Caspar, snatching Tarquin by the collar as he swept past to grab Caspar. He stood with a teenager dangling from each hand, scanning the rest of the audience for Rufus. The applause dribbled away into nothing, replaced by gasps of shock.

Rufus, reasoning that the game was up for his friends and perhaps retreat might be the better part of valour in this instance, had crept out of his seat and was trying to saunter unobtrusively to the back of the hall along the edge.

'Over there!' called Eliot, pointing. 'Stop him.'

Upon being discovered, Rufus broke into a gawky run, and might have made it to the door were it not for Noel sticking out his leg and tripping him up. While he was on the floor, Noel stepped over him and put him in an armlock as he helped him back to vertical.

'Ow!' Rufus whined, as Noel lifted him as easily as Carl was holding his two.

'Complain again, sunshine,' Noel whispered into his ear, 'and you'll wish you hadn't.'

Rufus wisely shut up.

'What is the meaning of this?' called Rosalind, now standing next to her seat near the doors.

'This lot were shooting at us,' said Carl, shaking each arm and eliciting groans from both boys. Perhaps he had a grip on them that was, strictly speaking, tighter than absolutely necessary.

'Acorns,' said Leroy, who had picked a few up from the floor. 'They're all acorns.'

'Anyone got a tissue?' said Irie, who was still bleeding. The drip had made it past her eye and was approaching her white shirt, which she knew her mum would be mad about.

'Oh God,' said Kayla. She walked over to Irie, reaching for a pack of tissues in her back pocket.

Tracie glanced at Irie's face, and then at Tarquin and Caspar, who were looking satisfied that at least one of their shots had drawn blood. She laid her trombone on her chair and followed Carl's path out of the orchestra, like a small, determined Rottweiler.

'Arseholes,' she said as she got near enough to aim a punch at Tarquin's stomach, seamlessly turning and delivering an identical one to Caspar. She knew from long Sunbridge experience exactly how much force to use to incapacitate but not cause any long-term damage. They hung from Carl's arms, winded. Tracie stared at them, nodded and turned to go back to her seat, muttering, 'Worth it – whatever,' as she went.

The entire orchestra gave her a spontaneous round of applause, and even Noel grinned from the other side of the hall. He could never condone violence, of course. But then, he *was* off-duty. He and Carl exchanged a look of huge satisfaction.

Anxious murmurs rose throughout the audience as people wondered where the next fight might break out. Mrs Ford-Hughes, in her accustomed front seat, looked especially nervous, and clutched her collarbone. Eliot decided to take charge.

'Ladies and gentlemen, please stay calm. As you can see, we've had a small, er, hiatus. But I can see Carl has it under control—'

'And Tracie,' called someone from the orchestra.

Eliot laughed. 'And Noel – thank you. I suggest we take five minutes to remove these people, check Irie's OK and that nobody else is hurt, and maybe, I don't know, pick up some acorns?' There was a nervous, tension-releasing ripple of laughter round the audience. 'Rosalind? Would you and some of your governors mind escorting Dr Irving and Sir Marmaduke into the foyer? Carl and Noel: shall we join her?'

He made his way to the back of the hall and through to the foyer, where the three Oakdean boys were standing in varying degrees of pain, still attached to Carl and Noel. Dr Irving and Sir Marmaduke were loudly disputing their ejection from the hall, claiming ignorance of any plan to shoot at the orchestra.

Noel was already on his phone, and turned to Eliot when he'd finished.

'On their way. If I could bag up all the acorns people are collecting, that would be great.'

Rosalind immediately dispatched Adrian to oversee that task. She then turned to Dr Irving. 'I want you out of my school. If this police officer doesn't take you himself, you must leave anyway. You too.' She nodded at Sir Marmaduke. 'You should be ashamed of yourselves.'

'Don't worry,' said Noel. 'They're going.'

The boys smirked to hear adults spoken to like that, which was pounced on by Noel.

'And you three can wipe those smiles off right now. Each of you has been carrying and using an offensive weapon in public without lawful authority or reasonable excuse. Which means you're going to the police station. Again.'

'And you'll be hearing from all our insurance companies,' said Eliot, 'about straightening out all the dents you put in the brass. Let alone Irie's head.'

It took a bit longer than Eliot's promised five minutes, but in the end the Oakdean boys – and Dr Irving and Sir Marmaduke for good measure – had been bundled into police vehicles and driven to the station. Noel requested that they be held pending his arrival. He didn't see why he should forfeit the rest of the concert on his evening off just to process them more quickly.

By the time they went back into the hall, Irie's forehead had a neat dressing taped to it, the floor was clear of acorn debris, and Mrs Ford-Hughes was regaling half the violins with a story about how she met Mr Ford-Hughes. She regarded herself as a fellow performer now, and was happy to shoot the breeze with her friends.

'Do you think,' said Rosalind to Noel, 'you could make some sort of announcement about this? To make it absolutely clear that this unfortunate incident was nothing whatsoever to do with Sunbridge Academy? I wonder, do I ask too much? This evening is of such importance to us.'

Noel smiled. 'I think someone should explain things to this poor audience. If Eliot's happy for me to, of course.'

'Sure,' said Eliot. 'I've no idea what I'd say. Never been interrupted by acorns before.'

So Noel accompanied Eliot to the front of the hall and faced a sea of expectant and slightly confused faces.

'I'm DCI Noel Osmar. Off-duty tonight: just here for the concert.' Warm laughter sounded sympathetic about his night off being interrupted. 'Just wanted to reassure you that all miscreants have been removed from the premises.' There was a small cheer. 'I can also confirm that Sunbridge Academy is merely the innocent host for this evening's excitements: no suspect is at all related to this school.'

'We all know which school they *are* related to,' said someone in the orchestra behind him, to laughter.

'Don't heckle me on my night off,' said Noel, half-turning and smiling. 'Or I'll clap you in irons. Anyway,' – he turned back to the audience – 'enjoy the rest of the concert. I know I shall.'

Eliot patted him on the shoulder and smiled, and Noel returned to his seat.

'Thanks, Noel,' said Eliot. 'And before we go on, I think we should show our appreciation to the kids in this orchestra, some of whom have never been in this situation before and have been stonkingly brilliant, as you heard in the Copland before we were so rudely interrupted by acorns. Firstly: the newly patched-up Irie on percussion!' There were wild cheers, led by her mum and brother. Eliot looked over at her. 'Feeling OK to carry on?' She nodded, grinning. 'Great. And next, our string players: from Oakdean College' – there were muffled pantomime boos – 'proving they're not all bad, we have Sebastian on viola and Rupert on cello.' More cheers. 'And our Sunbridge violinists, Danilo, Marina and Reece!' The hall erupted again. 'And to the brass: we have Hector on trumpet' – the clapping swelled again – 'and lastly, but by no means leastly, and I'm making that absolutely clear because she's *quite* capable of beating me up, we have Tracie on trombone!'

The hall went wild. The noise was doubled because the whole orchestra joined the applause, whooping and stamping their feet for Tracie, who was trying to style it out but failing to cover up how immensely pleased and proud she was. Kayla beamed at her and joined in the clapping. Carl punched her, affectionately and softly, on the arm.

'So,' said Eliot, when things had calmed down a bit, 'on with the show. Next we have some Mussorgsky for you: *Night on the Bare Mountain*. Just in case you hadn't had enough of hearing our brass section letting rip. And then to end the evening, we have one of the most beautiful symphonies there is: Sibelius's Second.'

He turned to the orchestra, raised his baton, and transported them all to the witches' sabbath.

Chapter 30

As the last D major chord of the Sibelius echoed from the hall's ceiling, beefed up by Irie's timpani roll, the audience started getting to their feet. Eliot acknowledged this standing ovation by stepping to the side and indicating it was all for the orchestra, and joining in with it himself. Tracie looked at Carl and blew the loose raspberry he had told her about: her lips were ringed with red and he knew she wouldn't have been able to blow another note that night. Hector's mouth looked the same. What they also had in common, however, was their utter commitment to doing their best for the piece and their fellow musicians. That kind of feeling of teamwork is rarely replicated anywhere else. But then any team would say that.

There were people milling about in the hall and foyer as chairs were stacked and moved to the side and stands folded and put away. Pearl collected the orchestral parts and sorted them. Rafael and David went up to Eliot to congratulate him.

'Been an eventful term,' said Rafael, 'but highly satisfactory in the end.'

'Quite,' said David. 'Don't mind admitting there a moment or two in the middle that I had my doubts, but this idea to get these kids involved – well, it really paid off.'

Eliot laughed. 'Thanks. I had my doubts too, David. At odd moments. Some were even this evening. But yes, great to do. Thanks for indulging me.'

Rosalind was back on duty at the door, taking her leave of the audience as they left. Henry stopped on his way past to thank her.

'Quite the evening, in the end,' he said. 'Do you know, even with all of Oakdean's wealth, I can't help feeling they're missing something we have here at Sunbridge. Well done, Rosalind. Top work.'

'Thank you, Headmaster,' she said, almost curtseying. 'I'll have the draft of our new cultural brochure on your desk next week.'

'No rush, no rush,' said Henry, walking away. 'And do call me Henry.' He knew she never would.

Erin, Charlie and Ann put their cellos in their cases and, with them slung over their shoulders, walked back from the dressing room-classrooms into the foyer.

'Do you think we'll ever do a normal concert again?' said Ann.

'God, I hope not,' said Charlie. 'This is far too much fun.'

'I could handle slightly less fun,' said Erin. 'You know, on a regular basis.'

Noel raised his hand to them as he came out of the hall. 'Nice one.'

'Have you got to work now?' said Erin. 'I was hoping you might come to the pub.'

Noel put on a glum face. ''Fraid so. I was hoping I might go to the pub too, but I'd better fill out a few forms.'

Carl and Kayla came out of the hall and walked towards the classrooms just as Tracie was coming out of them carrying her trombone case. Carl caught sight of Noel on the way and they paused. 'Drink? I owe you for nabbing that third little shit.'

'Can't, I'm afraid. Just telling this lot. Paperwork calls.'

'You work too hard.'

'I do.' Noel looked at Tracie. 'On second thoughts, you might not want to be a police officer. We work too hard.'

She laughed.

'Nice moves earlier,' said Charlie.

Tracie nodded.

'She's my bodyguard now,' said Carl. 'Nobody will dare mess with me.'

'Right, I'm off,' said Noel. 'Well done, everybody. For everything.' He twinkled one last smile at Tracie and was gone.

'I've got to get this bass back to the classroom,' said Kayla. 'Tracie, are you OK to get home? Your mum didn't come, did she? I don't think I saw her.'

'Nah. I'll be fine.'

'OK. See you on Monday then.' Kayla carried her bass down the corridor towards her music room.

'Gotta get the hooter case,' said Carl. He high-fived Tracie and went off to the classrooms.

'So what do you reckon, Tracie,' said Ann. 'You joining us permanently?'

'Oh, go on,' said Charlie. 'And it'll only be a couple more years before you can come down the pub too.'

'Charlie!' said Erin.

'Sounds good,' said Tracie.

The foyer slowly drained of people, until Rosalind judged it wasn't worth standing by the doors and moved towards her banners.

'Oh God, is she about to dismantle them?' said Ann. 'We might lose her altogether.'

'We could unroll her for our next concert,' said Charlie.

'Slightly flat,' said Erin.

'She could play flute with Brian,' said Ann.

Tracie laughed. 'Old people are mental,' she said. 'See ya.' And she left.

'Old?' said Erin.

'Now you know how I feel,' said Ann.

Eliot wandered from the hall still chatting and shaking hands with various parents and governors and Mr and Mrs Ford-Hughes. They took their leave of him in the foyer and went out into the night.

Eliot grinned. 'Well, we got through that. Thanks, guys.'

'Well done you,' said Charlie.

'How many pints do I owe everyone for this little experiment?' said Eliot. 'I might as well just put my entire fee behind the bar and let you get on with it yourselves.'

'But that wouldn't be half as entertaining as taking the piss out of you in person,' said Ann.

'Speaking of taking the piss,' said Charlie, 'we're going to have a lot of fun with this one.' He jerked his head towards the far end of the corridor from the classrooms, where the silhouettes of Carl and Kayla could be seen kissing.

'They're taking their time,' said Eliot. 'The pub won't stay open all night.'

'Come on,' said Erin. 'Leave them to it.'

Charlie yelled up the corridor. 'Last one in the pub's a sissy!'

Carl's arm detached from the double silhouette and threw a V-sign, before wrapping itself around Kayla again.

'They'll be along,' said Ann. 'Let's get them one in. Come on.'

Acknowledgements

As always, my first thank you is to Abbie Headon: commissioning editor and tireless supporter of my work, without whom the Stockwell Park Orchestra would never have played in public.

Books are a team effort. After Abbie, my words were scrutinised by project editor Claire Watts, copy editor Becca Allen and proofreader Abbie Rutherford. Their careful reading saved me from more than one embarrassing blooper.

Clare Stacey at Head Design produced the wonderful cover.

Tim Giddings was kind enough to look through my awful attempts at Latin and corral them into proper phrases. Bob Chapman allowed me to pick his trombonist's brain in case I'd made technical errors. Emma Crute checked over what I'd written about the police to make sure I wasn't talking rubbish. If any errors remain in any or all of my Latin, trombone craft or police procedure, they are entirely my fault and not because of Tim, Bob or Emma. Huge thanks to all three.

Ben Blackman is here as a consolation prize for there not being a Ben in this series. Yet.

The characters' names in this book were great fun to invent. Dave Trinket was invaluable. Eloise's help was brilliant, so a very special thank you to her.

About the Author

Isabel Rogers writes poetry and fiction, but never on the same day. She won the 2014 Cardiff International Poetry Competition, was Hampshire Poet Laureate 2016, and her debut collection, *Don't Ask*, came out in 2017 (Eyewear). *Life, Death and Cellos* is her first novel to be published.

She had a proper City job before a decade in the Scottish Highlands, writing and working in the NHS. She now lives in Hampshire, laughs a lot and neglects her cello. She is on Twitter @Isabelwriter.

Also available

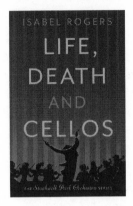

Classical music can be a dangerous pastime...

What with love affairs, their conductor dropping dead, a stolen cello and no money, Stockwell Park Orchestra is having a fraught season.

After Mrs Ford-Hughes is squashed and injured by a dying guest conductor mid-concert, she and her husband withdraw their generous financial backing, leaving the orchestra broke and unsure of its future.

Cellist Erin suggests a recovery plan, but since it involves their unreliable leader, Fenella, playing a priceless Stradivari cello which then goes missing, it's not a foolproof one. Joshua, the regular conductor, can't decide which affair to commit to, while manager David's nervous tic returns at every doom-laden report from the orchestra's treasurer.

There is one way to survive, but is letting a tone-deaf diva sing Strauss too high a price to pay? And will Stockwell Park Orchestra live to play another season?

The Stockwell Park Orchestra Series, Volume One

OUT NOW

Note from the Publisher

To receive updates on new releases in the Stockwell Park Orchestra Series – plus special offers and news of other humorous fiction series to make you smile – sign up now to the Farrago mailing list at farragobooks.com/sign-up.

Made in the USA
Middletown, DE
03 April 2023

28143726R00154